FESTERWOOD
AT FIVE

A "Novel" Approach
to TV News

mike ahern ◆ reid duffy

GUILD PRESS OF INDIANA, INC.
Carmel, Indiana

Published in the United States by Guild Press of Indiana, Inc.

ISBN 1-57860-061-8

Library of Congress
Catalog Card Number 98-72783

Printed in the United States of America

Cover art by Steven D. Armour
Text designed by Sheila G. Samson

to our families,

Sherry and Kevin
Loretta, Megan, and Matthew

acknowledgments

This novel was written over tons of power sandwiches, good beer, and other brain fuels of dubious nutritional value. So the authors must first acknowledge the providers of such nourishment, without whom none of this would have been possible. In addition, we are eternally grateful to Andy Murphy, our agent, motivator, and friend, who laughed at all the right places, and who knows all the right people. One of those is Della Pacheco, our first editor who took on the challenge of fine-tooth combing a manuscript from two television journalists long conditioned to pronouncing words correctly, at the expense of such petty concerns as spelling and punctuation. Later, the good folks at Guild Press of Indiana applied their keen editing skills to produce the finished product, which looked so professional that we didn't immediately recognize it as our own creation. Their efforts were indispensable, and we thank them all. And although he never knew it at the time, Stan Wood was a prime mover of this epic. His countless stories, anecdotes, and quick wit in so many situations are recalled several times in this book. They say to steal one idea is plagiarism, but to borrow several ideas is research. Stan, thanks for the research.

The authors also wish to thank several people for their professional assistance: Tom Maccabe, for his attention to detail; Gerry Inks, for his engineering technical advice so that we would not appear totally our of our depth; Rich Tirman, Ph.D., for making it possible for our characters to sound knowledgable in the mystifying world of psychoanalysis; and Joe Loughmiller, for showing us in terms we could understand that even a simple subject like road salt has a language all its own.

Special thanks to Julia Rhyne and Keith Bratton for helping whip our book and cover into shape in the early stages; and especially to Nancy Niblack Baxter, for making all this possible. And we offer a profound thanks to our families. Without their patience, support, patience, encouragement, patience—and *especially* their patience!—this project would still be a vague idea. Thank you Sherry and Loretta, and our children, Kevin Ahern and Megan and Matthew Duffy, who have promised to someday read this book in its entirety, without waiting for the video or resorting to Cliffs Notes.

Finally, we want to thank all of the very talented and colorful people with whom we worked over the years. Although all of our characters and situations are inventions of the authors, several real-life experiences inspired episodes in this novel. After all, fact is usually stranger than fiction; but in a television news room, it's often funnier, too!

Special thanks to Julia Rhyne and Keith Bratton for helping whip our book and cover into shape in the early stages; and especially to Nancy Niblack Baxter, for making all this possible. And we offer a profound thanks to our families. Without their patience, support, patience, encouragement, patience—and *especially* their patience!—this project would still be a vague idea. Thank you Sherry and Loretta, and our children, Kevin Ahern and Megan and Matthew Duffy, who have promised to someday read this book in its entirety, without waiting for the video or resorting to Cliffs Notes.

Finally, we want to thank all of the very talented and colorful people with whom we worked over the years. Although all of our characters and situations are inventions of the authors, several real-life experiences inspired episodes in this novel. After all, fact is usually stranger than fiction; but in a television news room, it's often funnier, too!

chapter one

"MR. FAGAN, PUT DOWN YOUR WEAPON! RICK ROBERSON IS COMING IN!"

As the voice of Police Chief Penny screeched through a bullhorn, I took my first tentative steps up the front walk, bundled in a flak jacket and clutching a six pack of beer. In front of me stood what was once a nondescript bungalow, squatting on a dead-end street. Tonight, this little house—bathed in the eerie glow of floodlights—was the epicenter of the biggest news story in the nation. Inside, an angry and frightened man was assumed to be holding his nephew at gunpoint. And, from all indications, he was ready to take out his fear and rage on the innocent child entrusted to his care.

Behind me, as far as the eye could see, was row upon row of police cars, their radios crackling and sputtering into the frosty night air. Helmeted and padded sharpshooters ducked behind each of the cars, with the shiny barrels of their rifles trained on the house. Behind them stood a stunning array of television satellite trucks, all of them powered up and feeding their signals back to their home stations and beyond.

Most of the reporters who were still hanging around had shivered through this whole ordeal, and they had long ago run out of colorful labels to describe the personality, mentality, and moral fiber of the man who had brought them all to this remote place, but only after accusing him of every unsavory human act short of chronic bedwetting. Ordinarily I would be back there with them, searching for words to fit the breathtaking televised image of a house where no one and nothing was moving.

They were my peers, but even I had to marvel at how they had managed to fill four hours of live TV coverage, armed with approximately thirty-five seconds of solid information. In so doing, they managed to alienate viewers who were no doubt royally pissed that *Wheel of Fortune, Seinfeld,* and *Buffy the Vampire Slayer* had been jettisoned for this very special, live version of *Men Behaving Badly.* In fact, by now all the major networks were here; CNN had even come up with some catchy theme music for its live reports, which were titled "Hostage in the Heartland."

Meanwhile, a squadron of helicopters—both of the news and police persuasion—circled overhead, operating in about twelve feet of airspace above Hostage Central, the little house that once was just the simple abode of one Norbert Fagan and his common-law wife, Marie.

The TV reporters who dug in behind me may have been my colleagues in another life. On this fateful night, however, I had been forced to cross the line between reporter and newsmaker. The gun-wielding madman inside the little house on Ralston Street had asked for me to intervene. I was to be the designated hostage negotiator. And that's how I found myself standing in this buffer zone among a collection of Barney Fife wannabes, known as the Festus County SWAT team; the even more threatening presence of the overly wired electronic media; and the man who had become America's Public Enemy Number One.

But how could this be happening? Just two days ago I was a small-town television reporter, covering a story in my own hometown about whether bonds should be floated to finance a sewer project. Now here I was, standing just a few feet away from the story that could make or break my career. As far as the rest of the world was concerned, I was about to risk my life in hopes of talking a deranged gunman into releasing his hostage and surrendering. What made this all the more incongruous was that I knew the man—I had known him since childhood. We were both raised in the same town and had attended the same schools. I'd driven down this street a hundred times, but now it all seemed foreign to me. In a few surrealistic hours, everything had changed.

As I started up the walk, I realized there was no way of changing my destiny. Events had spun out of control. The age of live, lurid news was here, and I was about to become an accomplice. But if only they knew . . .

"*Hold your fire, Fagan!*" Chief Penny's voice again cut the night air like a dull saw. I was on the porch now, facing a wooden front door that was well-gouged and flecked with pre-World War II green paint chips. The door was slightly ajar, then opened slowly to a slit big enough to show two wide, terrified eyes and the gleam of a double-barreled gun pointed directly at me, shaking uncontrollably. To make matters worse, I knew that on the other end of that gun was a disturbed man.

When last I saw Norbert Fagan, he was addressing a live television audience, his reddened eyes squinting into the lights under a wild shock of salt-and-pepper hair that jutted out beneath an oversized Army helmet with a chin strap that barely concealed a four-day growth of beard. His grimy shirt was covered with tomato sauce and beer stains; a pair of red suspenders barely held up his GI-issue camouflage pants that drooped from his small, shriveled frame as if they would drop at any moment. Comical, yes . . . but in the glare of those television lights, with his anger and confusion fueled by God-knows-how-many beers, I had to admit that my old friend Norb, or "Nutsy" as we came to know him over the years, cut an ominous figure. Even more so when he informed his captivated audience that he wouldn't budge until he could talk to me.

This was bizarre. I didn't know whether to laugh or cry. Suddenly, I was literally on the threshold of a story that the whole world was watching, and all I could think of was: *How did I get here, and why?* Just two days ago, no one had even heard of Festerwood, Indiana, and certainly no one knew the name Rick Roberson. Just two days ago, none of this seemed possible. Just two days ago . . .

chapter two

It was 4:40 p.m. and it seemed like everything but the clock was in slow motion. It was deadline time, just twenty minutes until *Festerwood at Five: Western Indiana's Most Complete News Report*. But I was stuck in mid-sentence, and my story was supposed to lead the newscast. By Festerwood standards, it was a pretty big news event. There had been a little domestic dust-up at the trailer park out on State Road 63 that turned ugly when the wife planted a letter opener in her husband's crotch. I was having some trouble coming up with just the right words to capture the drama of the incident without offending the dinner-hour audience. The producer of the newscast was in his usual state of near panic.

I turned back to my computer screen. My fingers tapped nervously on the keyboard, but nothing was coming out! There was a gnawing pain in my stomach, and I could feel the sweat pooling in the waistband of my shorts. Then the phone rang.

"No, not now!" I cried to myself. Of course, I had to answer it. Could be a tip on the crime. Maybe the one piece of evidence that I needed. I picked up the receiver. "Rick Roberson, news."

"Mr. Roberson, I'm Ann Rollins with Magic Media. Do you have a minute?"

"Who?"

"Ann Rollins. I represent the Magic Media Company?"

"Uh . . . sure. Sure! Of course! In fact, you caught me at a good time!"

Magic Media was a huge news consulting firm, a company that placed television news people in jobs all across the country. I had sent them maybe fifty tapes of my work but never got a reply. I had almost given up.

"Mr. Roberson, I have a client who loves your work."

"No sh . . . I mean, really? That's great." I couldn't believe my ears. Suddenly my story on the trailer park version of Lorena Bobbitt was the furthest thing from my mind.

"There's just one problem," she said. "My client doesn't want to get involved in any litigation. Do you have a contract where you are now?"

I didn't have a contract. The anchor people had contracts, but not the reporters who did the grunt work. "Well, yes, I'm afraid I do," I lied. "But there is an escape clause in it if I'm offered a job in a Top 20 market."

"Oh, that's too bad. My client is in a Top 25 market."

"Yeah, well, I have that, too."

"Oh, that's great! Now, I'm not sure about job description or salary, but most stations this size pay their starting reporters around fifty thousand or so. Would that be in the ballpark?"

"Fifty thousand would be . . . uh . . . interesting." I was about to jump out of my skin. Our *anchors* didn't make that much!

"Well, tell you what I'll do. I'll go ahead and—"

Bzzzzzzzzzzzzz . . .

The alarm clock jolted me out of my dream. I fumbled for the OFF switch and pounded it with my fist. I had this incredible headache, and my mouth tasted like rusted metal. A figure stirred under the sheets and moaned.

"Karen," I mumbled. "Get up. I gotta get to work."

"It's Carol," she murmured. "My name is Carol."

"Right." Carol something-or-other.

"Well, you're not the only one," she said as she kicked off the covers. "I'm supposed to be at work, too."

I had forgotten that. Carol was an intern at the station, one of the many students at Festerwood Community College who did slave labor in the newsroom so she could learn the business firsthand. I had no idea if she had any talent, but by the fourth or fifth round of drinks last night, I vaguely recall telling her that she reminded me of Jane Pauley.

That's when the evening began to come into focus, along with the familiar ripples of guilt. There had been a going-away party in the lounge of the Ramada Inn just off I-70. Dale Strackmeyer was leaving to take the job of chief news photographer at a station in Pittsburgh. No one liked Strackmeyer, but these going-away parties were something of a tradition at our station. Festerwood was not exactly the kind of place where you take a job and say, "Well, that's it. I'm set for life."

The Ramada Inn lounge was interchangeable with every other motel bar along the flat stretch of highway that cut across the bleak Indiana farmscape. The TV over the bar was tuned to ESPN, which was showing one of those late night reruns of a stock car race. No one was paying much attention, especially at our table, where photographer Lowell Loudermilk was holding court.

"Strackmeyer! Jesus, can you believe it? Pittsburgh!"

Lowell had several Black Russians under his belt, so there was no stopping him. "You know, we almost didn't hire Strackmeyer, but we needed someone for the weekend shift. He's the last guy I figured would walk out of here."

He turned to a sickly looking redheaded youngster in the seat next to him. "Hell, Freddie, every time I looked up, you were saving his ass in the editing room."

Freddie Klinger was too frail to carry a camera, but he was a whiz when it came to editing stories shot by other photographers. He forced a weak smile. "Goddam right, Jeff." Freddie was not a drinker, and the two Lite beer bottles in front of him had almost taken him out of the game.

"Besides," slurred Jeff, "Strackmeyer's a prick."

No argument there. But he was a prick on his way to Pittsburgh, while the rest of us did a slow burn in Festerwood.

Strackmeyer came over to our table. He was wearing the same filthy turtleneck sweater that he always wore, nubby with age and wear; and he had, as usual, pulled his greasy blond hair back into a ponytail. But instead of his traditional Chicago Cubs baseball cap reversed on his head, he now was wearing a newly purchased Pittsburgh Pirate cap, with the gold "P" in prominent display.

Strackmeyer momentarily lost his balance, then steadied himself by leaning on my shoulder. I shifted, but he stayed with me. "I'm really going to miss you guys," he whined. Strackmeyer had this annoying whine. "But you know something? You guys are good, and I know one day you'll be following right in my footsteps."

It was at that point that I ordered another round, and things began to blur.

Now, in the glare of morning, I looked out the bathroom window of my apartment. The November sky was the color of charcoal, and a light snow was falling on the flat roof of the apartment building next door. It was the fine, fresh snow of early winter, and it fell evenly on the bare branches of an old sweet gum tree in the yard below. The first snowfall of the season always made me feel anxious, another sign that time was quietly slipping away. But I had watched as snow dusted the leaves of that tree for years; and, every time, I couldn't help but be enchanted by the glistening white world that slowly took shape outside my apartment window. Then it hit me.

"Goddammit. This means we'll have to lead with a snow story!"

"What?" The voice in the bedroom sounded even younger than I remembered.

"Nothing."

I had a few repairs to make. A tired, sallow face looked back at me from my bathroom mirror. It was a face that was growing old before its time. The change was subtle. There was just a hint of gray in my unruly tangle of sandy hair, and only the first hint of laugh lines on my face, which, fortunately for me, is squared in a television-friendly way. My nose, which has always been too large, seemed to be pulsating in unnerving shades of bright red, and I looked stooped and small for a man who stood just under six feet tall. Part of that, I realized, was a result of my night of debauchery. But there was more to it. Every time I looked in the mirror, I saw a thirty-six-year-old man who was stuck in a premature midlife crisis.

In my business, television news, midlife doesn't sneak up on you. It arrives in a sudden, overwhelming moment of sheer panic. One day you're the up-and-coming young reporter with an unlimited future. The next day you're doing feature stories about old guys who repair grandfather clocks.

I knew if I didn't get out of Festerwood soon I'd wind up like Howard Tungle—the guy who used to give the early-morning farm-market reports on WHOE-Radio. Howard once told an interviewer for the *Festus County Fanfare* that he would never leave his job at the radio station no matter how many offers he had, because he loved the people of western Indiana, and they loved him. Not long after that, the station switched to a "Kick Ass" rock format, and exhibited its loyalty and love for Howard by showing him the door.

Today, Howard Tungle is a school crossing guard, and he occasionally speaks at Rotary Club luncheons about the good old days of radio. However, not as much as he used to—not since Howard put away one too many Old Styles during one luncheon and called the radio station manager "a little pussy." The station manager happened to be a Rotary member.

chapter three

I PUMPED THE ACCELERATOR TWICE AND MY '79 CHEVY NOVA GROANED to life. The one windshield wiper that worked swept a thin film of snow from the driver's side as I started down Hawthorne Avenue on my way to work. It was not quite 7:00 A.M., so there was little traffic as I drove past what remained of downtown Festerwood. There was a Walgreen's and a couple of clothing shops, a bank in an old red-brick building that had those turret-like towers at the corners, a shoe store where I had worked summers during high school, and vacant buildings that used to be shops and restaurants.

I passed by the remnants of the Savoy Theater, where I had fallen in love with Olivia Newton-John and had stood in line three times to see *Star Wars*. It was boarded up now, with one crooked red plastic "Y" still clinging to the marquee. There were a lot of For Sale signs in empty windows. If there had been a trickle-down economy in the eighties, it never trickled down to Festerwood.

The sorriest sight in town was the massive building that used to be Gilyard Enterprises. Until the late seventies, it was the largest employer in the area. Founded after the Depression by Colonel Frederick Gilyard, the factory produced a bewildering array of chemical products, solutions, and protective paints made to order for the war-effort industries. Gilyard adapted to the postwar industrial boom without breaking stride, except for occasional nuisance complaints about worker safety and air pollution. The acrid smoke, together with the perennial dull winter skies over Festerwood, did have one benefit: Festerwood residents usually were spared the downside of radiation that comes from a visible sun.

Gilyard industries prospered until 1978, when the elderly Colonel sold the business to a competing out-of-state conglomerate, J. V. L. Enterprises of Florida, which showed its faith in Festerwood by closing the plant down within six months. Suddenly thirty-five hundred people were without jobs. My father was one of them.

They tried to save the old building by converting it to a roller rink and, later, a bowling alley. There was even an effort to turn it into a convention center, but aside from the Festus County Apostolic Friends of Christ, no organization showed any interest in meeting there.

I passed by Norm Nordstrom's used-car lot, the stomping grounds of one of the durable merchants who never seemed to be phased by the economic vicissitudes. Norm was a community stalwart, past-president of the Chamber of Commerce, and a neighbor. He had hired my dad to manage his car-leasing operation when Gilyard folded.

Now in his third decade of selling what he advertised as "previously loved cars," Nutty Norm—as he called himself in his TV commercials—prided himself for selling vehicles with questionable engines but great heaters and working radios—made to order for Festerwood winters and working journalists whose knowledge of cars was pretty much confined to "forward on D and backward on R."

It was Norm himself who did a series of remarkably tasteless post-midnight commercials, in which he wrapped himself in a straight jacket and knit cap, and yelled into the camera, "I must be crazy! I'm practically giving these cars away!" Local mental health organizations finally gave up trying to talk WHOE-TV into dropping the commercial on the grounds of rampant insensitivity. But the commercial worked for me. Nutty Norm's is where I bought my "can't kill it with a stick" Nova for six hundred bucks.

WHOE's studios were located in a squat, cinderblock building in a fading industrial complex on the outskirts of town. Despite its nondescript appearance, station management insisted on calling the place Broadcast Park, even though a transmitting tower in the parking lot was the only visible clue that a television station might be located on the premises. Otherwise, the flat, gray building could have been mistaken for an auto repair shop, which is exactly what it used to be.

The Hubbard brothers, Ben and Billy, set up shop there back in the seventies. As a favor to my dad, they hired me for two excruciating weeks one summer, during which I tried and failed to master the concept of "multi-link suspension" and "anti-lock brakes." Bud and Billy were doing a pretty brisk business, since car crashing had taken on the stature of an Olympic event in Festerwood, especially on those Saturday nights when the third shift at the John Deere plant let out at about the same time as the St. Barnabas Bowling League.

Ben and Billy called their little shop Hubbard Brothers Auto Repair, which made sense. In fact, it seemed downright inspired when you consider what happened back in the mid-eighties. That's when Ben went into what Billy would later call his "patriotic fit" and renamed the shop America First. Ben appeared in commercials sporting a red, white, and blue sport coat and boasting that, from now on, only American-made cars would be serviced at the shop. Bud and Billy went out of business six months later.

As it so happened at about the same time, C. T. "Thumbtack" Thornton was looking for a place to put his TV station. C. T. wasn't really a broadcaster. He ran a family hardware store, with a timeworn oak floor, a patterned tin ceiling and huge counters. I never was good with my hands, but I liked to browse through Thornton's Hardware on Saturday afternoons.

As the story was told to me, back in the fifties, C. T. drew to an inside straight in a poker game with Bill Welliver—poker being a skill that C. T. honed on the front lines while keeping the communists from getting past the 38th parallel at Fort Leonard Wood, Missouri. Bill Welliver just happened to be vulnerable in two areas: he was a terrible broadcaster and a worse poker player. As a result, C. T. won the station in a card game. But to put a good face on it, he paid Bill fifteen hundred dollars. Bill was the mayor of Festerwood at the time, and losing the community's only television station in a card game could turn out to be a campaign issue.

Actually C. T. had his eye on the station for some time, as a way to advertise his hardware store. In fact, he chose the call letters W-H-O-E because a "hoe" was the only item in the store he could think of that had the three letters to follow the obligatory "W."

I opened the door of the station and immediately sensed panic. Helen Terhune was on duty at the front desk—just one of her many posts as the station's unofficial den mother. She also served as secretary to the general manager and sales department, and as part-time receptionist. As a result, Helen made it her business to know everyone else's. She possessed the longest blue-red nails in the Midwest, and she was tapping them against an empty Diet Pepsi can, a sure sign that the morning was off to a bad start. She glared at me and shook her head.

"You don't want to go in there."

She meant the newsroom and, as usual, she was right. I turned the corner and collided with Leon Heifitz, the producer.

"Jesus, where have you been? Hogan's furious!"

"Hogan's always furious. What's up?" I knew the answer, of course. The impossible had happened. An inch and a half of snow had fallen on western Indiana in November, a perfectly natural phenomenon given the geographic location and season. But in a television newsroom, especially this one, such an event was greeted with disbelief.

The newsroom was in a frenzy. Dirk Tubergen, the young reporter whose bed partner was a police radio, was rushing toward the door, followed very slowly by photographer Spanky McCallister, who obviously had not yet consumed his usual power breakfast of five doughnuts and two Mountain Dews. "Killer snow," he snarled as I stepped aside to give him ample room to negotiate the doorway.

The phones were chirping incessantly. I picked up a receiver. "Channel 49 News."

"Would you please announce that Westlane School is closed because of the unclement weather?" The voice on the other end strained for maturity, but cracked in a twelve-year-old way.

I thought this might be fun for a few seconds. "What kind of weather?"

The voice suddenly wasn't quite so assured, and not nearly as deep. "Uh . . . unclement. You know, like snow."

"Oh, you're calling to say there's no school because of the two-inch blizzard?"

"Yeah, that's it!"

"OK, what's the code?" The station had a special code number that school principals kept on file in case they had to call in a closing. It was a carefully protected number to guard against kids calling in false alarms.

"Uh . . . the code is . . . I forgot."

"Right. Well, tell you what. I'll just forget you called then, OK?"

Fred Hogan was on the phone, but he waved me into his office. I liked Hogan, although most of the newsroom staff considered him irrelevant. He was definitely from another time and place, a rumpled, balding man well into his fifties with a look of eternal exasperation on his broad, florid face.

Fred came to WHOE-TV right out of radio, but you got the feeling he would much rather have stayed with his original job as a newspaper city editor, from which he was fired after eighteen years of chronic alcoholism. The reason for his firing came as a surprise to just about everyone working at the newspaper, where chronic alcoholism often seemed to be a condition of employment.

But Fred carried the concept to unconscionable extremes, when, during the throes of his Christmas Eve depression, he re-edited wire-service copy on Christmas celebrations around the world, liberally using the word "alleged" with every reference to the Virgin Birth. As a result, readers of the *Festus County Fanfare* were greeted on Christmas morning with heresy from their morning paper. The enraged publisher stormed into the office and found Fred out cold atop his desk, clutching a bottle of Jack Daniels like it was a rosary. As Fred later recalled, the publisher bellowed something like, "Hogan, you sure as hell better be dead, 'cause if you're not, you're fired!"

"Rick, we got real trouble." Hogan's face was even redder than usual.

"Yeah, I know. Two inches of snow and you'd think the New Madrid fault has opened up."

"No, not that. Come in here."

Hogan's office was really nothing more than a cluttered cubbyhole stacked with newspapers and back issues of *Broadcast* magazine. He sank into his chair and flipped a letter across his desk. "Read this."

It was a stiff corporate letter filled with a lot of legalese, but the message was clear enough. Hogan, the man who sat before me, was being replaced. Fired.

"What the hell is this all about?"

"The ratings are down and I'm the scapegoat."

I couldn't believe it. "Thornton did this? He wouldn't know a newscast from a post-hole digger."

"Well, that's Thornton's signature. But it's the consultants."

That really floored me. I had no idea that old Thumbtack had hired consultants to size up our newscasts. The joke in TV news is that consultants are like the thief who steals your watch then tells you what time it is.

"Wait a minute. We never worried about the ratings before. Hell, we're the only goddam station in town."

Hogan sighed. "Fact is, the stations in Champaign and Decatur are getting more of our audience than we are. At least, that's what the research is showing."

That wasn't surprising. Hardly anything important ever happened in Festerwood. If the locals wanted their daily fix of fires and murders, they just tugged their rabbit ears into the right position to pull in stations in bigger cities. The news departments at those stations generally looked upon Festerwood as a suburb of Beirut. In fact, in my memory the only time any reporters from Decatur came to

Festerwood was to interview Dominic Demitri in 1983.

Dominic was a first cousin to Alexis Demitri, dubbed the "Grisly Greek" by the Decatur media after he entered a Beef Whiz fast-food restaurant where his wife worked, brandishing two machine guns and accessorizing with a bandoleer. When he asked where his wife was, a girl at the counter told him she hadn't worked there in over a year. The Grisly Greek opened fire, wounding twenty-three people. He then turned the gun on himself, only to find it was empty. This prompted the cashier to reach into her purse and shoot him dead with one shot from the .38 snub-nosed revolver that she had bought just the day before at the annual police auction. I heard later that when one of the out-of-town reporters asked Dominic whether he was surprised by his cousin's action, he replied, "Nope. Sounds like something ol' Alex would do."

There was an awkward pause as Hogan and I looked out at the chaotic newsroom: photographers bundling into padded vests that looked more like flak jackets, reporters screaming at them to hurry, and interns pouncing on every telephone as if it were a clemency call from the governor. It was frantic and foolish, and I knew Hogan was going to miss it.

"What will you do?" I asked.

"Oh, nothing for a while. Maybe take that PR job at the hospital. Hell, it's not like I haven't been fired before."

"Who's going to replace you?"

"That's the fun part." Hogan feigned a laugh. "I hear they've been talking to some young hot-shot producer from South Bend who walks around with a modem stuck up his ass."

"Why would he want to come here?"

"The scenery. How do I know? Probably wants to make his mark at a small-town station, then move on to something bigger."

I struggled to say something reassuring, but photographer Lowell Loudermilk came to my rescue. Never known for diplomacy when news was in the making, Lowell crashed through the door. "Rick! Come on! Big story at the city garage!"

Lowell might have his faults, but he knew the business; in fact, he was the best photographer we had. "You'll love this. All the snow plows have broken down, and you'll never guess what they're doing!"

I wanted to say that maybe they had an attack of common sense and realized this was no emergency, but I didn't want to spoil Lowell's fun.

"They're mounting the snow blades on garbage trucks! Can you believe it? You know how pissed people will be? Every time the truck clears ten feet of pavement, it'll have to stop to pick up trash. This could take forever!"

The last time I saw Lowell this excited was when he got to the scene of a burglary before the police, and he held the suspect captive in the glare of his portable light. Later, the suspect confessed that he was scared to death because the camera Lowell was holding bore a striking resemblance to a bazooka.

chapter four

"Take Sadler Drive," I told Lowell as we climbed into his Chevy Blazer with WHOE NEWS painted in garish red lettering on the side.

"Why? Hawthorne is faster."

"Because the mayor lives on Sadler, and whose street do you think they're going to plow first?"

Sadler Drive looked as if it had been polished by the melting snow, shiny but free of any accumulation. Lowell turned up the car radio. Aerosmith was wailing "Crazy," a song that would have been unheard-of a few years ago when WHOE-Radio was playing "Classic Country." We didn't talk much, but our minds were both working on the same idea: how to turn this story into the kind of feature that would wind up on a resume tape that would be our ticket out of Festerwood. I had been at WHOE-TV for ten years, the last six of which had been dedicated to a singular goal: finding another job.

Originally I had no intention of pursuing a career in television journalism, which, by WHOE standards, was often a contradiction in terms. But in my sophomore year at Festerwood Community College, I took a course in writing from Foster Labotte, the academic advisor for what passed as the student newspaper. Labotte put me on the paper's staff, which in time led to an interview with the chief editor of the *Festus County Fanfare*.

The editor immediately saw problems with my position. I was the son of Grace Roberson, nicknamed "Amazing Grace" after she somehow was elected to two terms on the Festerwood City Council, as a liberal candidate no less. No one could remember the last time a Democrat, let alone a liberal, had held political office in Festus County. In fact, it was a feat so extraordinary that it was rumored the *McNeil-Lehrer Report* almost covered it. The very prospect of that happening aroused the biblical wrath of the paper's publisher, Erb Hastings, who once was heard to sputter, "No creature plucked from the womb of that crazed council she-Devil, with her hippy-humping notions of halfway houses and abortion clinics, will ever work for this newspaper!"

Anyway, the editor knew that once Erb Hastings found out about my lineage, my chances of keeping a job with his newspaper were about as remote as the *Fanfare* winning a Pulitzer Prize. My application was rejected, and that's all Fred Hogan at WHOE-TV had to hear, since his entire post-newspaper career had been devoted to finding a way to get even for the consequences of his Christmas Eve rewrite.

I was hired immediately and discovered that I actually enjoyed the job. Fred insisted that he was impressed by my no-nonsense writing style, my on-air demeanor and straightforward delivery. And the fact that, as he put it, I was the only applicant he had interviewed who, "Didn't try to sound like goddam David Brinkley."

I soon discovered that Festus County was a smorgasbord of juicy stories. Up until then, I lived on a steady diet of small-town rumors, whispered in school hallways or boasted between innings of sandlot softball games. But now I was discovering that my hometown hid some dark little secrets. I broke the story about Council President Len Triggett, who had invited some Juvenile Center inmates to use a load of surplus gravel to practice their road-paving skills on his driveway. I tried to explain to Councilman Triggett that his insistence that, "Everyone does it!" didn't work for Richard Nixon and it sure as hell wouldn't work for him. Hogan loved that piece, especially since Trigget was a first cousin to Erb Hastings, who refused to run the story in his newspaper.

That led to a vicious campaign of name-calling between the

Fanfare and the TV station, which culminated in a full-page bogus ad in the Sunday edition which read, "WHOE-TV News . . . if it happened in Festus County, it's news to us!" Old man Thornton demanded a retraction, but the newspaper refused. Thornton retaliated by barring the *Fanfare*'s TV critic from the station. Hogan said that was like pulling your foot out of the ocean, since the critic, a Festus Community College drama teacher, almost never wrote about network television or local news, preferring to dwell on PBS documentaries, "because they contain substance." As a result, his was the least-read column in the newspaper.

My job also led to my short-lived marriage to Teri Tremont. She was a striking brunette who worked at Democratic headquarters, a warren of grimy rooms over an abandoned paint store in downtown Festerwood. But it wasn't her politics that attracted me to Teri. Let's just say that the designers of the miniskirt and the no-bra look pretty much had her in mind.

We hit it off one election night when I found her weeping softly in the corner of one of the rooms, with a tattered campaign placard at her feet. The Democratic Party's latest sacrificial lamb had just failed to keep the Republican incumbent, Wiley "Frosty" Foglethorpe, from capturing what had to be his seventy-third consecutive term. Foglethorpe had become so confident of victory that no one in the district had recalled seeing him in public over the past five terms, which is pretty much what his constituents preferred. At any rate, Teri was young and naive and actually thought her candidate had a chance to unseat Foglethorpe. He lost by such a wide margin that the *Fanfare* headline gloated the next morning, "Not since McGovern!"

I sensed that Teri needed a shoulder to cry on, and, as it turns out, a lot more. We wound up in bed an hour later and in church not long after that.

Teri got a job as an assistant public relations manager at Medi-Miracle pharmaceuticals, Festus County's biggest employer. Her timing was terrific, since the pharmaceutical's PR department was expanding as the result of lawsuits over its antidepressant drug, which supposedly caused some patients to grow a sixth toe on their left foot. After just a couple of months, she was promoted to the job of chief administrative assistant to the vice president of sales. I was proud of her instant success, and a bit curious, especially when I saw a blurb in the paper that her boss was being transferred to Muncie to head up a new plant.

That evening, I returned home from work to find her side of the closet liberated of all her clothing. A six pack of Budweiser later, I sat at the kitchen table as Teri explained that we had grown apart.

"Rick," she said, "I'm afraid that it's just not working out. I have an opportunity to advance my career, and I need to move on. It's for the best . . . for both of us."

I drained a lukewarm can and said, "In other words, Teri, you're screwing your boss and he's taking you to Muncie with him."

Teri looked surprised for a moment, then smiled meekly. "Something like that."

For some reason, I thought about Teri as the big, wet flakes of snow vanished on the windshield of Lowell Loudermilk's van. Peter Gabriel was crooning "Love Town" over the car radio and I stared out the window at the flat, featureless countryside as it blurred by. Lowell gunned the van onto a gravel drive toward the city garage.

As it turns out, the snow plow story wasn't worth the effort. Most of the plows were fixed before we got to the garage, so Lowell shot a few pictures and we headed back to the station. I could tell Lowell was upset. In his mind, I think he already had the story on his resume tape and in the mail.

Lowell saw himself as an artist. The rest of the photographers were just "shooters" who aimed their cameras, prayed for focus, and slapped their pictures together just before air time. But Lowell referred to himself as a "photojournalist"—a Picasso in a world of finger painters.

Reporters like me were just along for the ride. We could be useful to lug tripods or act as human microphone stands, but mainly we were accessories. Lowell put up with us only because he had to, and only if we stayed out of his way. Later, as we sat at our computer screens and clicked out our stories, he would stand behind us with a look of pained condescension on his face, emitting huge sighs of disapproval as we labored with our scripts. Once again, he knew he would have to rise above our pedestrian efforts to create a masterpiece of his own. But not this time. This time we had a thirty-second voice-over, a quickie that insulted his talents.

Our return trip took us down County Road 32, better known as the Duckaway Bypass because of its onetime main tenant, the Duckaway Motel, a winsome seven-room unit about three miles west of town. The interstate had long ago diverted all significant traffic from the road, which was now lined with the husks of gas stations and diners.

For a while, the Duckaway survived, mainly because of its lurid reputation. The motel had introduced the concept of "rent-by-the-hour" to Festerwood's rather meager public accommodations. So while businessmen and other travelers chose to spend the night at the Ramada Inn on Interstate 70, anyone with more amorous and less legitimate intentions usually booked a room at the Duckaway.

The hottest rumor making the rounds during my junior year at Festerwood High was that it was the owner of the motel who was responsible for its demise. He supposedly had a long-running affair with an eighteen-year-old maid, and they were discovered by the owner's wife when she walked in on them in Unit Six.

The story goes that his wife was able to share the Kodak moment, because he had forgotten to set the room's alarm clock. She drained her husband's bank account and left him on the verge of bankruptcy. Congressman Frosty Foglethorpe almost came to the rescue with a bill designating the Duckaway as a national historical monument, but when the crucial vote came up in the House, Foglethorpe was on a Foreign Affairs Committee junket, assessing the defense needs of Cancun. As a result, the Duckaway became just another in a long line of vacant buildings along the old two-lane highway.

"So, how was the intern?" Lowell asked with a smug look on his face.

"What do you mean?"

"You know. The intern—Karen."

"It's Carol. I mean, I think her name is Carol."

"Right. You were all over her like a dollar mop."

"Well, I was a little shit-faced, you know."

"So, how was she?" Lowell was having a really good time now.

"How the hell do I know? I drove her home after the party."

Lowell let out this obnoxious laugh. "Sure you did." Then he got serious, which was worse. "Listen, Rick, what you do is your business, but don't shit where you eat."

I thought that was a lovely metaphor. "I have no idea what you're talking about. I took the girl home and maybe I kissed her good night. I don't remember."

"She does."

"What's that supposed to mean?" Of course, I knew what that meant.

Lowell gave me one of his looks of self-righteous pity. "Never mind. It doesn't matter."

I sat upright. "Yeah, it matters. What did she say?"

"She said you're hung like a moose. Or was it a mouse? I forget exactly."

"That's an old joke. And besides, fuck you."

Lowell pulled into the station parking lot, and we started to unload the gear.

chapter five

ROLLIE WATSON WAS BESIDE HIMSELF AS HE PACED IN FRONT OF HIS WEA-
ther map. "Can you believe it? They called me in for *this*? I get more
snow on my TV at home!"

Rollie's forecasts might be hit-or-miss, but he was certain of one
thing: the people in the newsroom were hopeless fools when it came
to the weather. On slow news days, which were almost every day in
Festerwood, we pestered Rollie for long-range forecasts and projected
snow depths in hopes of contriving a weather emergency of some
sort. He winced every time a reporter entered his private domain.
This time, Rollie was frowning as he held a huge cutout snowflake
over the weather map, in the general vicinity of Indiana.

"Think this is too big?"

"No, Rollie. It's just right." I was in Rollie's weather station
looking for a story idea, something offbeat that I could turn into a
warm and fuzzy feature for my resume tape. But I could see Rollie
was going to be of no help. He considered the weather to be his prov-
ince, and I was just another newsroom poacher.

It was Merle Teel, the station manager, who was responsible for
hiring Rollie. Merle had attended one of those station manager conventions in Chicago. While dressing for dinner one night, he
watched the news on his hotel room TV and became fascinated by a
local weatherman. The weatherman was a folksy, balding, paunchy
personality with the memorable name of P. J. Hoff. His gimmick was

cartoons. Hoff had a cartoon symbol for everything: the sun, the rain, the clouds, the wind; and he had a character called "The Vice President in Charge of Looking Out the Window." Merle knew he couldn't lure P. J. Hoff from Chicago to Festerwood, but why not a local version?

Television station managers had a habit of doing this during out-of-town conventions. It usually happened after a night of drinking in some hotel bar. A small-town station manager—a guy who was raised as a salesman—suddenly becomes a talent scout. Watching a local newscast through bleary eyes, the manager will turn to his program director on the bar stool next to him and slur, "Hey, we oughtta do that!" The fact that it costs three hundred thousand dollars to do that in Chicago only becomes clear the next morning, but by then the Merle Teels of the world are on a crusade, dashing back to their stations with their latest burst of inspiration. And that's how WHOE came to hire Rollie Watson, who was working at the time as the political cartoonist for the *Festus County Fanfare*.

The fact that Rollie didn't know a cold front from a cold sore didn't matter. He could draw. And he was folksy. In fact, his overall appearance suggested to some viewers that Rollie must know something about the weather, because he dressed like a flood victim. At any rate, he was a huge success for a while, with his stick-on cartoon characters with names like Soggy Sam, Solar Sollie, Cloudy Cletus, and Freddie the Funnel. Actually, Freddie the Funnel didn't quite work out, since people in western Indiana have reason to take their tornado warnings seriously.

In time, Rollie learned enough about the weather to get by, but not without an occasional setback. I was on duty the night that Rollie was anxious to get home early for his daughter's twelfth birthday. Since it was a cool, pleasant April evening and the weather maps indicated no advancing fronts, Rollie decided to tape the forecast.

Leon, the producer, warned him not to, but Rollie insisted, bribing him with passes to the upcoming auto show, which Rollie had been given after he shamelessly plugged the event on camera:

"Tomorrow looks like a lovely day, a good day to take that new Ford Taurus out for a spin." Stuff like that. Anyway, Leon relented, and Rollie taped his forecast, calling for clear skies and mild temperatures, with Solar Sollie getting prominent exposure.

That night, as Rollie was capturing his daughter's birthday on home video, a freak storm swung up from the south and clobbered western Indiana. The Happy Trails Mobile Home Park on State Road 234 got the worst of it, with stunned survivors stammering into the camera, "Sounded just like a freight train, swear to God."

Rollie damn near lost his job after that one, but he saved it with an on-air performance that can only be called a masterpiece. With his magic marker, Rollie turned Solar Sollie's grin into a huge frown, and as Sollie and Rollie looked at the camera, he said, "Folks, we let you down this time. Maybe it's time for us to go. Sollie, start packing." And with that he walked off the set, leaving the audience in tears and the producer in a rage since Rollie had two more minutes to fill.

Of course the good people of Festerwood—while angry that Rollie hadn't seen a tornado coming—were still forgiving folks; they wrote and called in to plead with Rollie to stay. It was an apocalyptic moment in his career. From that point on, Rollie was a changed man. He took a course in meteorology at Festerwood Community College, even earned his American Meteorological Society Seal of Approval. Rollie hung on to a few of his cartoon friends, such as Sissy Snowflake, but from that point on he was a serious weatherman. And that explains why Rollie Watson was so upset on this day when the great November flurries struck Festerwood.

The phone was ringing when I got back to my desk. I ignored it at first, but it was too late for another bogus school-closing call, so I picked up. It wasn't the call that would lead me to Nutsy Fagan's house as designated hostage negotiator; that would come later, in a much more dramatic form. This was another crisis.

"Roberson, news."

There was a slight pause, then a hushed gravel voice at the other end. "You don't know me. But listen carefully. I got a tip for you."

Great. Just what I needed. A call from Festerwood's roadshow version of *Deep Throat*. But instinctively, I grabbed a pencil.

"Shoot."

"Check out a woman named Norma Flescher. Find out why she's been fired from her city job. There's something rotten going on. That's all I can tell you. She's in the book." Click.

Leon, the producer, shouted from across the room, "Rick! We need a thirty-second voice-over on the snow plows for the noon show."

"Right. I'm on it." Actually, I was having a private conversation with myself. *What the hell do you suppose that was all about?* Some disgruntled city employee trying to get even, I suppose. Still, on a slow day . . . even better, a story of corruption at city hall would look great on a resume tape. Every big city news director could identify with that. Maybe this caller had just punched my ticket out of here.

I looked through the phone book. *Farley . . . Fleenor . . .* there it was—*Flescher.* There was only one in the book. N. Flescher, 1235 Grant Street. I dialed the number.

A woman answered, "Hello, Flescher residence."

"Is this Norma Flescher?"

"Yes, who's calling?"

"Mrs. Flescher, my name is Rick Roberson. I'm a reporter for WHOE-TV."

A long pause. Her voice was thin, suspicious. "What can I do for you, Mr. Robertson?"

"It's Roberson. No 'T.' Uh . . . Mrs. Flescher, I understand you've lost your job at city hall."

"Who told you that?"

"Well, anything at city hall is a matter of public record, so it wasn't difficult—"

She cut me off. "I don't know where you're getting your information, Mr. Roberson, but I have been happily employed by the city for five years."

"Well, we have it on very good authority that you are being let go, and let me just add that we think the reasons for your department's actions are questionable, at best." I was good at this.

Her tone changed. "Mr. Roberson, I'm sorry, but you are wrong. I have had nothing but praise from the Purchasing Department for the job I've done. I was even Employee of the Month last year."

Well, that was a start, at least. "Exactly. And that's why we're as baffled as anyone. Does someone at purchasing have it in for you?"

Now she was angry. "I said, *I have not been fired!* Now, I'm afraid I have other things to do, so—"

"Mrs. Flescher, just let me ask you this. Why aren't you at work today?"

Another pause. "Well, if you must know, my boss called and said I wasn't needed today because of the storm. They're only working a half day."

Right. The storm. I guess two inches of snow would play havoc with city purchasing procedures. "Mrs. Flescher, let me just say if you need to talk with someone about this, you can reach me here at the station anytime—"

"Good-bye, Mr. Roberson."

It took forever for someone to answer the phone at city hall.

"Purchasing office, Sinclair speaking." A woman's voice, very officious.

"Hello, could I speak with Mr. Tyler, please?" Tad Tyler was in charge of the Festerwood Purchasing Department. I looked it up.

"Uh . . . could I say who's calling?"

"Yeah. Just tell him it's a call concerning Norma Flescher. He'll know what it's about."

A lengthy pause, then the voice of someone with a very serious nasal condition. "Tad Tyler speaking."

"Mr. Tyler, this is Rick Roberson with WHOE News. I'm calling about the Norma Flescher case. Can you tell me why she's been terminated?"

"Well, Mr. Roberson, Norma hasn't exactly been terminated.

She is on extended leave. We've been forced to make some cuts in our office staff, and Norma has less seniority than some of the other employees."

"I see. Funny thing is, Norma doesn't seem to know anything about this. I just talked with her."

There was a rustling sound at the other end, like someone fumbling with a receiver. "Well, we haven't had time to notify everyone yet. Norma will be informed of her situation when she arrives for work tomorrow. But I'm afraid I just can't elaborate. We have to cut back our staff, and unfortunately, Norma is on the list. Now, I really have to go." Click.

I had been hung up on twice in one morning. That was a new record, even for me. I started to redial Norma Flescher's number when the receptionist buzzed me.

"Rick, there's someone in the lobby to see you. And before you say it—no, I can't get rid of her. It's Clare Middleton."

chapter six

CLARE MIDDLETON WAS THE SELF-APPOINTED FESTERWOOD HISTORIAN, who pestered every reporter in town with her endless campaigns to turn eyesores into landmarks. She would take root in the lobby if I didn't show up.

Clare had been armed and ready. She was a large woman dressed in a gray suit and tie—all business from her wire-rimmed spectacles to her sensible shoes.

"Rick Roberson! I have a bone to pick with you!" Clare wasn't much for formalities. "You didn't return any of my calls last week, young man!" By now she had planted her considerable bulk between me and my only escape route to the newsroom.

"Sorry, Clare, but I was tied up—"

"Well, you can't escape me now! Just what are we going to do about our Dairy Maid?"

Dairy Maid, a dilapidated remnant from the fifties, was a boarded-up shack with broken windows on an apron of crumbling concrete. A ten-foot plastic ice-cream cone still teetered on a rusty pole fixed to the roof, just enough of it left to tell passersby that here once stood a really ugly drive-in restaurant. It was Clare's latest project to restore the building as an example of what she called "fifties roadside architecture." About the only historic value of the Dairy

Maid was how many postgame brawls occurred in its poorly lit parking lot.

"Tell you what, Clare," I said, "I have an important meeting right now, but I promise to call you when I get back to the office."

"Well, see that you do. I won't be given the runaround. We've already lost dear Colonel Festus."

She was referring to a statue in the city park. It was a hideous likeness of "Colonel" Grover Festus—the nineteenth-century farmer, trader, and liquor distributor—dressed in the uniform of the Union Army of the Civil War. His father was presumed to be the founder of Festerwood and the county that bore his name. Only much later did a twelve-year-old student at Festerwood Middle School, while researching the Festus family tree for a school essay, fail to find the name of any colonel named "Festus" on any of the lists of Indiana regiments in the Civil War. In fact, any letters he came upon suggested that if "Colonel" Festus thought about the war at all, his sentiments leaned decidedly toward the South.

Civic leaders tried to ignore the controversy, but the damn kid won the essay contest, and Paul Harvey picked up on the story. By then it was too late. Clare fought hard to save it, but on a somber morning in the late eighties, the statue of "Colonel" Grover Festus, discolored by pigeons and disfigured by local hooligans, was unceremoniously removed from the park.

A note was waiting for me when I returned to my desk. It was scribbled on one of those "while you were out" pads. *Norma Flescher called. Meet her at Dirkie's. One o'clock.* I recognized the handwriting.

"Rip 'n' Read" Morris was dozing at his desk, oblivious to the police radio chatter just a few feet away. Morris Chiles was our early morning and noon news anchorman, who earned his nickname at WHOE-Radio—his idea of "hands-on" journalism was to tear wire-service stories off the news printer and read them on the air, as is. This was probably wise in his case, since the one time Morris tried to inflict his own writing skills on a news story, it ended in disaster.

There had been a messy pileup on the interstate involving three cars and a semi. Three victims were rushed to the hospital, one in extremely critical condition. Not critical enough for Morris, however, who informed the radio audience that the motorist was "all but dead."

Not long after that, Morris switched over to television when it was learned he met two crucial job requirements: he worked cheap and he was the only reporter in town who would work the 5:00 A.M. shift. As a result, he was perpetually tired, with a permanent case of morning hair—the color of graying straw—which framed a wrinkled, baggy face.

I dialed his extension and did my best Fred Hogan impersonation. "Chiles, goddammit, get to work!" Morris spun around in his chair, and, for one delicious nanosecond, there was sheer panic in his eyes. Then he saw me hanging up the phone.

"Roberson, you're an asshole."

"I know. But the only difference between you and me is, I have to work at it. Hey, this note from Norma Flescher. When did she call?"

"I don't know. I sort of drifted off. Maybe ten minutes ago."

So, Norma was having second thoughts. Maybe there was something to this, after all. I walked into an editing bay where Lowell Loudermilk was in a frenzy, pushing buttons and turning dials as pictures whizzed by on the screen in front of him. He didn't look up.

"You write this snow plow story yet?"

"No, I was kind of waiting for inspiration."

He shook his head. "Right. Well, here's some inspiration for you. They're leading the noon news with this piece of shit."

"You've got to be kidding."

"I don't kid when it comes to bone-headed calls by the producer. Here, look at this."

He punched a button, and an image flickered on the screen. It was a low-level dead-on shot of a snow plow, its menacing blade approaching the camera like some mammoth creature. Suddenly, just as it looks like the blade will devour everything in its path, including the viewer, the camera tilts up to reveal the driver waving from the cab as the plow glides by. Lowell had done it. He had taken a worthless snow plow story and created art. Obviously, he wanted me to tell him that, so I did.

"Great stuff, Lowell."

"Well, it'll kill thirty seconds. The way I see it, you could just let the natural sound tell the story for this shot, then the anchor could start the narration right—"

"Sure, whatever you say. But listen, I need you to shoot something for me in about an hour. Some undercover stuff."

I knew that would get his attention. Lowell always talked about hidden camera stuff, or "Gotcha" stories as we call them, but he never could find anything in Festerwood worth the effort. For the first time, he turned from his work and looked at me.

"Really? What's up?"

I explained the Norma Flescher story and the fact that I had just received a call from her. "I figure she had second thoughts, so she called her office and found out she was being laid off. Now she wants to spill the beans."

"What beans? They're cutting back on staff."

"That's what they say. But how do you explain that *Deep Throat* call? Norma knows something, and she's being cut loose before she can talk."

"Well . . . maybe." I could tell I almost had Lowell's full attention. In his mind, he was already measuring his living room wall for a SPAM. That was the unfortunate nickname given to the State Photographer's Association Award of Merit. To the general public, the award meant nothing, but to a local television photographer, it was the Holy Grail. It meant that your peers recognized your abilities, but more importantly, it looked great on a resume.

Then I sprung my idea. "I'll call her back right now, and I'll set up a time to meet at Dirkie's . . . say, an hour . . . but you'll already be there, camped out across the street, with that new long-range lens on your camera." Lowell was looking positively transfixed. "You'll shoot the whole thing—me walking into the restaurant, sitting down, talking to her—and I'll be wearing a wireless mike. We'll get the whole thing on tape!"

There was a moment's pause. "What whole thing?"

"Everything! Why she was being laid off, what they're afraid she'll tell, who's behind this—"

"Wait a minute. You don't know jack shit about any of that. For all you know, she did a rotten job and happened to be expendable. You don't—"

"That's what we're going to find out! Believe me, she wouldn't want to meet if there wasn't something wrong. Trust me on this. This could be your ticket out of here."

That was my final card, and it worked. "OK, I'll just take my lunch hour then, so nobody around here will get wind of this. Oh, and be sure you're wired up before you leave."

chapter seven

THE LUNCH TIME CROWD AT DIRKIE'S WAS THINNING OUT AS I PULLED
into the parking lot and found a place at the rear of the building.
Dirkie's was Festerwood's fine dining establishment, which sought to
emulate Denny's by staying open round the clock and featuring lami-
nated menus with color-enhanced pictures of the cuisine. Dirkie's
was the traditional place for Sunday after-church brunches. Our family was no exception. Dirkie's was our regular stop after Sunday
morning mass; my older sister and I would devour our standard order
of buttermilk pancakes and link sausages. My sister eventually married and moved out of town, but when she visited with her family, a
trip to Dirkie's was considered mandatory.

The owners did try to make the surroundings as pleasant as they
could. There were green-checkered cafe curtains on the windows and
several potted plants . . . and clean restrooms. In fact, Dirkie's was the
only place in town that folks felt they could comfortably take visiting
relatives for all three meals.

By now Festerwood's fearsome snowstorm had disintegrated
into a steady, cold rain. I looked across the street and saw Lowell
Loudermilk's maroon Ford Tempo parked at a slight angle to the
restaurant's front door. We agreed he should drive his personal car so
as not to attract attention. I gave him a feeble wave and patted my
coat pocket to indicate I was miked.

I walked into a wave of stifling heat. For some reason, Dirkie's
management always set the thermostat at around ninety degrees. The
ladies from the Glory Bee Baptist Church Circle liked it that way,

and since they held their weekly Bible-study classes in Dirkie's ban-quet room, they pretty much had the run of the place.

There were six booths near the window. The first was unoccu-pied, but in the second I could see a bubble of blond hair rising above the seat back. I switched on the battery pack in my pocket and walked over. This must be Norma Flescher, I thought, but she was definitely not what I expected. I looked down to see a lovely, porce-lain-faced woman with impeccable makeup and a crown of flaxen hair that gave her an almost angelic appearance. Turns out that wasn't far from wrong.

"May I help you?" Her voice was soft, almost breathless.

"Uh . . . well, I think so. I'm Rick Roberson."

"Of course you are! Rick Roberson from the television!" Sud-denly she was animated, almost flustered. "Oh, I watch your news every night. Won't you join me?"

I had the feeling that I was sliding into the wrong booth, but it's not often that a beautiful young woman turns up in Festerwood, let alone one who is so eager to talk. Norma could wait a minute.

She held out a small, pale hand. "I'm Dawn Rae Hargis. We just moved here from Vevay."

"Nice to meet you, Dawn Rae. You say *we*. You mean you and your husband?"

"Oh, heavens no!" She giggled. "I'm not married. My father is the Reverend Billy Joe Hargis, the new pastor of the Festus Friends in Faith Tabernacle. You may have heard of it."

Friends in Faith was, in fact, one of the Sunday morning staples of WHOE-TV. For years, as I was growing up, the tabernacle pre-sented an excruciating half-hour program presided over by the Rever-end Floyd Fernicutt. On most Sundays, Reverend Fernicutt would just read from the Bible and sermonize; but occasionally, to spice things up, he'd invite other local clerics for a spirited round-table dis-cussion.

Father Blaise Malloy of St. Boniface Catholic Church was a regular guest until he and Reverend Fernicutt got into a heated exchange over the infallibility of the Pope. Father Malloy soon was replaced by the Reverend Claude Chastain of Glory Bee Baptist Church, who was more in tune with Reverend Fernicutt's fundamental religious beliefs. The program actually had a zero rating, a television phenomenon when you consider that some TV sets are turned on just for background noise on Sunday morning. But the Festus Friends in Faith Tabernacle had deep pockets, and its weekly check to the station guaranteed the tabernacle's television survival.

"Of course I've heard of it! Friends in Faith is a landmark in Festus County! It also sponsors one of our most popular Sunday morning programs." I couldn't help myself. She was absolutely gorgeous, and though her blouse was buttoned to the neck, it left almost nothing to the imagination.

"Oh, that's one of the reasons Daddy wanted to transfer here." She paused and lowered her eyes. "I don't mean he wanted to take advantage of what happened to the former minister, the poor man."

Dawn Rae was referring to the fact that Reverend Fernicutt's devotion was not limited to his church. He also developed a devout interest in Myrna Templey, the loyal church secretary who returned Reverend Fernicutt's affection with unusual zeal. That is, until they were caught in a compromising position by one of the women who arrived early to pass out the hymnals for a Wednesday night service. The resulting scandal—and the fact that the good Reverend and Miss Templey were found in the choir loft—led to a lot of newsroom jokes about how Reverend Fernicutt was finally caught by his own organ.

Dawn Rae looked up, her dewy eyes brimming with sincerity. "Daddy wants to start with a clean slate. He says whatever happened is in the past, and now is the time for forgiveness and healing. What do you think, Mr. Roberson?"

"Absolutely. Your father is right."

There was an awkward pause, but Frieda came to my rescue. She was a career waitress at Dirkie's, with the faded uniform and look of perpetual exhaustion to prove it.

"You want lunch, Rick?"

"No, Frieda, thanks." I looked back at Dawn Rae, who was picking at a pasta salad. "Listen, I need to talk with someone about a story, but I sure would like to continue our conversation some time."

"I'd love that, Mr. Roberson."

"It's Rick. Call me Rick."

"OK, Rick. Call me at the church when you can. I don't have many friends in Festerwood. Maybe you could show me around." She held out her hand and I caught a faint whiff of perfume. I was about to fall in love.

"I'd consider that a pleasure." I scooted out of the seat and continued my quest for Norma Flescher.

There were three more booths in the row—two of them vacant, the other occupied by a uniformed delivery-truck driver who was nursing a cup of coffee and exhaling a cloud of cigarette smoke. Norma was sitting in the last booth, scrunched down in her seat and hiding behind an enormous pair of sunglasses.

"Norma Flescher?" I startled her with my question.

"Yes, I'm Norma Flescher. Sit down, Mr. Roberson, I don't want to attract any attention."

As I resisted the urge to tell her that wearing sunglasses during a November snow shower might do just that, I slid into the seat opposite her and looked across the table at the small, frail woman bundled in an oversized stadium coat. There was a hood covering her head and a scarf wound tightly at her neck. She looked extremely uncomfortable.

Her hands fidgeted with a paper napkin. "Mr. Roberson," she began nervously. "I feel I must apologize to you. After you called, I checked with my office and was told that I was being laid off due to staff cutbacks. They said they were going to tell me tomorrow morning, but that some newspaperman called and seemed to know all about it."

That figures. The newspaper guys get all the credit, even when we get wind of the story.

"So that's all? No other explanation?"

"Oh, I didn't need one. I know what's up over there." Norma was suddenly becoming very agitated. I reached into my coat pocket to make sure the wireless microphone was still on.

I tried to sound nonchalant, as if I heard this sort of thing every day. "So, exactly what is going on?"

"You wouldn't believe it if I told you."

"You might be surprised, Norma," I said a little too quickly. "In my business, you hear a lot of things." For a moment there, I thought I sounded just like Dustin Hoffman in *All the President's Men.*

She lowered her voice. "Have you ever heard of paying one hundred thousand dollars for two thousand tons of street salt?"

I tried to sound impressed. "Really. Who did that?"

"You did. And I did—all the taxpayers of Festus County. That's what the purchasing department paid for its supply of salt for the roads this winter. Can you imagine that?"

I couldn't. "Norma, you'll have to forgive me, but I'm not exactly up to speed on the going price of road salt. Is that a lot?"

She looked around the restaurant, then leaned forward and whispered, "It's almost twice what it should be."

"Whew. You mean the county is paying one hundred thousand dollars for salt that should be only about fifty thousand?"

"That's exactly what I mean. And they've been getting away with it for years."

She definitely had my attention now. "Who has? I mean, somebody must be getting a hell of a kickback—"

"Not just somebody," she interrupted. "Tad Tyler."

I blurted out, "Tyler? The head of the department?"

Norma made a face. "Shhh . . . we don't want everyone in this place to hear us." She sighed deeply, then leaned forward again. "Tad Tyler's brother-in-law runs the company that sells road supplies to the county. There's no bidding for the contract. Tyler just sends him the money every winter and he sends the salt. I found out about it a few years ago, and now they're afraid I know too much and might blow the whistle on them."

"A few years ago? What took you so long?"

Even the sunglasses couldn't hide her embarrassment. Norma paused and the words came slowly. "Because Tad Tyler and I were . . . having a relationship."

"But you're not anymore?"

"No. Something happened. Tad is a married man, and his wife was getting suspicious. At least, that's what he said."

"But you didn't believe him?"

Now her voice was shaking. "I did at first. But later I found out that Tad Tyler carries on all the time. I was just one of his girls."

For some reason, I had a hard time picturing the man on the phone with the Mr. Peepers voice as a regular Lothario.

"So now you want to get even, is that it?"

"I suppose I do, in a way. Wouldn't you?" There was irritation in her voice. "I mean, I know too much about everything—the salt, the kickbacks, and Tad's personal life. I had to go. I suspected they were up to something, but I didn't know for certain until you called."

I looked out the window at the rain slanting across the parking lot. The wind had picked up, and the early afternoon sky was almost black with clouds. I thought we might have to make some radical changes in our snow story. A headline popped into my head: "Freak November tornado rips Festus County." I was always thinking in terms of headlines. It was an occupational quirk. I even had one figured out for my own death. I would be a passenger on a plane that crashed while carrying 134 persons, including one prominent passenger. The headline would read, "Quentin Tarantino, 133 others perish in plane crash."

"Mr. Roberson? Did you hear me?"

"Oh, yes . . . I'm sorry, Norma. Tell you what—I think you have a hell of a story here. I'd like you to go on camera with it."

"Oh no, I can't do that! I just wanted you to know what's going on and maybe you could put it in the paper or something . . . you know how you do, quoting 'anonymous sources.' "

"Norma, I work for a television station, not the newspaper. We depend on pictures for our stories. Without you telling your story to the camera, we have nothing to go on."

I didn't tell her about the microphone under my tie or Lowell's camera trained on her from across the street. That could come later. Right now I needed her cooperation.

She sighed. "Well, let me think about it. I guess I have nothing to lose but my job. And I've already lost that."

I asked Norma to gather whatever evidence she could—billing and shipping slips, correspondence, and any other relative records—and to make copies for me. She was crying softly now, and I sensed it was time to go.

"Norma, you'll be glad you did this. So will the taxpayers of Festus County." I shook her hand and was surprised by the firmness of her grip. "I'll call you tomorrow. Any news before then, and you know where to reach me. Take care."

chapter eight

THE REST OF THE DAY WAS PRETTY ROUTINE. OF COURSE, WE LED OUR five o'clock newscast with the non-story about the storm that never was, thanks to a shameless spin by Leon, the producer, who wrote the honest-to-God following lead: "Good evening, Festerwood. And congratulations. You have just dodged a bullet from nature's icy arsenal." Jerry loved theme shows, and it was obvious that his theme tonight was "Festerwood Goes to War!"

Evening anchorman Clayton Bodine continued, "A monstrous winter storm that closed schools and stranded motorists just west of here suddenly aimed its big guns to the north, and we caught only the ricochet. But don't say we weren't ready!"

At this point Lowell's "Here Comes the Snow Plow!" video came up on the screen, looking even more menacing than it did in the editing room. Bodine lowered his voice to its most euphonious range, and intoned, "All across Festus County, a small army of men— and women—" (he put added emphasis on mentioning women, ever since the Festus County NOW chapter threatened to sue the station over our use of words such as *mankind* and *firemen* instead of the more politically correct versions) ". . . mustered their strength to turn back the first assault wave, clearing streets for rush-hour motorists and school bus drivers. Finally, when the smoke had cleared, it was obvious that nature wouldn't trifle with us on this day. But just in case it had been worse, here's Rollie to tell us just how much snow we would have received."

My total contribution to the newscast was a short script to cover Lowell's snow plow footage, and a rewrite of the same story for the evening news. That bothered Karen Armstrong, a feisty little reporter who was the unofficial conscience of the newsroom.

"Worked your ass off, I see," she hissed. Karen was in a constant state of agitation, probably due to the fact that she couldn't quite believe that a woman with all her talent would be forced to work side-by-side with such incompetents.

"Yeah, Karen, I worked my ass off. I'm afraid there's not much left for you."

She was looking for something on her desk, but kept talking. "You missed the fireworks. Big Bob finally got into it with Leon."

"No! You're kidding me!" I had been waiting for months to see this happen, and I missed it.

Leon Heifitz was a scrawny little guy who produced the five o'clock news. He knew nothing about sports and generally looked on that segment of the newscast as three minutes of dead air. Bob Berlinski was the station's sports director, whose main qualification for the job was the fact that he was the starting center on the Festerwood High School basketball team for three years, leading the conference in personal fouls and attempted slam dunks.

He had been in insurance for several years, but when the sportscasting job opened up and no one in an eight-state area applied for it, someone suggested Big Bob during a sales meeting at the Ramada Inn bar. It turns out Big Bob had a deep, booming voice and a golly-whiz style that endeared him to Festerwood sports fans, even though he couldn't get through three words without tripping over the fourth. But he had enthusiasm, a local following, and a crew cut. What he didn't have was a clue about broadcasting, especially how to produce a three-minute sports segment that ran three minutes. His constant overruns drove Leon into apoplectic fits, and their post-newscast confrontations were legendary.

There was Big Bob Berlinski, all six feet and six inches of him—with his prodigious potbelly that put him roughly one hundred pounds over his playing weight, and his ruddy face bathed in sweat—looming over poor little Leon. But despite the difference in stature, Leon, with his thinning red hair and the enormous spectacles riding on his freckled nose, held his ground as he waved a bony finger in Big Bob's face and shouted, "If you can't time your show, then find someone who can!"

Big Bob always backed down, but we knew it was just a matter of time until he exploded. The time finally arrived, and I'd missed it.

"So, what happened? Tell me!"

Freddie Klinger, the tape editor, was only too willing. Freddie was almost as frail as Leon and had almost as much contempt for sports. But news producers and video tape editors almost never get along, so Freddie was anxious to unload the details.

Freddie rolled his chair out of an editing booth and was already into his story before he glided to a stop.

"This is great! Old Bob had this interview with Red Springer—you know, the high-school basketball coach. Red's team is off to a lousy start this season, so old Bob wanted to know why. Well . . ." Freddie gulped another breath. He was really into this. "Old Bob does the interview and rushes back here to get it on the air. Meantime, Sandy Kellerman is over at the Festus County Board of Health building, getting this interview for her medical series. Both interviews are coming back late, and, as usual, Leon is about to stroke out. But there's no sweat; we get both interviews edited—only Leon gets them mixed up when he takes them upstairs to the control room!"

By now, Freddie was about to come up out of his chair with excitement. "So Big Bob goes on with the basketball story, and he's saying, 'The Festerwood Wildcats are off to a disappointing start this season, having lost their first three games. In an exclusive interview . . .' You know, he's always saying shit like that. Anyway, he says, 'In an exclusive interview, I asked Coach Springer if he could give me some reasons for his team's poor showing.'"

Freddie waited a beat for dramatic emphasis, then said, "So the tape comes up on the air, and this guy in a white coat is saying, 'The sad fact is, herpes is up twenty percent and there is an alarming increase in the rate of gonorrhea.'"

Now Freddie lost it completely; he was laughing hysterically. "Can you believe it? The director panics and punches Bob back on the air and he's looking like a suicide waiting to happen! And you know how old Bob couldn't ad lib his way out of a phone booth. So he just sits there staring at the camera with this shit-eating grin on his face and says, 'We'll have more sports in a moment.'"

Freddie was out of his chair and staggering around the room in fits of uncontrollable laughter, screaming, "Isn't that great? And the best part . . ." Freddie found a chair and collapsed into it. "And the best part is, the coach saw the interview and called in to raise hell with Bob! Old Bob is taking all this shit from the coach over the phone and it's really Leon's fault!"

Karen finally interrupted. "Anyway, Bob had it out with Leon right after the show, telling him that he's just produced his last newscast, that tomorrow he's going to tell Hogan to fire him. Leon starts to give him some lip and Bob pushes him against the desk holding the police radios. The radios go flying across the room, breaking into about a million pieces, which means now Leon is in deep shit, 'cause screwing up a newscast is one thing, but costing the station money is something else."

I sighed. "You didn't get it on tape, did you?"

It was mid-afternoon and, by now, Lowell should have returned from Dirkie's with his pictures. I was about to call him on the two-way when I looked up to see the one thing no reporter ever wants to see: the sight of a forlorn photographer shuffling into the newsroom, muttering to himself.

"Lowell, what's the matter?"

"No sound. No fucking sound."

"You've got to be kidding."

Lowell flourished a plastic tape box. "Do you want to see this for yourself? I checked it when I got back, and I just double-checked in master control. There's no audio. Nothing. I thought we might be having problems, but I figured my audio gauges weren't working. Goddam wireless mike."

I sank into the nearest seat. My mind was racing. "Well, you got the pictures, right?"

"Yeah, I got the pictures. They're beautiful. But you can't hear a goddam thing."

When you work for a second-rate television station in a third-rate town, you learn to live with failure. In fact, you take pride in how creative you can be in such situations, since they happen all the time. When they hand out those television news awards, there should be a category titled "BSS" for "Best Shit Saved."

"No problem, we can save this," I said. "We have the pictures; we have Norma on camera; and I can paraphrase what she said if I have to. Besides, she may agree to go on camera anyway, so this stuff would just be for theatrical effect. Don't worry."

Lowell wasn't buying it, of course, since now we would have to depend as much on my reporter's skills to tell the story as his artful camera work. "I don't know, Rick. Maybe you should set up another meeting and we could do this right."

"Sure, that's the ticket. This time we'll bring along a stick mike with a big WHOE flag on it, and I can set it up on the table in front of her and ask her to speak slowly and distinctly. You know we can't re-do this. She's scared out of her mind the way it is. Our best bet is to try to win her confidence and get her to talk straight on. If that doesn't work, we always have your pictures and what I remember of our conversation."

Lowell just sighed. "OK, do what you want."

chapter nine

HOGAN'S OFFICE DOOR WAS AJAR, SO I LOOKED IN. HE WAS ON THE phone but motioned me inside.

"Yes, I understand," he was telling the caller, "we certainly did not intend to embarrass you in any way. It was just one of those regrettable mistakes."

Hogan's eyes rolled toward the ceiling as he waved me into a chair. "I sure will . . . yes . . . yes . . . I will, as soon as he gets in. And, again, please accept our apologies. Thank you for calling, Councilman."

Hogan hung up and sighed. "Just what I need today. That was Cecil Dennison, the town council president, and he's all pissed off about that graphic we ran last night."

"What graphic? He didn't make any news last night."

Hogan snapped, "No, he didn't. The story was about that serial killer in Nebraska being caught . . . you know, what's his name?"

"You mean Rabid Robert Dennison?"

"Yeah, that one. Only our producer got confused and guess whose picture we ran instead?"

"Don't tell me . . ."

"Right. There's the smiling face of Cecil Dennison looming over the anchorman's shoulder as he's talking about this crazy son of a bitch who killed eight people."

I knew Hogan was seething, but I couldn't help but laugh. "Jesus . . . that could be the best publicity old Cecil's had in some time."

Hogan shot me a look. "This may be funny to you, but you don't have to answer my phone. Anyway, I got other things on my mind."

Hogan sank into his chair and said, "Close the door."

There was always something chilling and ominous when Hogan told you to close the door. Usually he had an open-door policy so he could keep better tabs on the chaos in the newsroom, and to encourage anyone with a beef to come in and talk it out. Television news people are all a little neurotic, so Hogan spent most of his time listening to personal problems and complaints. After a while he started calling his office "the whinery."

But when he told you to close the door, then you knew there was trouble afoot. The last time anyone could remember a closed-door session in Hogan's office was several months ago, when he called one of the producers in to raise hell for missing the story of Ferdie Taylor's resignation. Taylor was the Festus County school board president who was stopped for drunk driving while en route to a school-board meeting.

This hadn't been the first of such incidents, but Taylor suffered a sudden attack of conscience on this occasion. Later, he showed up at the board meeting looking a bit disheveled, with fingerprint ink still on his hands. At the conclusion of the meeting, he made the stunning announcement that he was stepping down after fifteen years on the board to spend more time with his wife and kids. The fact that his kids were all grown and had moved out of state didn't seem to matter.

What did matter, as far as Hogan was concerned, is that somebody in the newsroom decided the board meeting would be another snoozer, and so no reporter was assigned to cover it. Hogan first heard the news of Taylor's resignation on the radio. But it hurt worse when he saw it on the front page of his daughter's school newspaper, but not a word on WHOE's ten o'clock news.

I shut the door and turned to look at Hogan; he was slouched in his chair. "It just gets worse." He seemed to be talking to no one in particular.

"What do you mean? They aren't even going to give you severance pay?"

"No, not that," Hogan said. "It gets worse for you and everyone else who will still be working here. I found out who hired the consultant. It wasn't old man Thornton."

"Then who? Not Bailey Thornton?" Bailey was the firstborn son of C. T. and Monica Thornton, a logical choice to take over the family business, since he was the current president and CEO of Hearth and Home, a hardware store chain in Michigan. The only trouble was, C. T. and his oldest son hadn't spoken in several years—ever since Bailey founded CANT, or "Christians Against Network Television," an activist group convinced that commercial television was the Devil's electronic workshop.

Hogan sighed. "No, not Bailey. Somebody further down the Thornton food chain."

Well, it couldn't be Denise, their second child who was back home for the third time after turning the hat trick in divorce court. That left . . .

"Not Looney Larry!"

Hogan grinned. "You're getting very perceptive in your old age."

I started whining. "C'mon, Hoagie. No way is C. T. Thornton going to turn this station over to Larry the Loon. I know the old bastard just turned seventy-six, but I see no signs of senility."

"Well, this isn't his call. It's Monica's."

So that was it. Monica Thornton was forty-two years old when she gave birth to Lawrence Montgomery Thornton. C. T. is two years older than she, so everyone assumed this was a surprise baby. However, Festerwood's more discreet rumor mongers couldn't help but notice how young Larry bore a striking resemblance to the station's longtime anchorman T. Clayton Bodine. It was, after all, Monica who had recommended to C. T. that Clayton become WHOE's first anchorman. That was back in the sixties.

Clayton Bodine was head of the high-school drama department at the time and had been Monica's leading man in many a summer stock production at the Festerwood Footlite Theater Barn. In fact, Festerwood theater buffs frequently commented on the searing energy that Monica and Clayton put into their romance scenes, leading some amateur critics to suggest that they weren't acting. When Larry came along a short time later, C. T. was more bewildered than suspicious. The regulars at the Festerwood Country Club said that C. T. spent long hours at the bar, asking anyone within earshot, "Can women still have babies past the age of thirty-five?"

Larry had grown up to earn his nickname. He was impulsive, dull-witted, and just plain silly. I tried to sound optimistic. "Well, how bad can it be, after all? Surely C. T. isn't going to let the Loon do anything remotely important with this station."

Hogan took off his half-moon specs and rubbed his eyes. Suddenly he looked like a very old man. "C. T. and Monica are living in Florida for good, and he doesn't give a rat's ass for anything north of Sarasota. He just wants peace and quiet, and the best way to attain that is to let Monica have her way on anything dealing with Larry's future. Monica wants Larry to run the station, and, based on my conversations with him, he's prepared to do just that."

A thousand thoughts swam through my mind, but something Walter Lippman said suddenly surfaced: "Television is for the vaguely talented." I had always thought that if I had a marketable skill, I would be doing something else with my life. But I had learned to love this business in spite of its contrived urgency, hyperbolized promotions, and monumental egos. There was something vital and dynamic about it. I actually enjoyed the breathless deadlines and instant gratification when one of my stories was up on the screen. And I knew that now and then we could even make a difference—that something we reported could do some good. After all, we had what amounted to a captive audience. People watch television—even the people who say they don't, watch television.

It was at those moments, when we transcended the day-to-day banality of our work, that I took pride in what I was doing. I kept such thoughts carefully guarded, but suddenly I had this overwhelming feeling that this was, after all, a pretty insignificant little endeavor. If a certified nincompoop like Larry Thornton could ascend to the front office of a television station, even in a two-bit town like Festerwood, Indiana, then how important could this be? I don't think I ever felt lower in my life.

Hogan sensed what I was feeling. "Look, Rick, don't take it so hard. Maybe Larry will come around. Chances are he'll grow tired of the place and let the department heads run it. Hell, this place damn near runs itself, anyway."

He was right about that. It's as if the whole station had been on autopilot for years. We had people whose jobs became redundant years ago, but because there was an office and a title for them, they kept hanging on. Hell, we even had a program director, and since the only stuff we cranked out were news and religious programs, he didn't have diddly squat to do.

Still, old Herb Stillwell had this way of looking important, strutting around the studio with this clipboard in his hand as if he was about to hit upon a really terrific programming idea. The fact is, the last good idea Herb had was back in the seventies when he decided to quit his disc jockey job and take his formidable skills over to television. Herb did have one awesome talent. He could clear a buffet table with the best of them. Actually, that was his chief assignment. Herb would attend every banquet and fund-raising dinner in town as the station representative, and now and then he'd show up to receive one of the rare awards we would win in categories like "Best Traffic Safety Awareness Spot."

The trouble is, Larry Thornton is the world's most consistent failure. He wants desperately to get out from under the shadow of C. T., so he enters into one doomed business venture after another. There was the combination pool hall and laundromat that went under two months after its grand opening. Then the semipro soccer team that was almost laughed out of town, although it did enjoy a brief cult status among members of the local Unitarian Church, where lost causes are something of a tradition. But Larry's biggest blunder was his awkward attempt to cash in on a novelty that was sweeping the country. Sad to say, by the time he produced his first batch of leashes for pet rocks, the fad had passed.

So this was our new general manager, a thirty-four-year-old loser who, his mother was determined, would find his rightful place in the business world by running a television station into the ground.

Hogan sucked on what had to be his first cigarette in three years. "I just had lunch with young Larry, and he has some very interesting plans for this station . . . and they don't include the general manager or me."

I couldn't believe it. "You mean he's cleaning house?"

"In a way, I guess so." Hogan exhaled a cloud of gray smoke. "He's getting himself a new news director, a new station manager, and something known in the trade as a promotions director. Oh, he also mentioned the 'C' word."

"Oh, Jesus, not a consultant."

"Damn, you're on a roll, Rickster."

"Hoagie, I don't know what to say. You and Merle Teele?"

Hogan actually looked relieved. "Don't worry about us. Merle was going to retire next year anyway. And I figure I got a few books and trashy novels in me . . . maybe I'll even go legit and take a job on the faculty of one of those journalism schools. Those kids need to hear from the real world now and then."

He reached into his drawer. "Here, you need a tissue."

I flopped into a chair. "So when does the proletariat find out about this? Can I look for this as the lead story at eleven o'clock?"

Hogan stared with unusual interest at the spiral of smoke coming from his cigarette. "Don't you ever read your memos?"

He flipped a sheet of paper in my direction, and there it was in black and white: *Staff meeting at 3:00 P.M. to announce some very important and exciting new developments at WHOE. Refreshments will be served.*

chapter ten

IT WAS COMMON PRACTICE THAT ALL OF THE STATION STAFF MEETINGS BE-gan two hours before the newscast, which meant that most of the newsroom reporters trying to make their deadlines weren't able to attend and were therefore unable to embarrass station management with pesky, annoying questions. But on this day, almost everyone was there to witness the second coming of Larry the Loon. The folding chairs set up in Studio B were filled by the time I walked in. In fact, the meeting was already underway, with C. T. himself holding court from the news set.

"So," he was saying, "this golfer gets back to the clubhouse . . ."

C. T., an avid golfer, was warming up his employees by telling exactly the same joke he told at the last station meeting a year ago. Of course, everyone pretended to be mesmerized by the story anyway.

"And the first guy he sees asks him, 'How did it go out there today, Fred?' And Fred answers, 'It was hell. I was playing with Harry, and on the fourth hole he up and dies of a heart attack.' 'No shit,' says his friend, 'that's awful.' 'I'll say,' says Fred, 'for the next fourteen holes it was hit the ball and drag Harry . . . hit the ball and drag Harry.'"

The employees all howled; Larry the Loon was doubled over in spasms of laughter in the chair next to C. T. I stood against a wall at the rear of the studio, next to Helen Terhune, who also served as the unofficial hostess of these events.

She leaned over and I caught a whiff of her almost-alluring per-fume. "Isn't it great about Larry? Or have you heard?"

"I heard," I whispered. "Hogan told me."

Helen had worked at WHOE for twenty years, and this had definitely destroyed some of her most important brain cells. She was as close to a company woman as you could get. "I just think it's about time that boy got a break. What do you think?"

I didn't answer, because I was suddenly fascinated by the strange grouping under the news set lights. There was Larry, looking out over his future employees with a kind of goofy, benign smile, now and then looking up at his father with the kind of respectful grin that you normally associate with politicians' wives as they endure one more of their husbands' boring speeches. Larry looked like someone who had de-evolved back to the fifties, with his crew-cut hair, horn-rimmed glasses, and pencil-thin tie. He just didn't look very smart. And, in this case, looks were not deceiving.

Merle Teele, the general manager, was up there, too, looking strangely serene, like a man with his bags packed and loaded in the station wagon.

Then there was Virgil Addison, the chief engineer, who every-one called "Edison." Virgil took that as a compliment, but the fact is, no one knew exactly what it was that Virgil did to keep the station on the air. That was one of the bonuses of being a television engineer. You could damn near say or do anything, because no one except your engineer buddies had the slightest idea what you were talking about. And Virgil took pains to keep it that way. That's why chief engineers usually keep their jobs till retirement.

The only time Merle had to call Virgil on the carpet was when the station finally put up a new transmitting tower on the edge of town a few years back. Somehow, the tower signal was on the same frequency as those remote garage-door openers that a lot of people have. Once the tower went up, quite a few angry motorists couldn't get their garage doors to open or close, but they sure as hell got a great picture on their television sets.

Merle was pissed because the *Fanfare* made a big deal out of it, and the station had to pacify all the angry callers by agreeing to have their remote controls fixed free of charge by Doors 'n' More, the company that installed them in the first place. Of course, in return for their services, the company got free commercial time on WHOE. A TV-station manager would rather give away six years of his sex life than a single second of air time. So Merle read the riot act to old Virgil, but he couldn't fire him because, as I said, no one really knew what Virgil did.

Actually, Merle probably was more irate over all the smart-ass jokes that floated through the halls of WHOE, especially in the news department, where irreverence was a virtue. A couple of days after the *Fanfare* story ran, Hogan saw Merle in the men's room and said, straight-faced, that he had this great idea how to keep everyone happy and not cost the station a cent. Merle, of course, was all ears.

"Here's the deal," said Hogan in a conspiratorial whisper. "We'll just sort of sneak little references to Doors 'n' More into our newscasts. You know, kind of subliminally, so it won't be too obvious that we're giving them a plug."

Hogan could tell that he had Merle's full attention. "Really? How would you do that?"

Hogan checked under the stall to make sure no one was eavesdropping. "Well, say we have a story about the cost of living. We could have Bodine say something like, 'The cost of living continues to go up and down, just like a Doors 'n' More garage door.' Or, you know that big murder trial in Festus County court? Bodine or Carol could say, 'Prosecutors insist that chances of an innocent verdict are remote—as remote as a Doors 'n' More garage door opener.'"

According to Hogan, Merle looked a bit perplexed, then said, "No kidding? Are you sure we could do that?" Hogan said he couldn't control himself any longer, that he burst into laughter. Merle supposedly hasn't said three words to him since.

So there they were—the past, present and future leaders of WHOE-TV. But who was that woman sitting at the end of the row, the one with the beatific smile on her face? I'd never seen her before, and I certainly would have remembered if I had. She was attractive in an officious sort of way, with her shiny black hair pulled back in a severe bun and the skirt of her tailored black suit falling a stylish two inches above the knee, exposing calves that suggested multiple episodes of jogging. She exuded the confidence of a woman ready to take on the world at the top of her game. She certainly didn't belong in Festerwood, and that worried me. Turns out I had reason to worry.

Meanwhile, old C. T. was droning on about how he took over the station a thousand years ago and turned it into a "dynamic force for the good of this community." Now, he said, it was time to move on and make room for the next generation of broadcasting leaders.

"You all know Larry, so I don't need to run on about his varied business career and his enthusiasm for taking on yet one more challenge. Just let me say that I hope you're as happy as I am that this station, which I've always considered my second family, will stay in the Thornton family." Larry rose to tepid applause and fumbled in his coat pocket for his speech.

Just for the record, Larry Thornton's first attempt at public disclosure was greeted by a booming, "We can't hear you!" from the back of the room. Virgil got up and fiddled with the microphone, producing a spine-grating screech of feedback that brought a groan from the audience and a scolding from old C. T. "Jesus Christ, Edison, what did you do?"

Larry grabbed the microphone as if it were a life raft. "First of all, I want to tell you that it took only two words for me to qualify for this job." He paused as if he had rehearsed this line about a thousand times, then said, "All I had to say was 'Thanks, Dad.'"

That was met with a thundering roar of laughter and applause, especially from Helen, who was laughing so hard I thought for a moment she might cough up something.

Now that his big joke had gone over, Larry the Loon was suddenly seized with confidence, and he launched into his little speech about how proud he was of the station that his father was passing on to him, and how he promised to carry on with only a few minor changes. I saw Hogan stiffen in his chair.

"First of all, I'm both happy and sad to announce that Fred Hogan, the man who built WHOE's news department in the tradition of Edward R. Morgan—"

Helen Terhune had worked her way to the front of the room and was tugging at Larry's trousers and whispering something that he couldn't quite hear. Looking extremely annoyed, Larry bent his head down, nodded, and continued, "I mean, of course, Edward R. Murrow."

I glanced at the woman seated at the end of the row, and her expression hadn't changed. There was a smug superiority in her smile, but it was also soft and strangely provocative. I felt a faint stirring in my loins.

The Loon continued, obviously upset that his rhythm had been interrupted. "Anyway, Fred Hogan is leaving us after many years of dedicated service. I think we owe Fred a round of applause."

Hogan grimaced and managed a feeble wave to his fellow employees, who were clapping their fool heads off—mostly out of relief that it was Hogan, and not them, who was getting the shaft.

Larry stumbled through the rest of his hit list, including Merle Teele, who just winced slightly and brushed some imaginary lint from his shoulder. There were several old-timers: people who remembered Larry from the days of his incorrigible youth, when he used to visit the station and play with the equipment. One of the engineers, Howie Dempsey, couldn't stand little Larry, and while everyone else walked on egg shells around the boss's son, Howie called him a "little bastard" to his face.

One day, a nine-year-old Larry Thornton gummed up a tape machine with a wad of taffy, stopping a soap opera in mid-scene. Howie screamed, "Look what you did, you little shit!" just as Monica was entering the control room, looking for her wayward son. Naturally, Howie was chastised, but he was an engineer, so he got off with a warning. But little Larry never went into the control room again.

Anyway, Howie was "retiring," as well as Helen Terhune, as it turned out, after "years of faithful service to my father and to this station." Helen was dumbfounded. There wasn't a sound in the studio. Here was a woman who had given the best years of her life to WHOE, and her reward was a public hanging. Of course, she was a loyal employee to the end, so Helen put on her best company face and smiled wanly to the smattering of applause from her co-workers.

Larry then went on about how some things wouldn't change. WHOE would not, for example, become a network station—as if we had a choice. We would stay independent, he said, because that is how we can best serve the good viewers of Festus County. To prove it, he introduced Herb Stillwell, who apparently would continue as program director.

Herb looked positively euphoric as he took the microphone. "I have some great news, Larry. And now's the perfect time to announce it." He took this dramatic pause and said, "I know that all of you will be thrilled to learn that WHOE has just purchased three full seasons of one of television's most beloved shows. We have exclusive rights in the entire western Indiana viewing area to encore episodes of the series . . . *Barnaby Jones*." There was a very long embarrassing silence, finally broken by frantic applause from Larry the Loon; a few stunned staffers joined in. I looked at the mystery woman. She just crossed her legs and adjusted her smile.

About that time, the studio door clicked open behind me, and someone slipped into the room. I had a vague feeling of déjà vu, a sudden rush of anxiety, as if a past chapter of my life had just reopened. I turned around, but the rear of the studio was swallowed in darkness. Herb made a few more announcements, which dissolved into this awkward little speech about how proud he was of WHOE and how he was looking forward to "carrying on the Thornton tradition" of excellent programming.

Even Larry looked uncomfortable as he took the microphone from Herb. "Thank you, Herb. I think I have really exciting news now. I know that every business needs an identity, especially a television station. That's why I'm announcing today that, from now on, our new team will be known as . . . Larry's Legionnaires." This time the silence was deafening, so Larry returned quickly to his notes.

"It is now my pleasure to introduce the newest Legionnaire, our new news director, a young man who will bring some much-needed changes to our news department."

Larry gave Hogan a quick glance and continued. "Not that we haven't stayed up to date under Fred Hogan. It's just that now we need some different kinds of changes . . . maybe. You know, more state-of-the-art stuff. So now, without further ado, I'd like you to meet . . ." Larry took a quick glance at his notes. "Bobby Nelson!"

Suddenly a little ball of human energy erupted from the audience. He was a lean, wiry youngster with intense, deep-set eyes and a stylish day's growth of beard. He couldn't have been more than twenty-six years old. He was about five-foot-seven, with a nervous body that seemed to stay in motion, even when he came to a complete stop.

He literally consumed the microphone. "Thank you, Larry! As Larry said, my name is *Boyd* Nelson and it's my privilege and honor to be a part of this new and exciting direction in which Larry is taking WHOE News, and I invite all of you—not just the newspeople, but *all* of you—to join me in taking WHOE News to the next level. Let me just say that the WHOE News of tomorrow won't look anything like the WHOE News today. Now, let's get to work!"

Lowell tapped me on the shoulder. "I've never had a used-car salesman as a news director before. Helluva concept."

Now Larry was back, introducing another of his Legionnaires. "Of course no television station can survive today without a full-time promotions director. That's why it's my pleasure to announce that WHOE is hiring the very best! Let me introduce—"

It was at that moment that I felt a sharp pain and jumped about a foot. Somebody had just goosed me! I turned to give Lowell some shit, when I saw a young woman who had just come into the room. She brushed by me as she made her way to the front of the room. Her hair was bleached blond and short; she was wearing a tailored red suit with a short skirt, and sheer hose that revealed a pair of legs that seemed oddly familiar, as did the wisp of perfume that trailed behind her. A spooky realization crept over me, just as Lowell grabbed my shoulder. "You know who that babe reminds me of?"

I didn't want to believe my eyes, but as she shook hands with Larry and adjusted the microphone, there was no doubt about it. Lowell stammered, "Jesus H. Christ. It is her. Oh my God." Then he lowered his voice. "Sorry, man, I wasn't pimping you. This one got past the grapevine!"

Teri Tremont—the ex-Mrs. Rick Roberson, the woman I last saw in divorce court—was now addressing my co-workers as the station's new promotions director. She was back in what was now passing for my life, and all I could do was mumble, "She cut her hair."

I didn't hear most of what she said. She cracked a joke about how surprised I must be to see her in this position, since we'd tried all the others. Then she launched into a Ross Perot-like spiel about demographics and target audiences, using a bewildering array of charts and graphs. From time to time, someone in the audience would turn and grin at me, just to see how I was taking all this. But my eyes returned to the woman in the front row. She was looking straight at me, with an expression that I can only describe as a cross between sympathy and passion. What I was feeling at that moment was pure and simple lust.

As a result, Teri was already walking by my seat before I realized she had wound up her presentation.

"Give me a minute after the meeting," she whispered. Then she winked and took a seat at the rear of the studio.

I was still in shock as Larry took the microphone and chuckled. "Wow! What goes around comes around, right, Rick old buddy?" Of course that brought gales of laughter from the surviving WHOE employees, who now realized they were charter members of Larry's Legionnaires.

Larry waited for the laughter to subside, then he got this almost-thoughtful look on his face. "Now, something really special. As you know, for years WHOE has prided itself in being a Midwest success story, without taking on any of the frills of the big-city stations. We did just fine without fancy gimmicks like . . . like, you know, those editing machines where you just punch a few buttons and all the pictures are stuck together in the right order. We never needed all that stuff. But times have changed. You just can't keep up with the big boys in Champaign and Terre Haute unless you are really up to date. So Dad . . . I mean, I . . . decided that what we need is a news consultant. And we found the right one. She's pretty . . . and smart, too! Meet our new news consultant, Jeanette Larmer, from Mangle and Associates."

The woman at the end of the row rose to her feet, spread a wide, condescending smile over the room, then glided to the microphone. Her voice was dark and dusky—straight out of an old Lauren Bacall movie. "Thank you, Larry. I'm sure we'll all get acquainted later on, but for now, just let me say that I'm here on a simple mission: to make your news department a giant in the field. But don't worry . . ." She paused with a throaty chuckle. "I'll try to be gentle." And that was it.

The rest of the meeting was a blur of frantic questions from the audience. There was a barrage of questions from Edison on how the coming changes would affect his retirement, pension plans, health insurance, and other life-defining topics that Edison expounded on with his fellow short-timers back in the shop. Most of us refused to allow such thoughts to cross our minds, because the idea of actually reaching retirement age at WHOE was about as appealing as being buried alive in a casket full of red ants.

chapter eleven

AFTER THE MEETING, I FOLLOWED TERI TO THE BACK OF THE BUILDING where she was already in the process of setting up her office. I had to admit, she did a hell of a job of redecorating. Teri had moved into what used to be a dingy basement vending-machine room that once was believed to be the largest source of Zagnut bars in western Indiana, not to mention the most wretched coffee in a tri-state area. Before that, it had been a storage room for all the studio cameras, videotape decks, and other deceased broadcast equipment that duct tape could no longer save. Not surprisingly, under Teri's guidance, the room looked like it had been given a fashion makeover by *Architectural Digest*, with breezy pastel colors brightening the walls, modern art prints festooned about, and a smoked-glass meeting table in the center of the room.

Teri, aware that I was gawking, looked a bit embarrassed. "As you can see, there was a lot of work involved, but only on weekends and days when I knew you wouldn't be around." She cleared a stack of videotapes off a chair. "Here, sit down."

She looked great, of course, but I was in no mood for reunion pleasantries. "Teri, what the hell are you doing here?"

She tried on her best pout. "You're still mad at me, aren't you, Rick?"

"Don't flatter yourself. I got over you as you were pulling out the driveway. Let me repeat the question. What are you doing here?"

She sat behind her gray modular desk. "Look, Rick, I thought long and hard about this, about how awkward it might be because of our relationship. But I've been given a great opportunity to do some really exciting, creative things here."

I got up and momentarily stumbled on the shag carpet. "Teri, I'm sorry, but what do you know about broadcasting, other than the alphabet—thanks to Vanna White?" That was the closest I could come to an insult, knowing Teri's passion for game shows, but my mind was working on more.

She became defensive. "I'll ignore that. If you will recall, I've been in public relations all my life, and I guess I know a little bit about the product. The fact is, this station desperately needs to promote itself. The competition is getting stiffer out there, and WHOE needs to grow."

I wasn't feeling very reasonable. "Right, your PR track record is legendary. You helped a political candidate to a whopping eight percent of the vote, and they're still talking about the great work you and Mr. Wonderful did for Medi-Miracle over in Muncie. By the way, has Medi-Miracle filed Chapter 11 yet? Just how is Mr. Wonderful these days anyway? I take it you didn't bring him with you." I could be a real asshole, and now I was outdoing myself.

Teri gave me a hard look. "I was wondering how long it would be before you brought that up. Well, you'll be delighted to know that Thad and I are no longer an item. He has found religion and is now back with his wife and children."

Sketchy details of the latest Medi-Miracle debacle were just starting to filter into Festerwood, but it involved a new wonder drug that was supposed to wipe out the discomforts of the menstrual cycle, called Ban-A-Cramp. Women said it did offer some relief, but after five days, many women found they were exhibiting facial hair of Rasputin-like proportions. Medi-Miracle scientists didn't help the situation; one of them revealed that Ban-A-Cramp, given in sixty-gallon doses to mice, resulted in the growth of whiskers that could only be described as spectacular. Medi-Miracle insisted it was a fluke; besides, facial hair naturally grows on mice, so the drug was simply accelerating the natural process.

And Teri didn't help matters either. In the midst of some pillow talk with Thad, she suggested that the company simply include a tiny tube of Noxzema shaving cream and a Bic plastic razor with each package of Ban-A-Cramp. Later, Teri insisted she was joking, but Thad, either through desperation or breathtaking ignorance, formally delivered this suggestion to an emergency meeting of the Medi-Miracle board of directors. One of Thad's more cutthroat co-workers then leaked the story to the business editor of the Muncie newspaper, who came up with this inspired headline for his story: "Medi-Miracle tells Ban-A-Cramp victims to flick a Bic!" Thad was fired the next day, got religion at a Promise Keepers rally, and showed Teri the door.

I turned around and found Teri standing about two inches from me. "Yes, Rick, Thaddeus found God. All I could give him was little snatches of Heaven." With that, she placed her hand on my crotch. "Does this bring back memories?"

There was a time when that subtle little maneuver worked wonders, namely on long car trips and at restaurant tables. This time, I just grabbed her hand and pulled it away.

"Sorry, Teri, you've turned me into a Trappist monk. I'm not interested, and while you're at it, please don't screw up this station . . . you or your new friends. This may not be anyone's idea of TV paradise, but there are too many good people here for you to turn this into one of your celebrated train wrecks."

Teri returned to her desk, her tone very businesslike. "Rick, I'm sorry you feel that way, but this station is in for big changes, and you're just going to have to deal with them. It's going to be for the best, and we're going to make it fun."

I turned and opened the door to leave. "Well, then, let the good times roll."

I returned to the newsroom and went to work on my big story for the day. There had been an accident on a county road involving a semi that was hauling cases of peanut butter to IGA stores. The truck just went off the road and into a ditch, and there were jars of the stuff all over. No one was hurt in the accident, so it made for some pretty breezy copy. But the best part was my interview with an eyewitness to the accident, a grizzled old guy wearing a Bash Seeds cap who happened to be driving his beat-up van just a few hundred feet behind the semi.

I stood in the editing booth behind Spanky, the photographer who shot the story; he was putting it together for the five o'clock newscast.

"OK, Spanky, here's the part, coming up right here . . ." I reached to punch the stop button.

"I got it, Rick. Christ, why don't you edit this and I'll write it for you?"

"Sorry. But this is what I want." On the tape, the old-timer was telling me, in a state of extreme agitation, how he saw the whole thing. "Yeah, I seen him. Way back two, three miles I seen that right rear tire on the semi just a-wobblin' like it was gonna spin right off any minute. I knew somethin' bad was gonna happen."

I jumped in. "You mean, you saw it coming? That wobbly tire— it was kind of an omen?"

"Naw, no way," said the old-timer. "That tire was a new one. Sure looked like it to me."

The interview ran on the five o'clock news, and everybody had a good laugh, except for the owner of the trucking company. He called to raise hell with us for implying that his trucks ran on old tires.

chapter twelve

THE NEXT MORNING, THERE WAS CHAOS IN THE NEWSROOM. I GOT THE first hint of trouble when I pulled into the parking lot and was almost run down by a news crew as they aimed their truck toward the street. Reporter Dirk Tubergen rolled down the window and shouted, "We got a Code Seven on Ralston!" Dirk talked like that all the time. It was the unfortunate result of living night and day with a police radio no more than six inches from his ear. Leon, the producer, translated for me when I walked through the newsroom door.

"Hostage story. Some guy is holding his wife at gunpoint in their home, says he'll shoot her if police make a move. Dirk's on his way."

As I walked by the police radios, something froze me in my tracks. I turned to one of the interns at the desk. "What was that address?"

She looked at the notebook in front of her. "Nine-seven-five Ralston. It's a house."

I knew that address. We had done stories there before. Of course—975 Ralston is the home of Norb Fagan, or "Nutsy" Fagan as we liked to call him. Old Nutsy did stuff like that all the time, ever since they put that plate in his head. Once, he even took his own dog hostage. Everyone knew that Nutsy was a few shingles short of a roof, so when he flipped out, we usually just checked with police to make sure he hadn't harmed anyone and let it go at that. But what the hell was going on now? Leon was new and hadn't dealt with Nutsy before, and Dirk probably had been sent out the door before anyone realized that it was just Nutsy acting up again.

There was a big conference underway in Hogan's office. Our new leader, Boyd Nelson, was in there pacing the floor and gesturing wildly. My former bride, Teri, was sitting in a corner scribbling in a notebook. And Jeanette Larmer, the consultant with whom I had locked eyes during the station meeting, was leaning against the wall taking it all in. I figured that no good could come of this.

I looked around for someone to fill me in on what was going on. As usual, morning newsman Morris Chiles was seated at his desk, devouring a Bear Claw and staring at his wall calendar. I startled the hell out of him. "Morris, what's happening around here? Do you know we're actually going out on a Nutsy Fagan run?"

Morris brushed some crumbs from his shirt. "Sure looks that way."

"Whose idea was this? You know as well as I do that Nutsy takes hostages like some people take aspirin. This isn't news."

Morris jerked his head in the direction of Hogan's office. "They think it is."

"Who? Not Hogan?"

"No, not Hogan. The three blind mice he's meeting with."

I headed for Hogan's office, with Morris shouting after me, "Welcome to the new WHOE, buddy!"

I rapped on the window to get Hogan's attention. He was slouched in his chair, looking a little bored by all the activity around him. He motioned for me to come in. I squeezed through the door, momentarily throwing Boyd Nelson off stride as he continued to prowl the cramped office. The former Mrs. Roberson was furiously taking notes as the new head of WHOE promotions, but she looked up long enough to say "Hi." Jeanette Larmer gave me a smoldering smile and crossed her arms. Boyd just looked terribly annoyed and continued his spiel.

"What we need to do is get some background on this guy. You

know—family, neighbors. Has he ever done this before? Does he have a violent past? Stuff we can use during the live shot."

I didn't wait to be introduced. "Whoa, wait a minute. You aren't, by any chance, talking about Nutsy Fagan, are you?"

Boyd turned on me. "If you mean Norb Fagan, that's exactly who we're talking about."

I looked at Hogan. "Hoagie, didn't you tell them about this guy?"

Hogan just sat there impassively, with a bemused smile on his face.

"Well, if you won't, I will. Look, guys, this Fagan character is not who you think he is. Many of us have known him since we were all kids. He's kind of the town fool, a running joke here in the newsroom. And he has a drinking problem. He doesn't mean any harm; he just gets drunk and wants attention now and then, so he calls the cops to tell them he's taken someone—or some *thing*—hostage. Believe me, this is not a news story!"

Boyd studied me for a moment, then said, "Maybe not in the old WHOE newsroom it wasn't, but beginning today, Mr. Fagan is most definitely news. And . . . ," he paused for emphasis, "I think we are going to make a statement with this story."

"No shit," I blurted. "We'll make a statement all right. Do you realize how screwed up this guy is? One look at a live television truck parked in his yard, and he might really go off the deep end. Right now he's harmless. The cops will talk him down, and tomorrow he'll be back at work reading water meters, or whatever he does. But just let him turn on the news and see all the commotion he's caused, and old Nutsy just might do something really weird."

Boyd shrugged. "In which case, we're doing a public service by getting him locked up."

"In which case," I exploded, "we would be guilty of being a public nuisance. This is bullshit, Boyd, and you know it."

"We don't have time for this, Rick. Let's get moving on the story." He turned to Hogan. "What do we have on this guy?"

Hoagie leaned back in his chair, looking as if he actually was enjoying himself. "Well, unless you count the day he hijacked that bus loaded with school kids and dropped them off at Sid's adult book store, not much."

Boyd had his faults, but he wasn't dumb. "OK, we can save the jokes for later," he said as he headed for the door. "I could use your help, Hogan." Then he turned to me. "And yours. But you both should know, we're going ahead with this—with or without you." He gestured to Teri and Jeanette to follow, then slammed the door behind them.

I took a deep breath. "Well, for an obnoxious little prick, he sure has balls."

Hogan leaned back in his chair. "I don't know. I kind of like him."

"Hoagie, you've got to be kidding! He just insulted the hell out of you and all you stand for."

Hogan laughed. "C'mon, Rick, I haven't stood for anything for years. Maybe there was a time, but, anymore, I don't know what's news and what isn't. Christ, maybe he's right. Maybe old Nutsy is one hell of a big story. Small-town madman fighting to escape the tyranny of his own soul. Shit like that. Who knows? All I know is, I'm tired and I'm out of touch and I'm being canned."

I suddenly felt very helpless and very alone. "Well, some of us have to deal with it." I walked out of Hogan's office and into the newsroom, filled with all the righteous anger of a true journalist who was about to confront evil forces that were very much out of his control.

Boyd was on the two-way radio with Dirk. "How many police cars?"

Dirk's voice crackled back, "Uh . . . none that I can see. You know, this guy has pulled this before—a lot."

Boyd ignored that. "Dirk, what can you tell us about this guy? Any past history? How about militias? Does he belong to any?"

I pulled up a chair. This could be interesting.

A long pause, then Dirk's voice: "No, not that I know of. I think he did belong to the National Guard though."

I thought that was kind of funny. Boyd Nelson didn't. "OK, OK, that's good. What unit and where? And do we have any pictures?"

That did it. "Boyd, you can't be serious," I said. "It's the Festerwood National Guard for Chrissake. Nutsy was a supply sergeant. The last time they called his unit up was for a paper drive."

Boyd ignored me and kept talking to Dirk. "Anything. Maybe an old picture of Fagan in his uniform."

Now I couldn't believe my ears. Dirk replied, "Well, yeah, we do have some file stuff of Nutsy when he was at summer camp with the Guard a few years ago."

Boyd turned to Jerry, the producer, who just stood there like a spectator at a five-car accident.

"Well, get me those pictures!"

Jerry hesitated and looked helplessly in my direction.

Boyd wheeled on him. "*Now!*"

This was getting out of hand. I tried reasoning with him again. "Boyd, don't go off on this. I'm warning you. So far we've cooperated with the police and kept Nutsy at arm's length. And in every case, no one got hurt. Besides, this is a pretty small town; everybody who lives here knows that Nutsy is harmless. They'd never believe us if we went live—"

Boyd interrupted. "Cooperated with the police? Is that what you've been doing? No offense, Ron."

"Rick," I said. "My name is Rick."

"Right. Well, no offense, Rick, but it's just that kind of attitude that has this station sucking hind teat when news happens. From now on, when it comes to getting the story, WHOE cooperates with no one."

The city hall salt scam suddenly loomed as a better story than even I imagined. "Somewhere, there has got to be some news happening," I muttered under my breath and headed back to my desk. I looked up Tim Facenda's phone number. Tim was a former WHOE weekend reporter, who now ran the Festus County Taxpayers Advocacy Coalition. Actually, he *was* the Festus County Taxpayers Advocacy Coalition, or F-TAX as it was known. Tim was one of those earnest people who was forever sending us news releases about such obscure matters as sewer overcharges at nursing homes. But he was dedicated to his work, and if anyone could help me with the Norma Flescher story, it was Tim.

chapter thirteen

I GOT HIS ANSWERING MACHINE. IT WAS TIM. HE HAD LOWERED HIS choirboy voice to a deep, serious baritone. "Hello. You have reached the offices of the Festus County Taxpayers Advocacy Coalition. All of our agents are busy right now."

"Tim, it's Rick Roberson. Pick up the phone, will you?"

There was a click at the other end. Tim was a little short of breath. "Hey, Rick, what's up?"

"Need some help. But did I catch you at a bad time?"

"No . . . no. I was just doing some legal work for a client."

I was a bit skeptical. "Sounds more like you were running laps."

"Well . . ." He lowered his voice to a whisper. "Actually my client is Evelyn Fastbinder."

"Don't know her."

"You might by her professional name. It's Angel Tripp."

Now that name was sort of familiar. "Angel Tripp . . . wait a minute! You mean the stripper at Babe's out on State Road—"

"Shhh," Tim whispered. "She might hear you. She's kind of sensitive about that. She's not exactly a stripper. She's an exotic interpretive dancer. She came to me 'cause she needs some advice on whether her tips are taxable."

Now I remembered her. In fact, I was pretty sure that I had contributed to her tax problems during one of our many going-away parties. "Is she the one with the great—"

Tim interrupted. "Hey, Rick, I'm kind of busy here. What do you need?"

"I need a favor. Got a call from a city employee, works in the purchasing department. She says she's being canned 'cause she knows too much. Swears her boss has a cozy deal with his brother-in-law on road supplies . . . you know, rock salt and stuff like that. Says he's getting a kickback on the runover. She's blowing the whistle 'cause he dumped her for somebody else."

There was a pause. Tim's voice was muffled, as if he were holding his hand over the mouthpiece. "Not there, Evelyn . . . a little lower and to the right." Now he was back. "Purchasing, you say? You don't mean Tad Tyler for Chrissake?"

"Yeah, Tyler—head of the department."

Tim sighed. "Well, it's possible. Mousy little guy like him . . . with just enough power and opportunity. Tell you what, I'll look into it."

"Great. But don't mention my name. My source is already a little shaky on this. I don't want to spook her."

"So who is she? Your source, I mean."

"Well, I'm not supposed to say, but just between you and me, her real name is Eleanor Roosevelt. Her professional name is Lotta Thighs."

"Fuck you very much," Tim said and hung up.

I looked up at the monitor sitting on the assignment desk. It was showing a closed-circuit picture of the front yard of Nutsy's house. Dirk was standing there, fiddling with his earpiece and talking to someone in the control room upstairs. "Right. OK. Just roll the National Guard tape when I say something about Fagan's military background."

Just then the phone rang. It was the receptionist. "Rick, your tour is here."

I drew a blank. Tour? What tour? I hadn't set up any tour.

"Sorry, I don't know what you're talking about."

The receptionist turned from the phone and asked, "Who did you say you're with?" There was a pause, and she was back on. "They're from Festerwood Community College. A radio and TV class. Here, wait a minute."

A different voice now. Younger. "Rick, it's Carol. Don't tell me you don't remember."

The trouble is, I was starting to remember all too well. It was hazy . . . but sometime in our moment of passion the other night, I had promised Carol, the intern, that I would take her class on a tour of the station. I hated giving tours, but as a very wise philosopher once said, "You can't reason with a man who has a hard-on."

"Of course I remember. Bring them in."

Carol led the six members of her class into the newsroom, like the seasoned three-week veteran that she was.

". . . very busy time of the day," she was telling her group as they came through the door, "so try not to bother anyone."

I started to walk over to greet them when an old bulletin slide—faded and smeared with thumbprints—popped up on the newsroom monitor. It had been so long since we used it that the slide still had the old Channel 49 logo on it, the one with the number "49" superimposed over a picture of the stunted Festerwood skyline. The taped voice of a long-deceased announcer intoned, "This is a bulletin from the WHOE newsroom."

"Oh look!" Carol cried, "We're in luck! There's going to be a bulletin!"

I took her aside. "Look, Carol, this is not what it looks like. I don't think these kids will get the right idea—"

"Hey, Mr. Roberson! Is somebody gonna get shot?" A future broadcast journalist with greasy hair halfway down his back had gathered around the newsroom set with the rest of his classmates. "Cool!"

I hustled them out of the newsroom just as Dirk came on camera and said in his most dramatic voice, "In this modest house, a tense drama is unfolding even as I speak . . ."

It was cool and dark in the main studio, vacant except for a dimly lit corner where Rollie was fussing over his weather maps. I pointed out the anchor desk with the fake skyline shot behind it, explained how the TelePrompTers worked, and I went through the signals that the camerapersons used to communicate with the newscasters.

Actually, it was going pretty well until one of the kids, a girl who was poking around behind the set, screamed, "Dog shit! I just stepped in dog shit!" Sure enough, she had.

Right there on the floor behind the interview set was a neat little souvenir of one of the most popular segments of our noon newscast, a weekly visit from the Festus County Humane Society and its Pet of the Week. In this case, it looked to be from a pretty good-sized dog that was looking for a home. I found some paper towels for the girl.

I wasn't sure if I should take the kids by Rollie's weather station. Knowing what kind of mood he was in these days, I thought it best to guide the kids around Rollie with just a brief acknowledgment.

"This is the hardest-working man in Festerwood," I said a little too cheerfully. "Just keeping up with our winter weather is a job in itself and as you can see. Rollie takes his work very seriously . . ."

Rollie looked up and glared at the intruders. "Carol," he said, "what the hell are you doing in here?"

Carol stammered, "Well, Mr. Watson, I thought I'd bring my class by the station and impress them."

Rollie looked down at his maps and growled, "Well, make up your mind, which is it?"

A television station control room, even in a one-coffeepot station like WHOE, is a pretty impressive place to first-time visitors. There are lights blinking, dials glowing, black screens flashing with spikes of jagged green lines, the constant squawking of intercoms, and the relentless high-pitched gibberish of rewinding videotape, sounding like confused munchkins on speed. And over it all, there is the chatter of the engineers, speaking in the arcane language that makes sense only to them.

"The video levels on the TBC are off—check the frame synchronizer!" From another corner of the room, a head popped up from behind a console. "Give me bars and tone! And somebody set up the chip chart for color balance!" Now a voice over the squawk box: "Your hue and chroma levels are way off. Check the vectorscope!"

One of the students, a pudgy girl with sandy hair and ornery eyes, turned to me and said, "Do you have to know all this stuff, too, Mr. Roberson?"

"No, not all of it," I lied. "I can pretty much hold my own in here, though."

Just then, chief engineer Virgil Addison wheeled his chair out of the sub-control room. "What the hell . . . ? Who punched up camera three?"

I looked up at the "On the Air" monitor, and there, filling the screen, was the enormous butt of Virgil's protégé, Steve Sabol, the maintenance engineer, who was bent over a TelePrompTer in the studio. Steve didn't know it, but at that moment his ass was entertaining thousands of viewers in the Festus County viewing area.

Virgil shouted at one of the students, the kid with the long hair and blank look. "You! Get off the fader bar!" I looked over, and, sure enough, Carol's classmate was leaning matter-of-factly against the control that activated the studio cameras. Virgil pulled him away, and I decided that perhaps the students had gotten enough technical instruction for the afternoon.

chapter fourteen

THE PHONE WAS RINGING WHEN I GOT BACK TO MY DESK. IT WAS TAX watchdog Tim Facenda, and this time he was all business.

"Rick, even a blind squirrel digs up an acorn now and then. You got one this time, buddy!"

I sat down. "You mean there's something to it?"

He almost jumped through the receiver. "Something to it? Christ, man, they're running a big-league scam downtown. Check this out: Last winter the City Fathers of Festerwood purchased two thousand tons of street salt for seventy-five bucks a ton, taxpayer money." He waited for that to sink in.

I was trying to remember Norma Flescher's figures. "That's more than it's worth, right?"

"More than it's worth? You've got to be kidding. This stuff goes for thirty-five dollars a ton, tops. And that's not all. They're buying the heavy duty stuff—the calcium chloride for the tough street-cleaning jobs—they're buying that for a buck a gallon. That's about three times what it's worth. This city is getting ripped off, man!"

I had to be sure. "Now let me get this straight. Purchasing is buying street salt for more than twice what it's worth, and the other stuff—"

"Calcium chloride. It's a liquid."

"Yeah, well, they're paying almost three times more for that? And no one caught the mistake?"

Tim's voice was growing more excited by the second. "There's no mistake! That's the point. You can be sure that whoever is doing this is getting one hell of a kickback from the supplier."

Norma's story was beginning to make sense. "And the supplier is—"

Tim finished for me. "Callico Chemical of Bushnell, Illinois. Managed by one Sander L. Fullington."

"Tyler's brother-in-law?"

"No, they wouldn't be that stupid. Fullington is the stooge, probably just a figurehead. But his boss is Graham Sendak, the brother of Mrs. Stella Tyler—"

This time I finished his sentence. "The wife of City Purchasing Director Tad Tyler!"

Tim let out a low whistle. "Finally, you figured it out."

"Jesus, Tim, how did you come up with this?"

"Just doing my job to serve and protect the good taxpayers of Festus County. Besides, there's a guy on Tyler's staff who owes me big. This dirty little business has been going on for some time."

Suddenly, Boyd Nelson and Nutsy Fagan and Teri Tremont and the whole ensemble that threatened to turn our little TV station into a kind of pale imitation of the tabloid show *Inside Affair* were pushed to the back of my mind. Somewhere out there, in the nondescript little offices of some small-town bureaucrats, there was news being made. Not major news, nothing to shake the republic to its foundations, but news that actually might make a difference in the lives of our viewers, many of whom just happened to be taxpayers as well. All I knew was that I had to call Norma Flescher.

"Tim, you're a pal. You don't know how much I need this story right now. I'll keep in touch."

Norma Flescher's phone rang five times before she answered. "Flescher residence."

I identified myself and, after a pause, she said, "I'm afraid I'm rather busy right now."

"Well, this will just take a minute."

Norma's voice was faint. "Look, Mr. Roberson, I've given this a lot of thought, and I . . . I just don't think I want to go public with my story right now."

Now was not the time to be pushy. "I understand, Norma. This must be very tough on you. But the fact is, I've been able to corroborate what you told me—"

There was genuine alarm in her voice. "You haven't talked to anyone at purchasing, have you?"

"No, no, I wouldn't do that. But I do have a source who says your information is correct."

There was a pause. "I'm sorry, Mr. Roberson, I just can't get involved in this. I made a mistake getting involved with Tad in the first place. I don't want to jeopardize my family in any way."

Time to change focus. "But what about your obligation to the public, to the taxpayers, Norma? Don't they deserve consideration? You could save them a lot of money and clean up some serious corruption at the same time."

Now her voice was more forceful. "I understand that. But I have a life to lead. Besides, if you have someone else willing to confirm what I told you, why can't you just use them?"

"Because it wouldn't be as compelling. You have the goods on these guys, Norma. You're the one who's been done wrong, all because you know what's going on isn't right." I was pressing now, but Norma Flescher had her mind made up.

"Sorry, Mr. Roberson. You'll just have to do this without me." Then she hung up the phone.

I sat there and stared at the wall opposite my desk. It was plastered with the run-of-the-mill citations that line the walls of every television newsroom in America. One from the Festus County Blood Bank thanked WHOE-TV for its "invaluable help in our annual donor drive." There was a plaque from the Festus County Pork Producers Association "for making our annual Pig-malion Festival a success." And directly in front of me hung a certificate for third place in the Indiana Press Association's "Best TV News Reporting" competition.

I won that several years ago for a series on rural gangs that we called "Crime Down on the Farm." At the time, I was certain that it was just the beginning, that in no time I would find the story that would deliver the two prizes I most coveted: a first place trophy and a ticket out of Festerwood. A moment ago, I thought that Norma Flescher was about to punch that ticket for me. Not to mention the fact that the people of this town were getting screwed, which had a tendency to piss me off, especially when the only person who could blow the whistle was refusing to put it to her lips.

chapter fifteen

THE PHONE STARTLED ME. MAYBE NORMA HAD CHANGED HER MIND! I picked up.

"Roberson, news."

I was greeted by the voice of a very angry older woman, raspy with rage. "How dare you interrupt my favorite program for this trash you're putting on now?"

I looked up at the newsroom monitor. Dirk Tubergen was interviewing someone. I turned up the volume.

"You've lived next door to Mr. Fagan for how long?" Dirk was asking.

An elderly man dressed in coveralls was deep in thought. "Ten years—no, nine. Now wait . . . let's see, Nutsy moved here in—"

Dirk interrupted. "That's all right, Mr. Ledford. What kind of neighbor is he?"

"Nutsy? The best. Stays to himself. He's a little odd maybe, but he don't make no fuss and he's always polite when you see him out in the yard."

"Hello? Is anyone there?"

For a moment, I had become engrossed in this "must-see TV" and I had forgotten the caller. "Sorry, ma'am. Uh . . . you are calling to object—"

". . . to this crap that's on the air right now!" she cut in. "Every day at this time I watch *Real Life Divorce* and now I turn on my TV and there's somebody yakkin' about God-knows-what. I want my program back on!"

"Well, ma'am, I'm afraid you need to talk to someone higher up than me. I suggest you call our program director with your complaint. He'd be only too happy to hear from you. Just call extension 144 and ask for Mr. Stillwell."

I felt a warm hand on my shoulder, and there was a familiar scent to go with it.

Teri cooed, "Rick, there's someone I want you to meet."

I looked up at a woman right off the cover of *Dressed for Success* magazine. She was tall with short, cropped black hair and an angular face that was softened by several coats of makeup. She wore a seriously tailored pin-striped suit, and carried an oversized notebook in her hand.

She studied me for a moment, then exclaimed, "Winter!"

I waited for a moment, but that was it. "Pardon me? You are . . . Miss Winter?"

Apparently, that was extremely funny. Teri and Miss Suit threw their heads back in uncontrollable fits of laughter, clapping their hands with glee. Teri finally found her composure long enough to wipe a tear from her eye, then she looked at me as you would a precocious child who had just used a very big word in the wrong sentence.

"Oh, Rick, that's so cute! No, this is Dixie Wells. She's our new color lady."

Now, I knew a "color man" was the guy who provides commentary during sports events, but I had a suspicion that I was out of my league on this one.

"How do you do, Mr. Roberson? May I call you Rick?" Her voice was deep, precise, a bit affected—definitely not the product of a Festus County education.

"Dixie is a colorist," chirped Teri. "She knows everything about skin tones and makeup and wardrobe. Jeanette Larmer, our new con-

sultant, wants her to give us some zip, some pizzazz. She was just dying to meet you."

"Wait!" Dixie suddenly looked alarmed. "This can't be! Wait a
minute!" And with that she tore open an enormous bag at her side
and started pulling out silk scarves like a magician in heat.

"Here! This is the one." She whipped out a bright red scarf and
held it under my chin, fixing me with a look of such urgency that I
was sure I had just made another ghastly mistake. Finally, she gave
this huge sigh, dropped the scarf, and said, "Thank God! You are a
winter, after all. For a minute there I thought I had you wrong. You
were almost an autumn!"

Teri just smiled and slowly shook her head with admiration.
"Dixie knows her stuff, Rick. If she says you're a winter, then you're a
winter."

"I know this sounds incredibly stupid," I said, "but indulge me.
What the hell are you talking about?"

Dixie stuffed the scarves back into her bag. "Well, Rick, we all
have our own color, our own season, if you will. It's based on skin
tone, your complexion, as well as your hair and eye color. In your
case, you'd show up as a winter on my color chart. So, you would
wear the appropriate makeup and wardrobe to compliment your
color."

I tried an expression of mock relief. "Well, at least I'm not a
nuclear winter."

Teri didn't smile. "This may be very humorous to you, Rick, but
Dixie is a real pro and she's here to help us."

Dixie snapped her bag shut and fixed me with an earnest look.
"That's all right, Teri. Rick is a newsman, a journalist. It's hard for
him to realize that television news is as much about how you look as
it is what you say."

I leaned against the desk. "Dixie, I'm no purist. I know that this
is part show biz. It's just that when you start talking about makeup
and wardrobe, you lose me. I have a stick of gunk I use to cover my
beard at five o'clock, and a couple of suits that make me look serious,

even authoritative if I remember to get them pressed. I just think you're wasting your time out here in the sticks. Our audience thinks you're color-coordinated if your socks match your undershirt. And believe me, there's nothing exciting about the word *winter* out here. I'm not sure—"

Dixie turned to leave. "Rick, no hard feelings, but you're dead wrong. This station is about to change its thinking about a lot of things. Give me two weeks, and you won't be able to tell if you're watching the news in Festerwood or Indianapolis. I'm sure you'll agree." And with that, the color lady and my ex-wife spun on their heels and were out the door.

chapter sixteen

THE FIVE O'CLOCK NEWS WAS JUST COMING ON, AND I REALLY DIDN'T want to see any more of Dirk Tubergen and Nutsy's neighbors. But there was more than the usual state of agitation around the producer's desk. I thought maybe someone had come to his senses and decided to back off the Nutsy story, so I walked over. Leon, the producer, looked up from a huddle of about six people and whispered, "Rick, you've got to see this. We're finally going to get old Clayton."

I knew exactly what he meant. Clayton Bodine had survived all these years as WHOE's evening anchorman for a lot of reasons. For one thing, he had the prototypical looks. There was his impressive shock of snowy hair. And his face, which was seamed with world-weary wrinkles, was a face that told the audience that here was a man who has seen it all. The fact that all Clayton had seen was a college drama department and a studio camera didn't seem to matter. Then there was his voice. It was a James Earl Jones-type voice, so deep and so commanding that anything he said sounded important.

His main drawback: Clayton wasn't extremely bright, and he was more than a little bored by current events. But he was very cautious. If the newscast he would be reading contained any word that might challenge his air of authority, he had the good sense to look it up in advance. Then he would carefully print the phonetic spelling of the word in the margins of his copy.

In all the years he reported the news for WHOE, Clayton Bodine never made a mistake. I mean, *never*. His infallibility was legendary in Festerwood. In fact, the *Fanfare* once conducted a poll of its readers to see who they thought was the smartest man in Festerwood. Clayton won, hands down. No one but Clayton and his co-workers knew of his little secret, of course. But as the years passed, there was a growing anticipation in the newsroom that one night, Clayton Bodine would not be prepared, that he would have to read his copy "cold" and would stumble on the air, exposing himself for the impostor he was. Once and for all, putting an end to his unblemished reputation.

From what I gathered, that moment had arrived. Leon brandished a bulletin off the Associated Press wire.

"Here," he said, "look at this."

I read the terse one-line story: *BULLETIN. Sources in the breakaway Russian Republic of Slovania announce that the country's foreign minister, Dimitri Dnepropetrovski has been assassinated.* That was it. Nothing more.

"You're about to watch history being made," Leon exulted. "Old Clayton has no time to read this one over. No phonetics tonight! We're going to slip this into his copy during a commercial. Then the fun will begin!"

I thought that was a bit cruel, but I understood Leon's excitement. He and the others who gleefully passed the bulletin from hand to hand were the newsroom grunts, the people who worked in the trenches, gathering and writing and editing the news for peanuts just so Clayton Bodine could go on the air with his mane of white hair and apocalyptic voice and read the result of their efforts. For this, he received roughly twice their combined salaries. Still, I never cared for their little game, since it not only would embarrass Clayton, who was essentially a decent man, but it would embarrass the station, which, last time I checked, employed us.

But there was no stopping them. Leon, flourishing the bulletin like a battle flag, rushed out the door and into the studio just as a commercial for Crazy Ed's Cars was ending. On the closed-circuit monitor, we saw him slip the bulletin into Clayton's copy before he had a chance to see it, and then, in a flash, the news was back on the air. Leon's co-conspirators eagerly gathered around the newsroom television set. They could hardly contain themselves.

Clayton glided through the stories that appeared on his TelePrompTer, then suddenly he stopped cold.

"This is it!" cried Leon.

Clayton glanced at the paper in his hands, looked at the camera with just a moment's hesitation and absolutely no hint of panic in his face, and announced, "Ladies and gentlemen, I've just been handed this bulletin: *Sources in the breakaway Russian Republic of Slovania announce that the country's foreign minister has been assassinated.*"

Then a pause. Clayton looked down at the bulletin, looked up at the camera, and said in the most authoritative voice I have ever heard him use, "We are withholding his name pending notification of next of kin."

"Shit!" Leon banged his fist on the monitor; the rest of his conspirators stared at the set in disbelief.

I just smiled and said to myself, "The man is a master."

Lowell Loudermilk was in his usual state of agitation. "I froze my ass for two hours out there, and now they're not even going to use it!"

I had just walked into Lowell's editing bay and found him staring at a still-frame shot of a tree limb encased in a sleeve of ice. "That's great, Lowell. Did you just shoot this?"

"Yeah, I just shot it, but it looks like it'll never get out of this room."

"What do you mean? Your stuff always gets on."

He punched a button and the screen went to black. "Maybe in the old days, buddy, but not now. Our new boy king says we don't have time for soft news anymore. No more features, no photo essays, no art. Especially if they run more than a minute-twenty."

I shook my head. "He doesn't waste any time, does he?"

Lowell reached into a drawer and pulled out a videotape. "By the way, here's the hidden-camera stuff from Dirkie's if you want it."

"I don't know. My source has dried up on me, and with everything else that's happening around here, I'm not sure I'm in the mood." Norma Flescher would have to wait for another day, if that day ever came.

Lowell put the tape back in the drawer and shut it. "Well, maybe you're right. As far as these new guys are concerned, what's a little scandal at city hall compared to a life-or-death hostage drama? Speaking of which, did you hear that the CBS station in Terre Haute is sending a crew here?"

"You're not serious?"

Lowell reached for his coat. "Serious as a heart attack. They picked up on the story from some viewer who couldn't get through to our switchboard to complain about our Nutsy Fagan bulletins. So she called Terre Haute in desperation. They figured it sounded pretty good. Besides, it's a slow news day."

"Jesus, our boy Boyd is a one-man wrecking crew."

"Not quite," Lowell said as he motioned me aside. "I'm on my way to join him. He wants me to shoot some sidebar stuff on Nutsy's neighborhood."

Lowell was out the door before I could respond.

"Don't say it, Rick! My wife and kids have this eating habit and I'm their main connection!"

"Hey Rick! Check this out!"

It was Morris Chiles; he was leaning back in his chair and staring at the newsroom monitor that was mounted in the wall above his desk. There, on the screen, was a grainy photograph of soldiers lined up on bleachers and squinting into the sun. The camera then zoomed in slowly and isolated one soldier, a scrawny kid in the third row, wearing an ill-fitting uniform. His face was obscured by a helmet that looked more like a large brown pot that had been emptied on his head.

Dirk Tubergen was saying, "Fagan's fellow Guardsmen remember him as a quiet man who kept to himself. But there were members of the 381st Tactical Allocations Unit who wondered, even then, what demons might lurk inside this intense young soldier."

Now there was another face on the screen, ruddy and bloated. The man's speech slurred from too many afternoon beers. "Yeah, you had to wonder about Nutsy." The graphics under the talking head identified him as Jake Tolliver, Ex-Guardsman. Jake obviously was enjoying the attention. "I mean, he was a good soldier and all that— don't get me wrong—but there was just somethin' about him . . . kind of secret, you know? I remember thinkin' at the time, *What's old Nutsy up to?* Of course, I never figured he'd pull anything like this. Hey, what time will this be on?"

Morris looked at me and laughed. "Great shit, huh? Nutsy Fagan, war-hero-turned-terrorist!"

"That does it!" Karen Armstrong shot out of her seat and charged toward the control room. At last! Someone besides me was outraged by this little sideshow.

"Unbelievable, Karen," I nodded.

She shouted back over her shoulder, "You're goddam right. I told them—Toliver is spelled with *one* L!"

chapter seventeen

IT WAS SEVEN O'CLOCK, JUST HOURS BEFORE MY DRAMATIC DEBUT AS HOS-
tage negotiator. I had decided to skip dinner, even though I drove
right past Dirkie's, where my digestive system normally would be
subjected to the house special: Yankee Pot Roast Normandy. Instead,
the Ramada Inn bar fit my situation. It was dark and almost deserted,
except for a couple who obviously started their own Happy Hour
much earlier and now were trying desperately to dance to the Clint
Black song playing on the jukebox.

I was well into my third beer of the evening in the only bar in
America that still serves Blatz on tap. Dex Feasal, the long-suffering
bartender, was dipping shot glasses into a sink filled with oily water,
trying hard to look interested in my monologue about the future of
television news.

On the television screen above the bar, Dirk Tubergen was doing what must have been his tenth update of the day, but it was clear
his supply of clichés was endless.

"It is now early evening, and as night fell on this once-quiet
neighborhood, one man holds his hostage, and this city, captive." As
he spoke, the screen filled with pictures of flashing red police lights
and yellow crime-scene tape that read POLICE LINES—DO NOT
CROSS.

I pointed at the screen. "Look at this, Dex—this is what I mean! Any other day, the cops would have blown this off, but now we've made a big deal out of it, so they've got to show up. And since they show up, everyone else does, too. There's a station from Terre Haute on its way here, and—"

"And by this time tomorrow, your little town will be on the map." The voice was vaguely familiar, but more sensuous than I remembered. I looked up and into the intensely green eyes of Jeanette Larmer.

"Hello," I said. "Don't tell me. Spring. You are definitely a spring."

She smiled. "I see you've met Dixie Wells. I'm impressed."

"Don't be. I don't think we got along that well."

She turned to Dex. "Scotch. On the rocks. And bring Mr. Roberson another—"

"Actually," I said, "scotch would be fine."

She motioned to a table in the corner. "I think our table is ready at last. Would you care to join me?"

I never noticed before, but the Ramada Inn could be a romantic setting if you put your mind to it. Even the squat little candle, burning in a plastic-webbed glass jar in the middle of the table, had a certain panache. And in its flickering glow, Jeanette Larmer was a bona fide knockout.

She lit a cigarette and exhaled a cloud of gray smoke. Never before had a carcinogen been so seductive.

"So, come here often?" she asked.

"Let's just say I'm on a first-name basis with the bartender. Actually, it's a little early for me, but I've been feeling very sorry for myself this week."

She feigned a look of pity. "Oh come now, it can't be that bad."

"Well, Jeanette, I guess I just can't help it. I hate to be a spoilsport for your little experiment," I nodded toward the television over the bar, "but if this is the direction you're taking our station, then it may be time for me to learn a skill and get the hell out."

Jeanette leaned toward me. "Rick, I think you should know something. Larry hired us—Boyd, Dixie, Teri, all of us—to turn this news department around. No offense to Fred Hogan, but we live in a new age, a new time. People turn on their television sets now and they expect to be entertained. They want tension, excitement, life or death situations. And I'm not talking about prime-time dramas. I'm talking about news."

I interrupted. "I'm not saying the news can't be all of that, but stuff like this—"

She jumped in. "Stuff like this is real! It's happening now! Not on a Hollywood sound stage, but right here in Festerwood. Rick, you're a purist, and I appreciate that. I cut my teeth in newsrooms like yours. But somewhere along the way, everything changed. Don't you see? People watch a story on TV now and they don't remember if they saw it on *CBS News* or *Geraldo* or *Hard Copy*. The lines have all been blurred."

I threw up my hands. "Christ, you're talking about tabloid news! You want us to become a tabloid news station!"

She gave me a condescending smile. "Rick, be honest. Aren't you already? Maybe just a little bit? I'm guessing now, but I'd bet that you guys led your newscasts more than once with stories about Lorena Bobbitt and Michael Jackson and Tonya Harding. And look at the O. J. trial. It's nothing more than a celebrity murder case, but the networks all had it staffed. More often than not, they led with it. Who are we to say what's news and what isn't? The whole world is wired."

I drained my glass and signaled to Dex to bring another round. "Jeanette, I know all of this. Even out here in the boonies we're aware of the global village. It's just that, somewhere, we have to draw the line. When guys like Nutsy Fagan drive legitimate stories out of our newscasts, then it's time to take stock of what we're doing."

She laughed. "Legitimate stories? You mean that interview with the councilman about the cost of bridge repairs?"

"Actually, yes, that's exactly what I mean. That's something people should know. It's their money that's being spent on bridges they have to drive over. But because of this Nutsy saga, we gave it thirty seconds instead of the time it deserved.

She leaned back in her chair and glanced out the window at the darkening winter sky. "It got precisely what it deserved. Look, Rick, it's the dinner hour. People are either making dinner or subduing their children. They only half-hear what we're saying. Anyone who's interested can read the bridge story in the newspaper tomorrow. It won't go away. But give them a hostage story, and you have their attention. Now they're watching. And later, if you have time, you slip in the bridge business. That way, everyone is happy, but at least we have viewers."

Dex placed two glasses of scotch on the table and asked, "How about some pretzels, folks?"

I looked up. "You never have pretzels at the bar, Dex."

"No, but at the tables we do. You should try them sometime."

I waved him off. Jeanette Larmer's eyes smoldered in the candle glow.

"Jeanette, you're missing the point. The fact is, Nutsy Fagan is not a news story—period. I've known him for years. He's an odd but harmless character who pulls this crap at least once a year. He's never hurt anyone. But suddenly we decide to take him seriously. We rush in with live cameras; the cops are forced to react with SWAT teams; and now TV crews are coming in from out of town. Now we've turned an annual domestic episode into a crisis. Don't you see what's happening? We're not reporting the news—we're *creating* the news! Without us, there wouldn't be any news here!"

She stubbed her cigarette in the ashtray. "But who's to say this isn't news? Just because you've ignored him in the past doesn't mean this Fagan character isn't worth a story. Who knows? Maybe he's a time bomb waiting to go off. The fact is, Rick, when it comes to deciding what's news and what isn't, the old rules just don't apply anymore. If it's happening, then we'd better roll on it or someone else will."

We were getting nowhere, but there was now a pleasant haze in the room, and the combination of scotch and Jeanette's sensuality was beginning to arouse more than my journalistic curiosity.

"What does a beautiful, obviously intelligent woman like you do in a dump like Festerwood?" I couldn't tell if I slurred the question or not.

"The same thing I do in every other dump that Mangle and Associates sends me to. I get a room at a local hotel and look for bright, sensitive reporters to beguile with my wisdom and charm."

"I see. Kind of like a challenge, right? You find the one guy who isn't buying into your little game, and you seduce him into seeing things your way."

She reached across the table and took my hand. "Exactly. Is it working?"

"The charm part is. I'm not sure about the rest."

She squeezed my hand and suddenly there was a sharp pain, a stabbing sensation, like a piece of metal in my palm. I opened my hand and found a key with the number 417 embedded in it.

Jeanette rose from her chair, feigned a yawn and said, "Oh my, it's almost 9:30. Where does the time go? I think I'll turn in. Good night, Rick." She glided from the room, leaving me with a half-glass of scotch and a serious dilemma. Should I give in and sleep with the enemy? Or should I stick to my principles?

I took my problem to the bar, where Dex had obviously been saving up one-liners for the occasion.

"Well, I see you have an appointment with the lovely Miss Larmer," he sneered. Dex's powers of observation were legendary. He made it a point to know who was staying in the hotel and why.

I raised my now-empty glass for a refill, and said, "I see you've been promoted to maid service again."

It was one of my lamer attempts to parry one of Dex's surgical strikes. Fact is, I kept my penchant for verbal abuse to a minimum with Dex. From his vantage point behind the Blatz beer dispenser, he was a major news source and clearinghouse for Festerwood scandal. I didn't relish the idea of becoming fodder for his personal rumor mill.

Dex slid a fresh glass of scotch into my hand and winked. "I have found her to be quite delightful, and I have reason to believe you will, too."

"Right. Tell you what, Dex, I'll come back later and we'll compare notes." I bought a six-pack of beer, slipped the key into my pocket, took one last swig of my drink, and started for the house phone in the hallway.

Dex shouted after me, "I'll look forward to that. You have a good one, and I mean that. I know it's been a while for you . . . at least with someone your own age."

I turned, paused for a second, and said, "Dex, can I ask a favor?"

"Sure, buddy, what is it?"

"When you die, can I watch?"

chapter eighteen

I DIALED NUMBER 417 AND SHE ANSWERED ON THE SECOND RING WITH what I thought sounded like a very matter-of-fact "Hello."

I unleashed the full measure of my telephone charm. "This is your favorite electronic reporter. I'm down in the lobby, and I found a room key that you must have dropped in the station parking lot. I just happened to be in the neighborhood, so I thought I'd drop by and return it. Are you decent?"

She laughed. "I'll let you be the judge of that. Get your lovely butt up here."

During my courtship with Teri, she was fond of answering the door in the nude as a way of jump-starting the evening. I found that to be an endearing trait, except for the night I forgot to tell her that, instead of meeting us at the restaurant as previously planned, my parents would be with me to pick her up. Which is why, to this day, Teri remains my dad's favorite daughter-in-law.

He would have been equally impressed with Jeanette, even though her greeting was a bit more demure, garbed as she was in a fashionable Ramada Inn face towel, supported solely by breasts that confirmed all of my expectations. Gone was the bun; it had been replaced by a splendid cascade of hair draping her shoulders, providing a perfect frame for that bemused, confident smile. The towel fell off as she approached me, revealing a stirring testimonial to the benefits of aerobics.

She grabbed me by the tie and kicked the door closed, while she engulfed me with a French kiss that nearly drove my breath mint into my esophagus.

"Is this decent enough for you?" she asked as she surfaced. But before I could reply, she had me flat on my back, disrobing me with the precision of an emergency-room nurse. Then suddenly, she was straddling me, holding up two condoms. "Which flavor would you like?" she teased. "Trojan or something from the Tickler persuasion?"

I gasped, "Extra strength!"

"Trojan it is!" she exclaimed, as she proceeded to apply it in a manner that suggested that I might not be her first. Then she climbed aboard and started her journey like a Pony Express rider under orders to deliver the mail to Dodge City by noon. It was all very exciting, but I felt like an exercise apparatus at Harv's Health and Fitness Center as Jeanette pumped away in apparent pursuit of her personal best. I really had no room to complain since she was getting the job done, but I couldn't resist making the point.

"You know, Jeanette, you don't have to feed the parking meters in this town after six o'clock."

She smiled amidst her feel-the-burn efforts and breathlessly replied, "Please don't spoil the moment for me. It's my first time."

I was about to reply when she cut me off with another soulful kiss that put us both over the top, complete with the requisite mating calls. For the record, at that moment, it had been two minutes and thirty-five seconds from the time I walked into her room.

"Well, so much for foreplay," I said as we discreetly uncoupled.

She brushed her hair back from her face and said in mock indignation, "What kind of girl do you think I am? I hardly know you. Foreplay before the wedding? Really, Rick . . ."

Jeanette reached over my head for what I assumed would be the postcoital cigarettes, or at least the pillow mints. But what she came up with was a small, black remote control, which she dramatically thrust toward the television. Soon, the room was filled with the sound of urgent martial music, accompanied by bright colored graphics of barely decipherable letters, which were twisting, turning, and somersaulting in space while a booming voice intoned, "This is *WHOE Fast Attack News*, with Clay Bodine and Melanie Farnsworth, Rollie Watson with your Accu-Doppler forecast, and Big Bob Berlinski on sports."

I was more than a little insulted. "What's this? Please don't tell me we just had a quickie before headlines."

Jeanette sat upright and pumped up the volume. "Oh, quit whining. Some of us work for a living. I need to see how we're handling the hostage story."

I leaned back against the headboard. "You guys didn't waste any time changing things around, did you? *Fast Attack News*? And that music sounds like we're about to invade Poland. And since when is it *Clay* Bodine?"

Jeanette waved her hand to silence me. "This has all been in the works a long time. It's part of our new image."

Well, it was new, all right. There was Clay—the new kid on the block, the former Clayton Bodine—with his jacket off, tie loosened, and sleeves rolled up. He looked, for all the world, like an actual working journalist, fixing the audience with his steely gray eyes and saying, "Festerwood Held Hostage—Day Two." And sure enough, right there behind him was a huge slide that proclaimed exactly that.

"Good evening, everyone. The eyes of the nation tonight are on Festerwood's far westside, where a man identified as Norb Fagan continues to keep police at bay while holding his common-law wife, Marie, and perhaps several others, hostage. Police believe Fagan, whose nickname 'Nutsy' now appears to be more prophetic than good natured, possesses an arsenal of weapons and explosives."

As he spoke, up came a photo of Nutsy wearing his Beetle Bailey helmet. By now it was clear that this picture was the only visual proof we had that Nutsy Fagan existed.

Now it was Melanie's turn to pick up the story. Melanie Farnsworth was relatively new to the station, a recent graduate of Indiana Normal University, where she had majored in radio and television. It was obvious that she had made a personal vow to rise above her degree and her chosen profession. She was pretty in a nonthreatening, Midwestern way, with her stylish brown hair and large, expressive eyes. Melanie was no dummy. She knew that her looks were important, but she made it clear more than once that it was not her face or her gender that mattered. Melanie was a serious newswoman, and at age twenty-four, she was on a fast career track. A couple of years in Festerwood to learn the ropes, a year or two in Evansville to polish her skills, then the big time.

Bodine hated her for all sorts of reasons. Mainly, she represented his first co-anchor, and Clayton—I mean, Clay—figured who the hell needed two people to read this drivel? Her age didn't help, either. He figured Melanie was young enough to be his granddaughter, and he resented the regulars at the Ramada Inn bar who kept asking him how he was getting along with the jail bait. But tonight, Clay and Melanie were the picture of teamwork.

"We have major new developments breaking at this hour, Clay. Norb Fagan has scheduled a news conference in just a few minutes, apparently to tell the world what he plans to do next as this tense hostage drama unfolds before our eyes. Our own Dirk Tubergen has been on the scene of this wrenching crisis since it first broke. Dirk, what's the latest?"

Dirk launched into his report with a ferocity that made it clear he considered this hostage crisis to be his ticket to the network. Any network.

"Yes, Melanie, at any second now we will hear the first words of a deeply troubled man. The man they call 'Nutsy' has kept this quiet, law-abiding community in his thrall for two days now, threatening to harm his common-law wife and who-knows-how-many others. Members of the Festerwood town and county SWAT teams have surrounded his home on Ralston Street; they are ready to riddle the structure with a fusillade of hot steel, once they are given a signal by Police Chief Fred Penny and Sheriff Myron Slope. *WHOE Fast Attack News* has provided police with a wireless microphone to give to Fagan, and he has put it on."

Dirk's voice rose noticeably as Nutsy, wearing a Festus Community College baseball camp, tentatively peeked out the front door.

"And there you see him for the first time since this ordeal began! Fagan is holding a police bullhorn and appears ready to speak. Let's give a listen."

"Excuse me, I need a beer," I said as I extricated myself from the tangle of sheets and headed for the bathroom. "Can I get you anything?"

Jeanette wasn't talking. At least not to me. She just sat cross-legged on the bed, staring at the television and repeating, "This is great!" over and over, to no one in particular.

I popped open an Old Style and stood before the bathroom mirror to assess the damage. I'd had a good time, and there were no visible scars, so I returned to the bedroom just as old Nutsy was addressing the masses.

There he was, with bullhorn and ballcap and what looked like a popgun in his hand, standing on his crumbling front porch steps as police cowered behind their cars, guns drawn.

"Now, I just want to say that I haven't done a goddam thing. I just want to be left alone here. I got a lot of things on my mind. But I'll be damned if I'm goin' to let you lock me up for no reason!"

I turned to Jeanette. "Since when did reason enter into this?"

"Hush," she whispered. "This is a classic."

I gave her my best lewd smile and said, "So are you. Did anyone ever tell you that you're cute when you're naked?"

She looked up for just a moment. "You're not so bad yourself, especially for an aging hunk. Now be quiet. I want to hear this."

Various reporters started bombarding Nutsy with the usual penetrating questions: "How many in there with you?" "Have you killed anybody?" "How long do you plan to keep this up?" "What are your demands?" And, of course, Dirk's stock question to anyone charged with a felony: "Why'd ya do it?"

But Nutsy was preoccupied with somebody in the house. "Horace, come here for a second. C'mon—it won't take long. Put down the goddam video game and come over here!"

A child no more than nine years old, wearing a No Fear cap and a Hard Rock Cafe tee-shirt moved into the picture, and Nutsy quickly wrapped his right arm across the kid's chest. You could hear an audible gasp from the reporters and cops, as well as the sound of SWAT team rifles being cocked, but the kid look unfazed by the whole business.

"Oh my God!" cried Jeanette.

"Interesting," I said. "I see little Horace is back for the season."

"What?"

"Horace. That's Nutsy's sister's kid. She drops the little terrorist off every fall while she and her husband follow the carnival circuit in Florida, selling elephant ears, corn dogs, stuff like that. Anyway, old Nutsy lets the kid run amok on his skateboard, up-ending old women and shoplifting everything he can get his sticky little hands on. Believe me, this kid is not in peril."

By now Nutsy had ducked back into the house, and all you could hear were his footsteps, a door opening and closing, and then the jarring sound of water hitting water.

"What's that sound? Is there a buzz in one of the cables?" Jeanette now was kneeling on her haunches, her eyes riveted to the screen, looking like Miss October taking a break from her centerfold photo-shoot to watch her favorite soap opera.

I took a swig of beer. "That, Ms. Larmer, is our own Norbert Fagan treating your viewers and mine to the lyrical sounds of the Ralston Street Ravager taking a piss. And it's all coming to us courtesy of our own WHOE wireless microphone. Another first, I'd say."

From the sound of it, Nutsy was disposing of all twenty-four cases of beer, the sum total of his first formal demand as a bona fide hostage taker.

Jeanette was impressed. "I think your medical reporter should do a story on Nutsy's bladder. He must have been a camel in a past life."

"We don't have a medical reporter, Jeanette."

She shrugged. "You will if I have anything to say about it. And Nutsy's bladder will be her first story."

Nutsy was talking very fast now, obviously scared to death but also a bit exhilarated by all the attention. "Look, I don't want to kill nobody, but I ain't goin' to jail for not doin' nothin'. So I ain't lettin' anyone go until I can give my story to a guy I can trust."

I could see Nutsy was starting to ransack his mind for a candidate. Then he found one. "I ain't gonna let these people go until I can talk to . . . Rick Roberson . . . of the television!"

I dropped my beer, adding a fresh stain to the Ramada Inn carpet, and just stared at the set.

"Holy shit! He wants to talk to me!"

Jeanette literally jumped out of the bed. "Unbelievable! Incredible!" She threw her arms around me. "Do you know what this means, Rick? Now we own this story!"

I sank into the bed. "I can't do this."

Jeanette wheeled on me. "What do you mean you can't do this? What kind of a newsman are you? Any reporter would give his right testicle for a story like this. And here it's dropped into your lap! Besides . . ." She looked away. "Now you have no choice! If you don't do what he says, two innocent people could be killed."

"There are no hostages, Jeanette! That's what I'm telling you! For God's sake, I've lived in this town all my life! I've known Nutsy all my life. Trust me, this is a non-story!"

"What about Marie? Has he ever taken her hostage before?"

I flopped on the bed. "Are you kidding? Marie outweighs Nutsy by two hundred pounds. If he gave her any shit, she would be feeding his remains to the dog. Or haven't you noticed? Marie has not made an appearance in this little human drama."

"So where is she?"

I sighed. "How would I know? She's probably down in Daytona for her annual sabbatical with some NASCAR racing mechanic she hooked up with at the Festus County Fair. In any event, Nutsy is holding zero hostages, so let's not have any of this put a damper on our evening. Shall I order the wine?"

I took in the foolishness of the situation. Here was a woman standing not two feet from me—a woman I didn't even know until two days ago—scolding me for not wanting to risk my life for a story that didn't exist until she entered my life. And she's doing it in the nude.

"Jeanette, if Nutsy decides to do anything, the blood won't be on my hands. I warned you and Boyd and the rest of your tabloid news team that there was no story here, that if we went in with cameras rolling, old Nutsy might just flip out. Now you're telling me that because you ignored my warning, it's up to me to go in there and save the day."

"No, not *save the day*, Rick!" She was shouting now. "Save two lives! I don't care how noble you are or how righteous you have become over this; the fact is, you have a chance to defuse a very dangerous situation!"

"And score a big win in the ratings?"

"Yes! And score a big win in the ratings! What's so bad about that? Or would you prefer to go on giving your little farm-market reports and tractor accidents to the few people who are still watching your pathetic newscast?"

I shook my head. "What tractor accident? Did we miss another one?"

She was dressing now, fumbling with the buttons on her blouse. "Goddam you, Roberson. I was wrong about you. I thought that you were a bright, ambitious reporter who was chomping at the bit to get out of this cow town. But it turns out you're part of the problem. Small-town boy with a small-town mind. Too bad."

It was quite a performance. In just a few seconds, Jeanette had made the transition from rage to pity. But then she hit me where it hurt the most.

"So," she said as she adjusted her skirt, "I guess we'll find someone else to talk to Nutsy. Maybe he'll take Dirk Tubergen, or even . . . who's that morning guy? Chiles. Maybe he'll talk to him. I just hate to see a story this big in anyone else's hands. A story this big could make or break a career. I hear that CNN is sending in a crew, and *USA Today* sent its stringer up from Evansville. Whoever gets this story has a one-way ticket to the big time."

That line was straight out of a made-for-TV movie, but it worked for me. She was right, of course. There was no value to the story—no reason for any of us to be there—but suddenly it had taken on a life of its own. Nutsy Fagan, town fool, was about to become a national celebrity, and there wasn't one goddam thing I could do about it. But if I did go along with this, maybe I could do some good. If, in fact, we had caused Nutsy to flip out, then maybe I could talk him down and get myself the one story that would jump-start my career. Lord knows I had waited long enough. As I sat there, it became easier and easier to rationalize the whole business. What can it hurt? If I do this right, everybody wins.

I began searching the bed sheets for my shorts. "OK, you're right. Rick Roberson, hostage negotiator, is about to swing into action. Where are my socks?"

chapter nineteen

LIKE EVERYTHING ELSE IN FESTERWOOD, NUTSY FAGAN'S HOUSE WAS only ten minutes away. It stood by itself on the south side of Ralston Street as the lone testimonial to a block of nine homes built before the turn of the century. They were torn down in the early seventies as part of a grandiose urban renewal project that, like everything else in Festerwood, never quite got off the ground.

That, in part, explained why the Fagan estate survived. It was once owned by Mildred Swithers, a spooky old lady who, in her dotage, had pretty much cornered the market on the Festus County cat population. She also kept several psychopathic dogs on the premises, whose howling could be heard long into the night. The house was dark and foreboding, with one eerie light shining from an attic window, day and night.

That's where old lady Swithers conducted her fiendish experiments on stray animals. At least that's what the Festerwood kids all said, especially on Halloween night, when they prowled outside the rusted iron gate and dared each other to "ding dong dilly ditch" the old woman's front porch. Such "rumors from the crypt" convinced demolition workers to save her home for last. As a result, she was spared when federal urban renewal grants and investment capital failed to materialize.

Miss Swithers died in 1973, and Nutsy moved in not long after his tour of duty in Vietnam, no doubt carrying his common-law bride, Marie, over the threshold. Marie was approximately eight years older than Nutsy. They met at Duke's Bar and Grill, which doubled as the Trailways Bus Station. She was a waitress, and he was the new bar fly on the block.

Marie was fascinated by Nutsy's Vietnam stories, even though he had just been a postal clerk at Cam Ran Bay, which was about as far from the fighting as you could get. And for his part, Nutsy was fascinated by anyone who would listen to them. They agreed to move in together, and Mildred Swither's home was available. When they moved in, the place would have been described by realtors as "a good starter home" or a "handyman's delight." Nutsy and Marie pretty much saw to it that the house maintained that status, a place where everything came off in your hand.

But on this night, it was a showplace. In the glow of floodlights, the little house on Ralston Street looked like something out of a Stephen King movie. Police cars were lined up three deep in a semi-circle facing the house. A few of them I recognized—they were the familiar tan and silver colors of the Festus County Sheriff's Department, but they had plenty of company. A police helicopter circled overhead, and perhaps a dozen units from surrounding cities and counties had joined the militia. The policemen who belonged to those cars were all dressed in their chic SWAT ensembles: bullet proof vests and official SWAT team baseball caps from the Cooperstown collection. All of them were poised for some serious shooting, bracing their rifles on the hoods and trunks of their police cars.

Behind this front line were the television satellite trucks. I counted seven in all, representing TV stations from Terre Haute, Champaign, and even as far away as Indianapolis—all of them running at full power, sending their pictures from Festerwood out into television's global village. The only station missing from this formidable display of space-age newsgathering was WHOE. We hadn't gotten around to investing in a satellite truck, so we made do with a tired-looking van bearing a microwave transmitter that allowed us to bounce our signals off various places, people and things to a transmitter high atop downtown Festerwood's tallest building, the six-story Union Bank. It didn't work half the time, but it was working just fine tonight in what the new regime was confident would be WHOE's finest hour.

"Nobody allowed beyond the tape." My path to Nutsy's house was blocked by a burly cop wearing a uniform I didn't recognize. He must have been one of the many lawmen from the outside counties who were brought in at taxpayers' expense to keep the peace.

"I'm Rick Roberson," I explained. "The guy Nutsy wants to see."

The cop didn't budge. "I don't care if you're Dick Tracy. Nobody gets beyond the tape."

"Look, I'm a reporter." I searched my wallet for the press pass that I hadn't used for ten years. "Here. WHOE-TV."

The visiting policeman squinted in the darkness. "I dunno. This sure as hell doesn't look like you."

He was right. The picture was ten years old and my hair was about ten inches longer. "Well, this is old, but it's me . . . and if I don't get inside that house in the next few minutes, all hell could break loose!"

"Roberson! Over here!" It was Myron Slope, the Festus County sheriff, who was about the last person in the world I figured would come to my rescue. Slope was widely regarded as the most corrupt sheriff in Indiana, but he was a reasonably savvy cop when he put his mind to it. He had held onto his job for twenty-four years, which put Sheriff Slope in the enviable position of knowing a lot of things about a lot of people, especially those who were inclined to sit on grand juries.

As a result, my periodic exposés into his creative theories on how to turn law enforcement into a personal profit center never blossomed into indictments. But this year, the good sheriff was actually facing a primary challenge from none other than Chief Fred Penny of the Festerwood Police Department. Fred was a nervous, cautious leader whose conciliatory ways served him well on most days in the

Festerwood urban jungle. Of course, he was clearly over his head here, and Slope knew it. Both men stood facing the real Ralston Street terrorist, WHOE News Director Boyd Nelson.

"I don't like this a goddam bit," Sheriff Slope was saying. "This is just too dangerous. We got a real tense situation here."

Young Mr. Nelson just shook his head. "Sheriff, if that little boy dies because you wouldn't let our best man come in and defuse the situation . . . well, I certainly wouldn't want that on my conscience."

Sheriff Slope's normally florid features turned a deeper shade of red. "Look, goddammit, I wouldn't let Roberson wash my cat. The only reason that Nutsy wants to talk to him is so he can blow his wise-ass face off!"

I thought this might be a good time to join the discussion. "What's the problem, Sheriff? Having a Maalox moment, are we?"

They all turned and looked at me like I was Jimmy Hoffa.

Boyd shouted, "Jesus, Roberson, where have you been? We've been trying to get ahold of you for hours!"

"I was getting a bikini wax in preparation for my Caribbean cruise, but I understand Mr. Fagan has invited me in for pizza and beer. How could I refuse?"

Slope shook his head violently. "You stay out of this, Roberson. I'm not going to let you foul this up."

I tried to look puzzled. "Oh, does this mean Fagan has pulled ahead of you in the polls? Or do you want to throw him in jail so he can help you pave your driveway?"

This stirring debate was abruptly terminated when I felt two very firm hands on my arm and shoulder, spinning me away from the action. I looked up, way up, into the face of Festerwood Deputy Police Chief Dennis Fronzman, all six feet-six inches of him; he'd been my friend since nursery school.

As he firmly led me away, he said, "Rick, we've got to talk. Please join me in my office."

It was freezing inside Fronzman's police cruiser. Freezing and noisy.

"Jesus, Fronz, can you turn that thing down?"

Fronzman faded the volume on the police radio and turned to me with a look of amused exasperation, culled from his experience of having known me too long and too well—through twelve grades of education and more bar-hopping expeditions than our kidneys cared to remember.

"Rick, how the hell did this happen?"

"I should ask you the same thing, Fronz. What's with this SWAT team bullshit? You know Mister Rogers is more of a threat than Nutsy Fagan. Why don't you do what you've always done with Nutsy: walk in the house and hit him upside the head till he sobers up?"

Fronz looked at me like a fourth-grade teacher looks at a student who's trying to explain that his hamster consumed his homework. "Excuse me, but I don't recall that horseshit station of yours ever responding to a Nutsy Fagan run with satellite trucks and helicopters, attracting the media of the entire free world to our little town. What's going on with you guys, anyway? We've had everybody but Barbara Walters here."

I just sighed and looked out the window at Nutsy's little house, all lit up like a supermarket grand opening.

"What can I say, Fronz? It's the millennium and anything goes. The main thing is, right now, how do you think I should handle this?"

"Christ, Rick, this has gone way beyond you and Nutsy. You and I know he's harmless—nothing that a detox center couldn't cure—but thanks to your blanket coverage, we have our two favorite candidates for sheriff trying to out-macho each other. Does the campaign phrase *soft on crime* ring a bell? And look out there. Every squirrel hunter in both departments is itchin' for the word to open up and turn Nutsy into hamburger helper." Fronz gripped the steering wheel in his celebrated "true grit" mode. "I'm not going to let that happen. I'm not going to let them drag Nutsy off to prison."

"So," I said, "let me repeat: How should we handle this?"

Fronz looked away. "I suggest you accept Nutsy's invitation. Go in there and try to get him calmed down."

I had a feeling that would be his answer. "And what about the first lady of the Nutsy household? She can be quite a handful, too."

"As far as we know, she's not home. Somebody said she's down in Daytona for the stock car race. So that leaves Nutsy and the kid."

"And a weapon," I added. "What about that gun he was holding at the kid's head? That made quite an impression on my new boss and our audience."

"It's a toy, for Chrissake. I bought a bunch of them for my boys last Christmas." Fronz opened the car door. "Now let me handle the troops. Just remember, the sheriff and the chief are way out of their depth here. Like all of us."

Chief Penny just stood there in full befuddlement, looking like a man trying to think deeply about where he might have left his car keys. Fronz took him out of earshot and began what looked like some earnest diplomacy. Fact is, without the Fronz, Penny was a lost soul amidst the modest intrigues of the Festerwood police force, and he knew it. Fronz was the brains behind the department and was so good at his job that the good folks of Festerwood were convinced that Chief Penny was a leader of considerable wisdom and insight. Now his chief deputy was paving the way for him to demonstrate this skill in the election year's most compelling setting—within full range of a television satellite truck.

Meanwhile, Sheriff Slope was introducing young Boyd Nelson to the realities of small-town law enforcement.

"Look, son, I don't give a rat's ass if that lunatic in there blows Roberson's head off and tosses it back on the lawn in a Hefty bag. Hell, he'd probably get off for justifiable homicide. But I'm not going to let Roberson jeopardize the life of innocent hostages just so you can get more people to watch your horseshit newscast!"

Boyd didn't have time to reply, because suddenly a voice boomed out of the night. "We're going to let Roberson go in."

Slope looked stunned, for he had never before been in the presence of Police Chief Fred Penny in the process of actually making a decision. The chief, still giddy from what must have been a massive dose of testosterone administered by the Fronz, looked Slope in the eye and said, "Myron, this is my call in my jurisdiction. Your boys are here for backup."

Sheriff Slope turned a violent shade of purple. "Fred, you're out of your mind. You're not fit to run the dog pound!"

I joined the fray. "Well, Myron, when Chief Penny is elected Sheriff, you'll at least have the consolation of knowing Festerwood won't be his primary jurisdiction."

Now it was Boyd Nelson's turn to pull me away from the crowd. Our new leader was the picture of controlled agitation. "For God's sake, Roberson, please take this situation seriously. Look, they're going to let you go in there, and here's how we're going to handle it. We're going to put a wireless mike on you, and maybe a directional mike, and we'll see if we can pick you up live. The wireless we gave Nutsy earlier crapped out—"

I stopped him right there. "Boyd, I know this is the nineties, but no live shots. Let me figure what's going on in there first, and if Nutsy wants an interview or wants to make a statement, then we'll have Lowell come in and set up a camera. We can tape it."

Boyd shook his head. "Look out there, Roberson. Every satellite truck in the free world is parked on Fagan's lawn. They're expecting to go live. Their viewers and ours are expecting us to go live. We have to do it!"

By now, Larry the Loon and several of his WHOE Legionnaires had joined the party. I continued talking to Boyd, but my message was for Larry. "By all means, let's go live, so we can treat our audience to Nutsy's colorful vocabulary. Or did you not know that variations of the word *fuck* can be used in place of almost any noun, verb, or adjective? Then they can all hold their breath as Nutsy decides whether to wrap up this spectacle by blowing the head off a nine-year-old kid or yours truly.

"Now, I agree, this is no big deal in my case, especially if this turns into a ratings spectacle, but there may be a problem if in fact he does pull the trigger and WHOE becomes the first TV station in history to show a live execution—uncut, uncensored, and commercial-free!"

It worked. Larry pushed his way through the crowd and said, "I don't think we better go live right now. Let Rick go in and talk to the guy—see what he wants, settle things down."

Our leader had spoken. Boyd grumbled something under his breath, but whatever he said was lost in a perky voice from another WHOE staffer. "Here, you'll need to wear this!"

It was Teri. She was smiling brightly as she handed me what appeared to be a navy blue flak jacket. It was brand new, state-of-the-art; I was impressed. Then I turned it around and saw the inscription on the back. In bold orange letters across the top were the familiar call letters of the station, W-H-O-E, and under that, in a semicircle of smaller letters, was the phrase, "Your Festus County Fair Station." And just below that, at roughly the middle of my spine, as a helpful guide for the sheriff's SWAT team sharpshooters, were large cartoon drawings of a smiling cow and a maniacally grinning pig.

A voice from the crowd: "Rick, I'll be happy to step in for you." It was our man on the scene, Dirk Tubergen. "I've been here from the first, and I know where this guy is coming from." There was an urgency in his voice, as if Dirk feared that I might become a special guest star on his resume tape.

But this sudden outpouring of concern was touching, in a way. "I appreciate that, Dirk, I really do. But Nutsy did ask specifically for me. I'm sure that you would have been his first choice, but maybe he couldn't pronounce *Tubergen*."

I took Dirk aside and lowered my voice. "Look, Nutsy and I go back a long way, and I know he's just a harmless drunk. This looks bad, but we're part of the problem here—a big part. So do me a favor. Go easy on the tabloid stuff, OK? You know, 'Festerwood Held Hostage' and 'Ralston Street Ravager'—it's not helping the situation a bit. I'm afraid Nutsy is hearing all this and it may be getting to him. If it does, he could do something drastic, after all."

Dirk looked confused. "But Boyd said—"

"Forget what Boyd said. Please, just play it straight, at least until I get my ass out of that house."

Nelson walked over. "We better get going on this." He handed me a cellular phone. "Here, see if you can keep in touch with this. Our number is taped on the back."

As it turned out, I had an even more portable, folding cell phone in my pants pocket that was linked with Fronzman's personal cellular, so we could more or less discreetly chat in the unlikely event that one of us actually came up with an inspired idea as to what the hell to do next.

I turned to Chief Penny. "Chief, I think I'm ready. Would you care to announce me to our host?"

chapter twenty

IT WAS TIME NOW FOR THE DUELING BULLHORNS.

Chief Penny began. "Fagan! This is Chief Penny. Do you hear me? Fagan! Do you hear me?"

Nutsy's bullhorn started its reply with an ear-splitting squeal, followed by, "Yeah, Whaddya want? Did ya bring the beer? I'm runnin' low."

Now it was the chief's turn. "We got Rick Roberson here, and he's willing to talk like you wanted. He's coming up, OK?"

"All right. Have him come in the front door. And no funny stuff. Is he bringin' beer?"

I started my trek to the front entrance as Penny assured Nutsy that more brew was on its way. I tried to remember Fronz's assurance that the menacing-looking double-barreled gun pointed at me was actually a toy. Nutsy's rheumy eyes looked out from the crack in the door. It slowly opened and I walked in with studied nonchalance. My host slammed the door, only to see it fly back at him due to a faulty lock. Nutsy kicked it four times before he got it to stay in place.

"How are you doing, Norb?" I launched my hostage-negotiating career with the most sympathetic tone I could muster.

"I'm fucked, man. I gotta be dreamin' this. I think they wanna kill me."

"No, they don't," I lied. I decided to change the subject. "Hey, look, Norb, they made me wear this stupid flak jacket, and it's real uncomfortable. Mind if I take it off?"

Nutsy nodded. "Yeah, go ahead. Hey, man, I wasn't goin' to shoot you."

I wrestled out of my bulletproof cocoon and tossed it on the coffee table, next to two pizza boxes from Pepperoni Pete's.

Nutsy gave a quizzical look to the designer cow and pigs on my flak jacket. "Is the county fair already started? Man, it's a little early this year, ain't it? Boy, Marie will be damned disappointed if she misses it."

"Uh, no, Norb, it doesn't start for another seven months, but my station is planning to cover it like a beer fart."

There was an awkward pause, then I said, "You know, Norb, I'd feel a lot better if you would put that gun down."

Nutsy seemed somewhat surprised by my request; he brought the weapon up to his face, as if to examine and confirm that he was actually holding such a thing in his hands. I was also giving it a closer inspection. Turns out Chief Deputy Fronzman knows his firearms.

"Excuse me, Norb, but does that say 'Mattel' on the barrel?"

Nutsy looked stricken. His lower lip started quivering, then he threw the gun on the floor, producing a tinny clank. He sat down on the couch, put his head in his hands, and started sobbing. The sight of a grown man crying has always made me uneasy. It seemed like every time I looked up, there was some brawny athlete announcing his retirement on TV and sobbing uncontrollably like a third grader who screwed up in a spelling bee. Now here I was, in the company of one of the community's most erratic citizens, as his flimsy allotment of the American dream was unraveling amid a fortress of pizza boxes and empty beer cans. The thought was not lost on me that the last time I dried a grown adult's eyes was on Teri's magical election night; I was not exactly in the mood for another life-defining moment.

I sat down next to Nutsy. "Look, Norb, things are not so bad as they look. But you got to work with me. Let's clear up a few things. Where's Marie?"

Nutsy looked at me with the saddest eyes I'd ever seen. "Oh, she went to Florida with that mechanic fella. I don't know why she does this every year. Just up and takes off with hardly a good-bye. And this time I'm thinkin', *Damn, she ain't comin' back*. I don't know what I'd do without Marie. So I start feelin' real sad, and then I start drinkin' too much and feelin' sorry for myself, and then I kind of blackout. Next thing I know, the place is surrounded by cops, and all these big trucks with these big round things on 'em—"

"Satellite trucks," I said.

"Whatever. So here I am, wonderin' whether they're gonna kill me or take me away to where I'll never see Marie again—"

I put my hand on his shoulder. Physically, Nutsy was as hopeless as his situation. His matted, graying hair hadn't been subjected to a comb in some time; it branched off in all directions. His camouflage pants were torn in both knees, and his pizza-and-beer-stained tee-shirt bore a faded inscription that paid tribute to that cutting-edge rock band of the seventies, The Cowsills. He was barefoot, the soles of his feet as black as coals. His bloodshot eyes showed the full effects of two sleepless nights filled with bouts of self-pity.

I tried to get the conversation back on track. "Norb, do you remember calling the police and telling them you were taking people hostage?"

He looked as if he was trying to remember. "Well, I kind of lose track of what I'm doin' when I have too much to drink. I kind of dream stuff like that, but I know I done it before and they never made a big deal about it. Seems to me that Deputy Fronzman—he's always nice to me—he just lets me sleep it off and then drives me home the next mornin' and tells me to stay here till Marie comes home."

I stood up and looked out the window at the blinding lights and the shiny gun barrels trained on Nutsy's home. "Well, Norb, things have kind of changed around here, and I'm afraid you got a lot of attention this time. And you know you don't help things a lot by pointing that toy gun at Horace's head."

Nutsy shrugged. "Hell, Horace knows I don't mean nothin' when I do that."

I sat down again. "I know Horace knows, but everybody watching out there doesn't know. So you, me, and Deputy Fronzman got to figure something out here before things get out of hand. By the way, where is Horace?"

With that, Nutsy rose to his feet. "Where is that little shit?" That was followed by an ear-splitting bellow. "*Horace!* He was supposed to be cleanin' up after the cat. I'll bet he's outside."

I was, to say the least, astonished. "Say what?"

Nutsy went to the front window and peaked out through a slivered opening in the shade. "Goddammit, there he is!"

chapter twenty-one

I LOOKED OUT THE WINDOW AND, SURE ENOUGH, THERE WAS HORACE ON his skateboard—weaving around various reporters and technicians, deftly leaping over cables and wires—oblivious to the fact that his well-being was a matter of universal concern. Of course, the reporters and police were equally oblivious to the fact that the object of their concern was hanging ten—or whatever it is you do on a skateboard—right in their midst.

Granted, Horace had changed his looks considerably from his hostage cameo appearance by removing his cap to show off his sandy-colored hair that was done up in the popularly hideous kitchen-mop fashion—long on top, burr cut along the sides. He was wearing the "Fab Five" shorts just below the knee and a winsome orange tee-shirt that shouted the enduring shorthand philosophy, *Shit Happens.* No doubt that was a present from his grandparents, commemorating the ninth year that Horace was being allowed to live.

Horace's journey through satellite city was suddenly blocked by one of Chief Penny's finest, who was shouting, "Hey, stop that kid! It's long past curfew!" To that, Horace did a nifty pirouette on his skateboard, ducked under the cop's groping arms, pushed off with his right foot, and zipped under the officer's legs. The cop spun around, took two steps in pursuit, and tripped over a thick cable, courtesy of CNN. As the cop yelped in pain and grabbed his shin, Horace made a beeline for the house.

Moments later, the door burst open, and Horace, carrying his skateboard as if it were a trophy, walked past us like we were coat racks. Then he sat down in front of the television set to immerse himself in the video of some Cro-Magnon rock ensemble. As his temporary guardian, Nutsy took another crack at imposing adult supervision.

"Goddammit, Horace, what did I tell you about leaving the house while the cops still had it surrounded? Your mother's goin' to be pissed when she gets back and finds your head blowed off."

Horace stared blankly at the television. "There's nothin' to do around here. Any more pizza left?"

"I'm goin' to order more in."

"Well, tell 'em not to put any more of them dead fish on 'em, those antosies."

Nutsy nodded. "I'll have 'em put 'em on half the pizzas."

"OK," Horace agreed. "Just so they aren't on my half."

I didn't want to interrupt this quality time between hostage and hostage-taker, but I sensed that the central point of Nutsy's little speech was being buried under the mozzarella. "Uh, Horace, your uncle is right. It's dangerous out there, and until we get this all straightened out, please don't go outside again."

Horace, his eyes still riveted on the TV, inquired, "Who are you?"

"I'm a good friend of your uncle's, and I'm trying to get him out of this mess. But I need your help. Promise me you'll stay put until this is over."

"How're you gonna make me?"

Suddenly the thought of taking a hostage started making sense, but I tried another tack. "Horace, see that poker leaning up against the fireplace?"

For the first time since he sat down, Horace exhibited head movement; he looked at the well-rusted iron poker next to the grungy fireplace, which, judging by its condition, must have been used more than once by Nutsy and Marie to cook animals that had thought themselves exempt from the American food chain.

"Well," I continued, "if you give me any more trouble, I will take that poker, ram it up your ass, and pull it out your ear. And don't think I won't. I've done it before. Do I make myself clear?"

"Whatever," he said, turning his head back to the screen. I chose to interpret this as a sign of his full cooperation.

Nutsy and I sat at the kitchen table. The situation was so foolish I didn't know where to start. Here was Nutsy, armed with nothing more than a toy gun, while his alleged hostage was out in the street playing demolition derby with the cops and reporters. There was even less to this than met the eye.

I propped my elbows on the table. "Norb, why don't you just give yourself up?" I said in my best coaxing voice. "I can tell the cops that Marie's not even here, that Horace is in no danger unless he trips over a camera tripod, and that you can't do any harm with a gun that shoots cork pellets. Let's just—"

Nutsy sat up in his chair. "I got another gun. A real one. And it's loaded, too."

"Where is it, Nutsy?"

He looked hurt. "I ain't tellin' nobody, not even you, Rick. And I sure don't trust them cops out there. I ain't never done nothin' to hurt nobody before, but now they're callin' me the Ralston Street Scavenger—"

"That's *Ravager*, Norb. And it's not the cops who are calling you that; it's the reporters. They just made that up so this would look like a good story. Don't pay any attention to them. Why don't we just go out there and explain what happened and it will all go away."

"Nothin' doin', Rick. Not now. They want to kill me. I know they do. I ain't gonna give up without a fight."

I leaned back in my chair. "Norb, you have nothing to fight with. You're outnumbered. And besides, what do you want from all this? What exactly do you want me to do here?"

Nutsy gazed off toward the kitchen window. "Hell, I don't know what I want. I didn't want none of this to happen, I can tell you that.

I figured you were about the only guy I could talk to. You're one of the few guys in town who's been nice to me, especially that time you put me on TV."

God, I had forgotten about that. I had known Nutsy since my childhood, but about eight or nine years ago I was responsible for giving him his allotted fifteen minutes of fame. I drew the short straw and was sent down to the town dump on the hottest day of the year. The dump had been operated by three generations of the Flanders family with a dedication that was fierce, bordering on disturbing.

Flaky Floyd Flanders represented the second generation and looked for all the world like a crazed pirate. He had a right eye made of glass that allowed you to see through into the socket. Apparently, no one thought about the effect that would have on anyone meeting him for the first time. He had a permanent three-day-old beard stubble, and his head was always wrapped in a sweat-soaked red bandanna that looked as if it might have been used for general clean-up around the yard.

Floyd was usually in a rage, bellowing indecipherable words—presumably profanities—at assorted Sanitation Department garbage haulers, letting them know in no uncertain terms that he would decide when, where, and how their trash would be deposited on his property. The haulers always complied, mostly out of respect for the Flanders' prize collection of Dobermans which had been recruited from the Baskerville estate.

Nutsy was a valued employee of the Flanders' dump. He never missed a day of work; he toiled hard without any complaint; he functioned as a handy sounding board for Floyd's volcanic eruptions—especially after his sons, Ferdie and Faldo, started tuning him out or responding in kind. And the reason I wound up interviewing Nutsy on that hellacious day is because I couldn't understand a damn word that Flanders said in his interview. In comparison, Nutsy came through like Charles Kuralt. He projected a sweet innocence as he earnestly assured me that the heat "wasn't all that bad, especially when you compare it to Vietnam, where it got real hot and sticky." I guess that

Nutsy was quite thrilled to see himself in my report, which otherwise was the usual insipid mid-August heat-coping story that was a staple of local television news. All I remembered from that journalistic effort was how tenaciously the stench from the dump clung to my clothes, skin, and psyche.

"Yeah, you're one of the few people who's ever been nice to me. Even back in school when all the kids made fun of me—you and Father Mike and Deputy Fronzman never called me names or nothin'."

His listing of patron saints brought me up short. "Who did you say?"

"Uh, Deputy Fronzman—he was real nice to me when I was arrested—"

"No, no, before that. Who did you mention before that?"

Nutsy thought for a moment. "Well, you and Deputy Fronzman . . . and . . . Father Mike."

"Father Michael Roarke?"

"Yeah, I guess. You know, over at St. Bonnie's."

Of course! The Reverend Michael Roarke! Suddenly I spotted one of those thousand points of light at the end of the proverbial tunnel. I whipped out my cell phone and made contact on the first ring.

chapter twenty-two

"FRONZMAN HERE. PLEASE TELL ME YOU HAVE SOMETHING RESEMBLING good news, Rick."

"Indeed I do, Deputy Dennis. It seems Nutsy has strong diplomatic ties to our good friend, the Pope."

Fronz answered immediately. "Oh for Chrissake, of course. Mike Roarke! Why didn't we think of him before? He's perfect. Hell, I was just out drinking with him last week."

"Where? How come I wasn't invited?"

"It was right after the K of C banquet. I guess we didn't notice you up at the head table."

"Good try, wise ass. I didn't make that one. The *Gilligan's Island* reunion show was on that night."

Now Fronz was a little less enthusiastic. "Trouble is, Mike is up in Minnesota conducting one of those retreats for Parents Without Partners or something like that. I think he told me there were no phones up there."

"Damn. What town is he in?"

"Dunno. All I remember is that it's in Minnesota. I'll go ahead and call the church to see if Father Bonnie knows."

I wasn't thrilled. "Oh, he'll be a big help."

"I know," Fronz said, "but we got to start somewhere. Wait a minute. Why the hell are we going to all this trouble, anyway? Nutsy isn't even holding a real gun. We could just—"

"Save it, Fronz. He says he has a gun, all right. An honest-to-

God firearm hidden somewhere in the house, and with all the ruckus you and my colleagues are making out there, he's about as paranoid as you can get. I don't want to take any chances that he might go postal on us."

"OK, we'll play by your rules. I'll be in touch."

I hung up and turned to Nutsy. "Deputy Fronzman is going to try to locate Father Mike. He thinks Father Bonnie might know."

Suddenly Nutsy took his anxiety to a new level. "Oh, God, please, not Father Bonnie. No, don't call him—please!"

Father Boniface Mulcahy was a longtime symbol of churchly intimidation. He became pastor of St. Boniface Catholic Church in the early sixties. His parishioners, my family included, widely believed at the time that the bishop of western Indiana, Bishop Ignace Perkowski, sentenced Father Bonnie to his new parish just to get rid of him.

At the time, Mulcahy was pastor of Our Lady of Eternal Anguish, or some name like that, over in Bedford, and he also served as head of the diocesan seminary, where he infused his students with the full measure of his intensely conservative dogma, which was in total disagreement with all the changes coming out of Pope John's Second Vatican Council.

In addition, he wrote and edited his own newsletter, called *The Catholic Clarion Call*. In it, he lambasted all the demons that he saw dividing the church: the English-speaking Mass, the roles of women in the Church that went beyond the cleaning of the sacristy, and any subtle suggestion of sex outside of marriage. He issued lengthy diatribes against birth control, married and/or guitar-playing priests, and nuns who wore street clothes.

But Father Boniface Mulcahy finally went one step too far when he denounced virtually all things relative to Vatican II, which put him on a collision course with the bishop, whom Father Bonnie privately referred to as the Polack Prelate. But there wasn't much the bishop could do, seeing as how Father Bonnie's little newsletter was a big hit among some very well-heeled church members. However, when Mulcahy, in a particularly inspired editorial on the evils of drink, seemed to take Christ to task for turning water into wine at that wedding at Cana, His Eminence decided it was time to make his move.

He summoned Mulcahy into his office and informed him that *The Clarion Call* was no longer in business, because its editor would find himself collar-deep in his new responsibilities as the pastor of St. Boniface in Festerwood. The bishop appealed to Father Bonnie's considerable ego by reminding him that very few parish priests were fortunate enough to be assigned to a church bearing their name. And he had no trouble selling the idea to the always-compliant parishioners, since we had been without a pastor for five months following the death of our longtime leader, Father Derek O'Grady.

When the eighty-five-year-old, partially deaf priest failed to show up for 6:30 A.M. Mass one Sunday, the head usher, two altar boys—including yours truly—and all twelve of the early-Mass regulars conducted a search. Finally we found Father O'Grady in peaceful repose in his confessional, where he had apparently been since the previous Monday—another sign that his role as visible parish leader had somewhat diminished over the years.

Father Boniface Mulcahy, ever the staunch traditionalist, had no intention of changing his ways—no matter where he hung his cassock. He was especially fearsome in the confessional, where his assigned punishment for even the most casual sins fell just short of lethal injection.

Nutsy was mumbling, "Not Father Bonnie . . . not Father Bonnie . . ." as I sat him down on the couch and opened a couple of beers.

I tried to sound reassuring. "Norb, I understand what you're going through. But what's wrong with Father Bonnie? Why don't you want to let him help?"

Nutsy just sat there trembling. He muttered something that sounded like, "Wesnay Cufezzun."

I leaned closer. "What's that, Norb? I couldn't hear you."

Nutsy looked me in the eye this time. "Wednesday confession," he said. Then he started shaking again.

"Oh, I see. Wednesday confession. Exactly what happened—"

Nutsy didn't let me finish. He was on his feet now, waving his arms wildly as he paced the floor. "Wednesday confession! Wednesday confession!" he shouted, his face contorted in an angry pout. "Every Wednesday the sisters made us go to confession!"

I figured Nutsy was back in his grade school days now, probably at the old St. Boniface school. He just kept pacing and shouting.

"Every Wednesday," he ranted, "the sisters made us line up in church in front of the confession box, and we always got Father Bonnie. He always smelled bad and he was mean to us kids. If we didn't speak right up and have all our sins memorized, he'd get mad and give us a big penance . . . like maybe ten Our Fathers and ten Hail Mary's and five Acts of Contrition!"

Nutsy was really agitated now. There was no stopping him. "I never knew what to say! I was just a kid, and Sister Agnes made us come up with at least five sins to tell in confession. She said disobeyin' your parents was one, and so was usin' the Lord's name in vain. You know, like cussin'. But it was tough comin' up with sins every week, 'cause I wasn't old enough to do real bad stuff yet.

"Then one day I was first in line to go in, and I was scared 'cause I didn't have any really good sins. I heard one of the older boys who was a class or two ahead of us. He was in the confessional sayin' to Father Bonnie, 'And one sin of self abuse.' Hell, I didn't know what he was talkin' about, but it was a new one and it gave me all five sins that I needed, so I went in . . ." Now Nutsy was really in a state, his face all flushed and wet with spittle. "And I said to Father Bonnie, 'Bless me, Father, for I have sinned. My last confession was one week ago. I disobeyed my parents two times, teased my sister one time, used the name of the Lord in vain two times . . . and one sin of self abuse.' I said that kind of fast. I started in sayin' the rest of it . . . you know, 'I am heartily sorry for these and all my sins'—only he didn't let me finish.

"There was a big thud like he bumped his head or somethin', and he said real loud, 'What did you say, boy?' Man, he scared the shit out of me! 'Did you say self abuse? How old are you, son?' Well, I told him I was seven and a half years old, and then he got real pissed! Old Father Bonnie just got up, and next thing I knew, he was out in the aisle raisin' hell with Sister Agnes . . . askin' her what kind of kids she was teachin' and where did we learn stuff like that?

"Later on, she grabbed me in cafeteria and, man, I got reamed! She went on about how awful it was . . . you know, *self abuse* and all . . . and how I was goin' to Hell if I kept it up. Then she asked me which one of the older boys told me about it. I told her I didn't know, that I just heard it somewhere. The thing is, I didn't have any idea what the hell it was all about! It just sounded like a good sin, and it was easy to remember. I'll tell you what, though, I never used that sin again when it was time for confession. Not even when I started jerkin' off for real."

I assured Nutsy that Father Bonnie would not be brought into these proceedings. But even I had no idea how little help he would be. When the Fronz called the rectory to find out the location of Father Mike's retreat, Father Bonnie responded with a terse, "How the hell should I know? I've got a sermon to write!"

Fortunately, I remembered that Fred Hogan's wife, Mary, was a pillar of the church, a member of all the parish committees and, even better, she possessed an encyclopedic knowledge of all Catholic retreat houses in the continental United States. It took just one call to her to pinpoint Father Mike's retreat. He was at Our Lady of the Pond outside of Remer, Minnesota—a remote, can't-get-there-from-anywhere former fishing camp. Naturally, Hoagie had a contact in the area—an old Army drinking buddy turned police chief in a nearby town—who tracked Mike down and drove him to the nearest phone, where the Fronz apprised him of the situation and transferred the call to my cell phone.

Father Mike greeted me with his usual concern for my spiritual well-being. "Rick, I sincerely hope this call involves your last rites.

You know my ability to perform miracles ends at midnight. So . . . how can I help?"

"A miracle would be great, Mike, but what we really need is your soothing presence down here. Unless you want to see two members of your flock get their asses blown to pieces."

Father Mike said he would be there as soon as he could, which unfortunately was thirteen hours by car, assuming he could find his way out of the woods. At that point, I convinced Fronz that we should take advantage of the media air force that had assembled in front of Nutsy's house. And that's how—on a dark, windy November morning—a helicopter rented by the tabloid TV show *Inside Affair* was scheduled to lift off from Ralston Street in Festerwood, Indiana, heading for Bigfoot country on a journey to retrieve a priest from his mission in the wilds of northern Minnesota. Of course it came at a price. The show's intensely blond reporter, Lisa LaBonte, insisted that she and her photographer be on board to interview Father Mike during his return flight.

There was a time, back in the carefree days before his ordination, when young Mike Roarke would have taken advantage of a sure thing like this. But just in time to save the honor of Festerwood's female population, Michael Roarke discovered he had a calling, after all. In fact, he was the most popular priest in the area, with the ability to relate to all generations of parishioners. The older folks thought he was kind and patient, and he reminded many elderly women of the good son they wished they had. The kids saw another side of Father Mike; to them, he was hip, funny, and he understood their problems. At any rate, he was the perfect man for the job. All I had to do now was wait and try to keep Nutsy calm through the night.

chapter twenty-three

"HEY, UNCLE NORBIE, LOOK! WE'RE ON TV!" AS IT SO HAPPENED, Horace had punched up a 3:00 A.M. rerun of *Inside Affair*. We were all wide awake. For some reason, sleep was hard to come by in the Fagan household. We sat down to watch, just as a reporter was finishing up his story from the front yard.

"So there is no field of dreams in this little Indiana town tonight." He confused Indiana with Iowa, but what the hell. "Here, you will find no legends walking out of corn fields and onto baseball diamonds. In this town, you will find only the harsh realities of small-town America left in the dust of industrial progress. And here, in this modest home, is one man who may symbolize all the frustrations, all the broken dreams of a vanishing way of life. His name is Norbert Fagan, but in fact he is Everyman.

Nutsy looked confused. "Who's he talkin' about? *Everyman* don't live here. I do!"

I reached down to turn off the set, but Horace already was clicking through the channels with the remote.

"Wait, Horace! Stop it there!" I shouted. He had landed on Channel 49, which was showing an exterior shot of Dirkie's restaurant. An announcer, who sounded like he had balls the size of muskmelons, was saying, "You won't believe what we found in this restaurant. WHOE, the station that was first to capture the drama of the Ralston Street hostage crisis, is now working on a report that no taxpayer can afford to miss! Coming up later this week, the story of the city hall beauty who blew the whistle on her boss and got a pink slip for her efforts. Don't miss our investigative report, 'Skimming the Salt' later this week on the new WHOE News!"

I just stared at the set. "Christ, I don't believe this!"

Lowell's camera had zoomed in through Dirkie's front window and focused on a woman seated in a booth talking to me. Only the woman wasn't Norma Flescher. There, on the screen, was a perfectly framed picture of a beautiful young blonde. I was looking at the stunning profile of Dawn Rae Hargis, the minister's daughter!

I called the cell phone number that Boyd Nelson had given me.

"Creative Services Department," Teri answered the phone.

As angry as I was, that stopped me cold. "Teri? Is that you? They put you in charge of the hotline?"

"Rick? Are you OK?"

"What do you think? And what the hell is the promotions director doing out on the front lines at this hour?"

Teri sounded hurt. "Just doing my job. Boyd wants plenty of promos on the air by morning. This is a big story, Rick."

"And apparently not the only one. I just saw your promo for my Norma Flescher story—"

She jumped in. "Oh, good. Rick, you've been holding out on me. This is really great stuff!"

"Teri, would it make any difference if I told you that the woman you're showing on the screen is *not* Norma Flescher?"

There was a pause at the other end. "Really? Who is Norma Flescher?"

I was quickly losing control. "You mean you didn't bother to find out the identity of the woman whose picture you're spreading all over the city?"

"Well, no . . . I mean . . . you know, Lowell said it was her."

"*Lowell put you up to this?*" Now I was shouting.

"No need to scream at me," Teri said. "I just went around the newsroom and asked if anyone was working on a promotable story. Lowell sort of said that you guys had shot a hidden-camera story on a woman. So he showed me the tape and it looked great, and since you're all tied up with the hostage thing, I just figured we'd go ahead and kill two birds with one stone, you know, reach the big hostage audience with this promo, and—"

"Teri, stop!" One thing hadn't changed since our short-lived marriage: Teri's mouth still went into overdrive when she was nervous. "You have to take that spot off the air right now. Not only do you have the wrong woman, but the right woman hasn't even agreed to do the story. We could get sued in every court in Festus County."

"OK, Rick. But how did Lowell get so confused?"

"That's what I'd like to know!" Then I remembered—he had no sound! The wireless microphone didn't work, so Lowell assumed that the first woman I talked with in the restaurant was Norma Flescher. In fact, it was Dawn Rae Hargis. Lowell must have shot video of our little chat, then shut down his camera, figuring there wasn't anything else to shoot. He was probably in his car heading back to the station when I started my conversation with Norma.

So that's why Spanky gave me a thumbs up in the hallway yesterday, and said, "Way to go, Rick! You got a real looker this time!" He had seen Lowell's pictures of Dawn Rae Hargis and assumed she was the subject of my story. I thought he was blowing me some shit because Norma is definitely not a looker. But now it all came together.

"Teri, you have to do something about that spot. And tell wonder boy in the news department that if he puts anything on the air that even remotely concerns this story, I will personally shove Lowell's battery pack up his tight little ass."

I punched the END button on my cellular phone. At least it had come in handy in this emergency. I looked over at my host, who had been catching a nap on the couch. "You want another hostage, Norb? I got someone in mind."

chapter twenty-four

A NUMBING PAIN SHOT UP MY ARM. I MUST HAVE PASSED OUT ON NUTSY'S couch and bumped my funny bone on his splintery end table. My eyes were almost crusted shut, but I could detect a rare hint of November sunlight in the room. It must have been just after dawn. Time to make some business calls.

Morris, the morning newsman, as usual answered the phone on the sixth ring. "News, Chiles."

"Hostage hunk, Roberson. Morris, get me Loudermilk."

I waited for that to register. "Rick, is that you? Hell, I figured old Nutsy would have you tied to a chair and you'd be begging for mercy by now."

I was in no mood for Morris's feeble attempts at humor. "Just get me Loudermilk."

"He's not here. He's there—with you."

"What are you talking about?"

"It's Lowell's turn on the Nutsy shift. He's parked right outside your door, shooting pictures and beaming them back home. By the way, tell Nutsy his house needs a paint job."

I thought it was about time that Nutsy and I had a chat.

"Norb," I asked, "got any more of that beer?"

"Couple," he said as he opened the refrigerator door, filling the kitchen with the unmistakable stench of spoiled food.

Nutsy produced two green bottles with unfamiliar labels. I looked closely and saw that in response to his first demand as a serious hostage taker, Nutsy had been rewarded with a case of nonalcoholic beer. I showed Nutsy the label.

He just shrugged and popped the cap. "Well, hell, I didn't know. I seen it on TV."

We sat at the kitchen table as Horace ran his Nintendo game at full volume in the next room.

"Norb, you know you got to stop doing this. How many times have you called the cops to say you've taken Marie hostage or one of your neighbors or even the dog, for Chrissake?"

Nutsy took a swig from his bottle. "Yeah, but I just got drunk and did that. Cops took me downtown and then I was all right. But there ain't never been nothin' like this. Look at all—"

My cell phone beeped and Nutsy jumped about a foot out of his chair.

"Roberson."

"Rick, it's Karen at the station. Turn on the morning news. You'll like this."

I grabbed the remote from Horace, who immediately tried to bite me on the wrist. "Hey! I was usin' that!" he screamed.

I zipped to Channel 49 and caught the tail end of a story.

"It's feared the death toll in that avalanche will go much higher." Peggy Carnowsky, our forever-chipper noon anchor lady, was finishing a story of Alpine tragedy. But even now, her voice sounded like she might break into a cooking tip at any moment.

"Now," she chirped, "here's Morris with a very special guest."

The camera cut to Morris Chiles a bit early and caught him as he was still brushing away the remainders of the show's last guest, the Pet of the Week. This was the most popular segment of the morning newscast, but it was one that Morris despised—not so much because it insulted him as a journalist, but because he was allergic to almost every animal ever featured.

Morris looked a bit startled to see the camera pointing at him, but he recovered smoothly. He cheerfully nodded to his co-anchor across the room. "Thank you, Peggy."

Then, suddenly, Morris Chiles was transformed. In a heartbeat, his mood darkened. Gone was his cheerful, fishing-buddy demeanor that made Morris such a favorite at Kiwanis luncheons. His voice and his expression deepened as he looked into the camera and asked, "Who is Norbert Fagan? Is he a dangerous man who must be stopped or a desperate man crying for help? Is he a ruthless terrorist determined to avenge social wrongs or a tragic victim of circumstances that are beyond his control? Is he, in short, our neighbor in need or our own worst nightmare?"

It beat the hell out of me, but it was clear that Morris was here to help.

"Today, we have with us a man who can answer those questions."

The camera cut to a frail, gray little man in a tweed sport coat, whose eyes darted around the studio behind an enormous pair of horn-rimmed glasses.

"Our guest is Dr. Colin Merriweather, professor of clinical psychology at Festerwood Community College. Good afternoon, professor."

With no warning, Dr. Merriweather replied with a voice that literally shook the glass figurines on Marie's coffee table. From somewhere deep within his fragile body came a booming baritone. "Good afternoon, Mr. Chiles." The professor may have looked like Don Knotts, but he had the voice of Darth Vader. I could just see the engineers in the WHOE control room dropping their Krispy Kremes as they reached for the audio controls.

A very concerned Morris Chiles leaned forward in his chair. "Doctor, what sort of man are we dealing with in Norbert Fagan?"

The professor paused thoughtfully and said, "I would say, given Mr. Fagan's behavior so far, that he suffers from paranoid schizophrenia that is manifested in brief psychotic episodes induced by stress, perhaps concurrent to an underlying personality disorder."

Obviously that was not the answer Morris expected. Certainly it wasn't one he understood.

"Uh, professor, does that mean that Mr. Fagan is, in fact, dangerous to others?"

Another thoughtful pause. "In this case, he could be, if he also suffers from manic depression, which could explain why he escapes reality on occasion. He could also suffer from a histrionic personality disorder manifested by manipulative behavior such as—"

Morris knew he was getting nowhere and the clock was running. "Professor, excuse me, but in laymen's language—just as simply as possible—can you tell us what would cause a man like Mr. Fagan to turn to violence?"

Dr. Merriweather straightened his glasses. "Childhood trauma."

Now there was something Morris could jump on. "Something in his childhood, then? Like abuse at an early age?"

"Exactly. Mr. Fagan could be striking out at all the pain he suffered at the hands of his parents or his childhood friends. Whatever the case, he blames others, not himself."

Nutsy was fascinated. "Damn straight!" He shouted at the TV set. "It ain't my fault!"

The camera cut back to Morris. "Are you saying, Doctor, that Norbert Fagan's hostages are, in fact, surrogates for those who inflicted pain in his childhood?"

"Perhaps, Mr. Chiles. If that is the case, then we are dealing with a highly disturbed man who might stop at nothing to exact his revenge."

"Thank you, Doctor Colin Merriweather."

Now the camera was back on Peggy, who obviously had already taken a few acting lessons from Jeanette Larmer. Slowly shaking her head, she looked deeply into the camera and half-whispered, "A tragic story, Morris." Then, magically, her radiant smile reappeared and she bubbled, "Now stay tuned. Next we'll meet the newest residents of the Evansville Zoo. If you'll pardon my pun—it's a story with a real porpoise!"

I handed the remote back to Horace.

"Well, Norb, there's more to you than I thought."

Nutsy looked almost pensive as he stared at the rug. "What does he know about me growin' up, anyway? None of his damn business."

I tried for an opening. "Right, Norb. But is there anything to what he said? Anything that may have happened in the past . . . ?"

Nutsy shrugged. "Sure. I mean—I'm, like . . . gettin' even for stuff that happened when I was a kid, I guess. That's what he said."

"But Norb, the point is—"

My cellular phone rang. "Roberson."

"Rick? It's Hogan. I think we need to talk."

chapter twenty-five

I CLEARED A PILE OF BEER CANS FROM THE COUCH AND SAT DOWN, TURN-
ing my back so Nutsy couldn't hear me.

"I could use some advice, Hoagie. This whole thing's got Nutsy
paranoid now, and the longer he stays in here the more nervous the
cops get—"

"I don't mean that crazy business," Hogan said. "I'm talking
about the promos that are running on the air right now, the ones
showing that blonde with her face digitized."

He was talking about an overused process that we'd apply in order to disguise someone's face when we didn't want to reveal the
person's identity on the air—usually an alleged prostitute or someone
who might sue us if we got our facts wrong. It must have been infuri-
ating for the viewers, because all they would see was a block of tiny
electronic squares dancing over the screen where the subject's face
should be.

The crack two-man law firm that represented the station—Barrows, Tinker, and Barrows—suggested that we use this digitizing
method all the time. Actually, there was no second Barrows, but it
looked more impressive in the phone book that way. As a result of
their advice, almost any event that was deemed newsworthy got the
treatment. Our finest moment may have been the Boy Scouts Annual
Pancake Breakfast; we digitized an entire troop of scouts after word
got out that some people got sick on an undercooked batch of link
sausages.

I had this sinking feeling in my stomach. "What's the story they're promoting?"

"Hell, Rick, you should know. It's your baby. Blonde rats on her boss and now WHOE is going to blow the lid off city hall. You know, promo shit. They hid her face pretty well, but you can see she's blond, and they sure didn't hide her figure."

"Christ, Hoagie, they've done it again. That's my Norma Flescher story! I told Teri that they had the wrong woman the first time around. She wasn't listening, as usual. The blond isn't Norma Flescher. It's—"

"I know damn good and well who she is," Hogan interrupted. "She's the daughter of Reverend Billy Joe Hargis, who is about to sue old man Thornton for every dime he's worth. Since everyone else in charge around here has made a field trip out to Nutsy's house, the good Reverend decided to spend the past hour giving me hell."

"Wait a minute, Hoagie. How does he know it's his daughter if we digitized her face?"

"That's just it. We didn't hide her face on that first batch of spots, and after they ran on the air, a crew from *Inside Affair* decided that little old Festerwood must be a Midwest version of Peyton Place, with a crazy bastard taking hostages on one side of town and the beautiful daughter of a minister telling city hall secrets on the other. They did a little digging and found out who the blonde really is. So now they're snooping around the church, ambushing people as they leave, asking them what they know about the minister's daughter. They haven't run a story yet, but Reverend Hargis is pissed. He wants to know how this got started."

"Isn't that pretty obvious, Hoagie? It's this dream team: Boyd, Jeanette . . . all of them. They'll be here just long enough to dazzle Larry the Loon with some big-city graphics and slogans, hype a couple of stories, and jack up the ratings, then they'll blow town with another notch on their resumes. But what I don't understand is how they got their anxious little mitts on my Norma Flescher story."

I heard Hogan take a deep breath. "Well, that's easy enough to explain. When Teri came through the newsroom looking for stories to promote, Lowell showed her your tape—"

"I know all about that. We didn't have any sound, so he figured Dawn Rae was Norma. But where did they get enough information for even a promo?"

There was a familiar tone of exasperation in Hogan's voice. "Rick, you took notes. Lots of them. That's the old-fashioned reporter in you, the one I always liked. But you shouldn't leave your notebook on your desk in full view of everyone in the newsroom, including a young promotions director with no experience and an ambitious photographer who's on the make.

"Lowell knew enough about the story to give Teri an outline. Then they found Tim Facenda's number in your notes and called him. I guess he figured you had given them his name, so he filled in the blanks. Since you're busy doing your slow waltz with Nutsy out there, they went ahead with what they had on their own. Hell, they had the pictures, even if they were the wrong ones, and enough copy for a promo. Under the current regime, that amounts to TV news."

I collapsed on the couch. I couldn't help but think this whole thing was my fault. If I hadn't been so all consumed with getting the hell out of Festerwood, I wouldn't have set up that hidden-camera meeting with Norma Flescher and none of this would have happened. If I had just stuck to my guns on this Nutsy Fagan business, I wouldn't be sitting here now with Nutsy passed out on the floor and Horace out running the gauntlet on his skateboard. But no, I had just enough ambition to rationalize my way into big trouble.

In a way, I was just as guilty as Boyd and Jeanette and the rest of them. Maybe more so. I knew better. I also knew deep down inside that if I really wanted to, I could bring this fiasco to a halt. But the thing was, in some perverse way, I didn't want this to end, not just yet. I suppose it was the reporter in me overpowering whatever humanitarian instincts I possessed, but I had this morbid curiosity to see just how this was going to be resolved with as little intervention by me as possible.

I might be Nutsy's designated friend, but I was also an observer by profession. Besides, there was always the chance that in the end, a hero would emerge from this bizarre situation, a hero who just happened to be a television reporter looking for a big city job. The fact was that all of us—Slope and Penny, the politicians; Boyd and Jeanette, the new age journalists; and me—all of us were here to serve our own purposes. Nutsy Fagan was just the unlikely vehicle.

chapter twenty-six

It was almost noon, and by now the morning sun had been reduced to a cameo appearance in the skies over Festerwood. The sky was smudged with gray clouds, probably from the exhaust of TV news helicopters and satellite trucks. The commotion on the front lawn had settled into a kind of steady hum. Luckily, Nutsy's latest pizza delivery from Pepperoni Pete's had come with a complimentary six pack of beer. The delivery boy was shaking when Horace answered the bell, but he did manage to ask for and get Nutsy's autograph before he left. I popped the top on an Old Style and settled back with the remote control. It was time for the noon news.

Bedlam. Edgy music and crazed graphics, followed by a talking head I didn't recognize. It was a "cold open," a quick sound bite to get the viewer's attention before the newscast actually began. A young man with soap-opera features was saying, "I really feel that the eyes of the world are on your town this week. Festerwood, Indiana, is one place we all will remember."

Clay—the erstwhile Clayton Bodine—now sporting a Dan Rather V-neck sweater, looked thoughtfully at the monitor, then turned to the audience. "A reporter for *Inside Affair* confirms what we already knew. Festerwood, Indiana, is a city on the move."

I turned to Nutsy. "Congratulations, Norb, you got the station's A-team out of bed to do the noon news."

Nutsy just looked at me blankly.

"Good afternoon, Festerwood. I'm Clay Bodine."

"And I'm Melanie Farnsworth. Welcome to Channel 49's noon news, the highest-rated newscast in western Indiana."

Well, that didn't take long. Larry the Loon must have sprung for some overnight ratings.

Clay's turn now: "Melanie, the news is not good from the siege on Ralston Street. For another day, Norbert Fagan remains holed up in his fashionable Festerwood home."

Now that was news. Nutsy's joint had gone from "rundown" to "modest" to "fashionable" in less than a week.

The anchorperson ping-pong match continued. Now it was Melanie: "This marks the fourth straight day that Fagan has refused to give up his hostage—"

Clayton broke in. "Uh, actually, Melanie, it's been three days now."

Uh-oh. Trouble in paradise? The first sour note in the Clay and Melanie show?

Melanie ignored Clayton's correction. "Before we join our man on the scene, Dirk Tubergen, we want to know what you think of the way the hostage crisis is being handled by police. So we've opened up our TelePoll lines to take your calls. The numbers are on your screen. Just dial HOSTAGE—that's 467-8243—to give us your opinion. After the tone, punch the star key if you'd like to see police use force to end the hostage incident; punch the pound key if you believe they should continue to negotiate. Results of our TelePoll will be announced on tonight's *Festerwood at Five Fast Attack News*."

I was hoping there would be a third number to call if viewers wanted the station to give Nutsy a rest and return to some honest-to-God news, but no such luck. I turned off the set.

It was one call I did not want to make. There were two rings, then Norma Flescher answered. "Hello. Flescher residence." She didn't sound angry, at least not yet.

"Norma, it's Rick Roberson. Listen, I'm sorry—"

"Well, I wondered when I would hear from you. What's going on, Mr. Roberson? Somebody said they heard there was going to be a big story on *Inside Affair* about a woman telling city hall secrets in Festerwood. So I turned on the TV to watch. I was afraid you had decided to show my story without my permission."

"Norma, I'm so sorry. This was all a big mix-up, and I couldn't be there to fix it because I'm stuck here with Norb Fagan—"

"Oh yes, that poor man. Does he need anything? I was thinking about bringing a casserole over—"

"No, Norma, that's nice of you, but I'm more concerned about your story. Look, I hope this doesn't cause you any trouble."

"Not for me, Mr. Roberson. But I do feel sorry for that poor blond girl, the minister's daughter, who they showed pictures of. I didn't realize she even knew Tad Tyler . . . but he was a scoundrel—"

"Wait a minute, Norma. You mean they ran that story and showed Dawn Rae Hargis?"

"Well, no, not a story. One of those little teasing things you TV people do. You know, you say you're going to do something, then you say you're not going to do it until tomorrow. I just hate it when you do that. They did that on a Michael Jackson story last week—"

"Norma, try to remember. Did they actually show Dawn Rae Hargis on the screen?"

"Is she the blonde in the pink sweater?"

"Yeah, that would be her."

"Well, they showed her all right, coming out of church with her father—you know, he's the minister of the Festus Friends in Faith Church over on Hillside."

"Yes, Norma, I'm familiar with it."

"That's all. They just showed the minister and her greeting people after Wednesday services, and said something about how you wouldn't expect to find two sensational stories in a little town like Festerwood. Then they said something about Mr. Fagan and what he's done, and said that tomorrow night they'll talk about how the minister's daughter got city hall in trouble. Only . . . she never worked there, Mr. Roberson. I think maybe there's been a mix-up."

Deep shit. I was in deep shit. "Norma, listen. I have to go now. I wouldn't worry about this if I were you. Just a little misunderstanding. If I can help it, your name will never come up. I promise you."

"Well, all right, Mr. Roberson. I just don't know how this Dawn Rae Hargis woman knew anything about city government. I hear she's new in town, so—"

"Norma, like I said, it was a big misunderstanding. I'll see what I can do about it. Listen, try not to worry."

I hung up and looked at my watch. I figured I had maybe four or five hours to derail this *Inside Affair* story. But how? And even if they agreed to dump it, how much damage had already been done?

I was startled out of my thoughts by a sharp ring—louder than before. Instinctively, I flipped open my cell phone, but there was just a dial tone. Another ring. Then Horace shouted from the next room, "Uncle Norbie! It's for you!"

It was Nutsy's wall phone in the kitchen. It hadn't crossed my mind that, in this age of satellite and microwave communication, someone might actually be calling on a regular household telephone.

Nutsy started to unfold himself from the easy chair where he had collapsed hours ago.

"Wait a minute, Norb," I said. "You don't know who this might be. You don't want to say the wrong thing and give them an excuse to do something rash. Let me—"

"I know who it is!" Horace ran into the living room, breathless with excitement. Aside from a person-to-person call from Beavis and Butthead, I couldn't imagine what would be so stimulating to young Horace. "It's Kathy Kellogg from that TV show!"

chapter twenty-seven

Of course. Somebody at the station was having some fun. Probably one of Karen's sick jokes, or maybe Teri was getting bored and decided to amuse herself. Kathy Kellogg was the ace anchorwoman at NBS, the leading network news operation. She made three million dollars last year—at least that's what I read in *People* magazine. She interviewed people like Yassir Arafat and Lee Iacocca. In fact, she and Iacocca sang a duet on her last show. She sure as hell wouldn't be calling Nutsy Fagan in Festerwood, Indiana.

"I'll get this, Norb. You just sit tight."

I picked up the receiver, and it immediately slid out of my hand. It was covered with a strange brown slime, as if someone had smeared peanut butter and bananas all over it. I figured that Horace had thoughtfully decided to share some of his lunch. I wiped the receiver with a paper towel.

"Hello. This is Rick Roberson. Who's this?"

"This is Kathy Kellogg of NBS News. I would like to speak with Mr. Fagan, if that's possible."

"Right. Actually, I'm Walter Cronkite, and I got him first. This is some coincidence, I'd say."

The voice on the other end was decidedly more brittle. "Look, I don't know who you are, but this is Kathy Kellogg, and I'm calling for Norbert Fagan. Is he in?"

"Oh, yes, he's in, but he's sort of busy right now torturing a pack of Cub Scouts. Can you call back in, say, ten years?"

Now the voice took on a more urgent tone. "Pissed off" might best describe it. "This isn't funny, whoever you are. I want to talk to Norbert Fagan, and I want to talk to him now!"

There was authority in that voice. And a familiar cadence. Suddenly I had this sinking feeling in my stomach. It did sound like Kathy Kellogg. You don't suppose . . .

"Karen, is that you?" I almost pleaded the question.

"This is Kathy Kellogg! Put Norbert Fagan on this phone immediately, or I will . . . well, I will do something drastic!"

It *was* her. I couldn't believe it. Kathy Kellogg was on the Nutsy Fagan story!

"Wait just a minute, Miss Kellogg—I mean, Ms. Kellogg—I'll get him."

Nutsy was passed out again on the couch. I stood there for a moment staring at him, listening to the traffic in his front yard. I was remembering something Jeanette Larmer had said during our brief courtship in the Ramada Inn bar. Something about how the line between legitimate news and tabloid entertainment had been blurred. How it all ran together now. I didn't want to believe her. I still didn't. But here I was, news reporter turned hostage negotiator, about to make the connection that would turn the town drunk into a national celebrity. Jerry Springer, call your office.

"Norb, you'd better take this call. It's Kathy Kellogg."

Nutsy wiped a strand of drool from his chin. "You mean from the TV?"

"Yep, the very same. She wants to talk to you. Now, be careful. Don't say anything. Wait a minute—you wouldn't happen to have an extension phone, would you?"

Horace was eager to please. "Yeah, we have one. Up in Uncle Norb's bedroom!"

"OK, Norb, now you get on the kitchen phone and I'll get on the extension. You just let me answer for you. Got it?"

"Sure," Nutsy said as he hoisted himself from the chair and stretched, suddenly rejuvenated by his famous caller. "I like Kathy Kellogg. She's my favorite."

I found the extension phone under a pile of soiled clothing on Nutsy's bed. By the time I excavated it, the famous newswoman and the soon-to-be famous Ralston Street Ravager already were engaged in conversation.

"The way I see it, Norbert—may I call you Norbert?"

"Sure," Nutsy said. "That's my name."

"Great. Well, the way I see it, I could bring my crew right into your home, and we could have a one-on-one interview about all the tensions building up inside you, all the pressures of our society that caused you to go over the edge."

I thought it was time to join the conversation. "Excuse me, Ms. Kellogg . . . may I call you Kathy? I'm Rick Roberson, a local television reporter, and Mr. Fagan invited me here to talk this all out. Look, I'll be honest with you. The fact is, there's no real story here—"

It was amazing how her voice could change from sincere compassion to controlled hostility. "Look, Mr. Roberson, I don't mean to be insulting, but Mr. Fagan's story has grown far beyond your little town. Have you read *USA Today*? Your Mr. Fagan is becoming a national hero. Here, let me read a paragraph:

> *If Henry David Thoreau were to choose his modern-day successor, chances are he would not turn to the obscure town of Festerwood, Indiana, or to a disturbed Vietnam veteran named Norbert Fagan. But the similarities cannot be ignored. Mr. Fagan, now holed up in his modest home for a third day, has chosen to wall himself off from the rest of the world, a world that he no longer embraces; indeed, a world that no longer has any need for him. Mr. Fagan—*

I had heard enough. "Wait a minute! This has gotten out of hand. Norb, no offense, but Kathy, you've got to know that Norbert

Fagan's house is about as far from Walden as you can get. What he's done here, he's done before—many times. It's just that this time, my stupid station decided to make a big deal out of it, and—"

"And," she interrupted, "you are watching your story slip away from you. I understand, Mr. Roberson. Carrie Fowler over at ABC did the same thing to me when I thought I had that exclusive with Norman Schwarzkopf."

"But Nutsy—I mean, Norb—isn't Norman Schwarzkopf! He's a nobody! Don't you see —?"

"I am too somebody!" For a moment I had forgotten that Nutsy was on the other phone. "And I would sure like Kathy Kellogg to visit me! I never met anybody famous before."

She jumped in. "Then it's done! I'll get my crew together and we can be there in two hours. And, Mr. Fagan, remember: this is *our* little secret. You don't want to tell anyone else about this."

"Don't worry, ma'am. I won't tell nobody."

"Oh, Mr. Fagan, one more thing. I think you should know that you'll be in good company when this runs on the air. You'll be part of my monthly celebrity special. We have Dolly Parton, Keanu Reeves, and Henry Kissinger already lined up."

I was literally struck dumb. Henry Kissinger and Nutsy Fagan on the same show. Well, why not? It was about time that the world heard another authoritative opinion on the tensions in the Gaza Strip.

"Gotta go, Mr. Fagan. Oh, can I bring you anything? Carl Sagan always liked it when I brought him some chocolate truffles."

"Beer," Nutsy said. "Only not that kind that comes in the green bottles."

"Brown bottle beer it is. See you soon!" And she hung up.

chapter twenty-eight

I MUST HAVE BEEN EXHAUSTED. I STARTED TO DRIFT OFF TO SLEEP ON Nutsy's spring-loaded couch as WHOE News continued to torment soap opera lovers with its round-the-clock coverage of the "Ralston Street Ravager."

Our new receptionist had spent most of this saga reassuring callers that Tiffany on *The Young and the Reckless* had not had her baby and that it still wasn't clear that Ridge was the father. Dirk was interviewing cops and medics and hostage negotiators and neighbors and anyone else he could get his hands on. Clayton and Melanie were breathlessly giving results of the TelePoll, which revealed that more than eighty percent of the God-fearing folks in Festerwood would like to see the cops storm Nutsy's house and let the Devil take the hindmost. Through glazed eyes I could see that Jeanette Larmer had been one busy girl. Clayton Bodine had re-invented himself again and had traded in his Dan Rather sweater for a pair of stylish red Larry King suspenders. I was almost asleep when, in my half-dream state, I heard a pounding at the front door.

"Roberson! Open up! It's Tubergen!"

I jumped up so quickly that I pulled something in my groin. "Wait a minute! Who? Who is it?" Man, I had this incredibly sharp pain just to the right of the crown jewels.

"Tubergen! Godammit, open up! These cops are making me nervous!"

I was bent over like Quasimoto as I dragged myself to the door and opened it a crack.

"Jesus, Dirk, it is you! What the hell—?"

"Just let me in! I'll explain when I get inside."

I opened the door just wide enough to allow Dirk to squeeze through.

Dirk's greeting was, "Christ, it smells in here!"

I kicked a soggy pizza box out of the way. "Sorry, buddy, but it's the maid's month off. What the hell are you doing here, anyway?"

Dirk shook his head. "Look, I don't know where to start. This Norma Flescher thing has gotten out of hand."

"Tell me about it. I hear *Inside Affair* is snooping around the church.

Dirk looked around. "Where's Nutsy?"

"Sleeping off a few beers, probably."

"Then why don't you just tell the cops to come on in and we'll get this fiasco over with?"

I opened the refrigerator door. "What? And give up all this free beer? Are you crazy? Look, I explained this to Fronzman already. The way things are going, I'd make a move and Nutsy would come out of his stupor long enough to find the one gun he has that fires real ammunition. Then God knows what would happen. And you guys aren't helping any. Nutsy is convinced that every gun and every camera in the country is trained on him, and he can't figure out why."

Dirk opened a beer. "Well, I might have the solution to all our problems. That's why Chief Penny decided to let me come in."

"Let me guess. You are the designated hostage negotiator. Roberson out; Tubergen in."

"Nope. Better than that." Suddenly Dirk was into his reporter mode, fixing me with a look of smug sincerity. "I know this Norma Flescher thing must be driving you crazy. Hogan tells me the station really screwed this one up, and here you are, joined at the hip with Nutsy with no chance to get this straightened out. But I've been schmoozing with some of the *Inside Affair* people out there. And here's the deal. *Inside Affair* has agreed to drop the Flescher story— never mention it again—if you can convince Nutsy to do an exclusive one-on-one interview with them. He can have up to three minutes, unedited. He can tell his side of the story to a nationwide audience. No strings attached. If that happens, this Norma Flescher business never sees the light of day." Dirk looked extremely pleased with himself.

I collapsed into the nearest chair. "Tubergen, where were you when the baseball talks were going on?"

Dirk just smiled. "Brilliant, if I do say so myself."

"Just one minor problem," I said. "It won't work."

"Why the hell not? It's perfect."

"It would be if you had been a little earlier. It so happens that Kathy Kellogg schmoozed Nutsy into an exclusive interview on her show."

"Right. Was that before or after Larry King called?"

"I'm serious, Dirk. Kathy Kellogg has decided that our friend Nutsy here is one hell of a story, and she's due here at any moment to make him a household word."

Dirk wasn't smiling now. "Jesus. Is there any way you can talk him out of it?"

"Probably not. Nutsy is a little star-struck right now. Of course, I could appeal to his sense of loyalty and to our good will."

Dirk brightened. "You could? I mean . . . could you do that?"

I laughed. "Sure. I'm betting that Nutsy would quickly give up any chance at fame and glory just to bail WHOE out of trouble and save my ass. Get real, Dirk. Nutsy is no Rhodes Scholar, but he does watch television, and he knows the difference between some half-ass TV station in Festerwood, Indiana, and a glamorous network anchorwoman who suddenly is showering him with attention. You don't need a TelePoll to know that when it comes to choosing between saving our ass and having Miss Kellogg in for beer and pizza, we come in third."

"Right, I know that." Dirk was pacing the floor, agitated. "But that's not the point. You don't need to tell him anything about the Norma Flescher business. Just sell him on this interview. I'll bet he watches *Inside Affair* just like everyone else. So it's just a matter of you convincing him to go on this show instead of some boring Kathy Kellogg special."

"Kathy Kellogg's not boring. She's my friend." It was the voice of Festerwood's own Henry David Thoreau standing in the doorway and looking a bit disheveled after his nap. "You shouldn't talk about her like that."

I got up to make the proper introductions. "Norb, this is Dirk Tubergen—"

"I know who he is." Nutsy interrupted. "He's the guy that's been callin' me the Ralston Street Scavenger and names like that. But he shouldn't talk about Miss Kellogg that way."

Dirk made his pitch anyway. "Nutsy, I know how you feel—"

"My name's Norbert. I don't like people callin' me Nutsy."

"Sure, sure . . . I'm sorry. But Norb, the thing is, more people are watching shows like *Inside Affair* these days. Kathy Kellogg is a fine reporter and a wonderful person, but stories like yours are lost in those network news shows with all those other stuffy stories about the Mideast and taxes and those long interviews with people like Alan Greenspan—"

Nutsy became very defensive. "Dolly Parton's goin' to be on. Miss Kellogg said so."

That stopped Dirk for a moment. "No shit? I hear Diane Sawyer's been trying to get her."

I thought it was time to step in. "Dirk, forget it. Norb is going to be interviewed by Kathy Kellogg and that's it."

Then Dirk went for the gut. He locked eyes with Nutsy. "Even if it means our TV station—Rick's TV station—could be sued for every penny it's worth?"

"Dirk, don't go there. I warn you—"

Dirk was in Nutsy's face now. "Did you know, Mr. Fagan, that if you refuse to go on *Inside Affair* and you talk to Kathy Kellogg instead, a story's gonna be run on the air that could result in a lawsuit so big that our TV station—the one you watch Rick on every night—could be forced off the air? I would lose my job, but I don't care about that." Dirk cast a wounded look my way. "Rick here—who has gone to bat for you, who came running to your side when you needed him most, the one guy who you can really call your friend right now—Rick would lose his job, too. Did you know that? Could you live with yourself knowing that?" Dirk dropped onto the couch. "And all because you were selfish when Rick needed you most."

Actually I thought Dirk did a pretty good job, even if he was full of shit. I waited for Nutsy's response. Nutsy just stood there in the hallway, looking either thoughtful or confused; it was hard to say which. Then he started nodding his head very slowly.

"You're right. I seen Dolly Parton on that other show last week. I know 'cause she talked about how she went to the doctor to make her boobs bigger."

I smiled and turned to Dirk. "Anything else?"

Dirk got up, shook hands with Nutsy, took one last pull on his beer, and opened the door. "Thanks for the beer, buddy. And good luck. I mean it."

chapter twenty-nine

THE CELL PHONE AGAIN. I WAS IN NO MOOD FOR ANY MORE BAD NEWS.

"Talk to me," I barked.

"Goodness, aren't we irritable?" It was the one voice of sanity in my life.

"Mother . . . how did you get this number?"

"Well, dear, you do recall that I am a member of the city council. If memory serves, you even voted for me in the last election. I simply threatened to cut Chief Penny's budget if he didn't tell me how to reach you." Her tone softened. "Seriously, what's happening? Are you in any real danger?"

"No, things are under control here. Where are you calling from?"

Mother sighed. "I'm out here with all the other circus performers from your chosen profession. What about that shotgun Mr. Fagan was brandishing on television?"

"A toy, Mom, but a good one. Made by Mattel."

"I'll remember that when I file my next gun control bill. But seriously, Rick, how can I help?"

"Well, Father Mike is on his way here. He's going to try to talk Nutsy into surrendering. After that, I don't know what will happen."

Her voice brightened. "He'll need an attorney, won't he?"

"I suppose so."

"Then this looks like a case for Harold Fenneman."

"F. Lee Fenneman? Isn't he a little out of Nutsy's price range?"

"It's Norbert Fagan, dear," she pointed out, as a way of gently reminding me of her role as chairperson of the Festerwood County Mental Health Association. "No, I think Harold will be willing to waive his usual outrageous fee for a chance to showcase his courtroom skills on a national stage."

Harold Fenneman was now in his tenth year as Festerwood's most prominent attorney. He came to our fair city from somewhere in New Jersey. He always said that the name of the town isn't important. Then he'd follow that with his standard joke about two guys from New Jersey who meet in a bar: *One says to the other, "Where you from?" The second guy answers, "Jersey." Then the first guy says, "Oh yeah? What exit?"* The joke grew stale very quickly, but eventually we got wind of Fenneman's past.

Seems that he fled to our little corner of the world in lieu of an indictment for his creative handling of various probate proceedings. But it was his East Coast attitude, his brashness, that alarmed and fascinated the good folks of Festerwood. I doubt if the aliens who landed in Roswell, New Mexico, stirred up things in that town as much as Harold did in Festerwood. His manner infuriated judges, totally unglued then-Prosecutor Ted Lemmons—just five years out of law school—and mesmerized many a Festerwood jury. His theatrical cross-examinations and his tear-stained closing arguments produced an alarming number of hung juries.

By far his biggest score—and the case that earned him his nickname, "F. Lee"—was the Theodore McKnight case. Mr. McKnight was found dead in bed with six bullets in the back of his head. An open-and-shut case against his wife, Darlene, who happened to be lying in bed next to him. That is, until Fenneman informed the jury that it was one of the worst cases of suicide he had ever seen.

When Prosecutor Lemmons wondered aloud how Mrs. McKnight couldn't hear the shots, as she claimed, Fenneman pointed out that the revolver had a silencer, that Mr. McKnight had fiendishly shot himself in the back of the head to make it look like murder in order to deprive the saintly Darlene her rightful claim to his insurance and inheritance. Fenneman explained that a six-shot suicide was possible, because the first five bullets lodged in that part of the brain that doesn't instantly produce death or unconsciousness when penetrated by gunfire. Lemmons was so demoralized by the resulting hung jury that he didn't re-file charges against Mrs. McKnight, now the current Mrs. Harold Fenneman. After that, Nutsy's case would be a piece of cake. I told Mother to give F. Lee a call.

No sooner had I hung up than the phone rang again.

"Don't worry, Mom, I'm getting enough sleep."

There was a pause. "That explains everything. I wondered what the hell you were doing in there." It was Boyd Nelson. "Think you might have time to generate a little news between naps? I mean the whole world is sitting on this story like it's a time bomb and, so far, you haven't given us squat."

"Hi, Boyd. Good to hear from you, too. Fact is, we're working on it. Deputy Fronzman is fetching the local priest to talk to Nutsy, and I think there's a chance—"

"I know that. But how about our viewers? We sent you in there to get us an exclusive with Mr. Fagan, and—"

Now it was my turn to interrupt. "Whoa, wait a minute, Boyd. To begin with, you didn't send me in here. Nutsy—I mean, Norb—asked to see me. There's a big difference. That makes me responsible for his well-being and that of everyone else connected with this squirrely story. I told you there was no news here, but you went ahead and alerted the free world, and now we've created a monster. I personally don't give a shit whether we get an exclusive with Fagan or not. I just want to bring this sideshow to a peaceful conclusion."

"Are you through," Boyd snapped back, "because if you are, then I should remind you of something. You are still a reporter covering a story. And you just happen to be in a position to own that story. I don't care what noble cause motivates you right now. What I'm interested in is the story. That's all. Or maybe you would prefer that the *Festus County Fanfare* gets it first. Their reporter is out here drooling all over the lawn."

That was a low blow, and it hurt. Actually, I was a little surprised that I still had any feeling down there at all. But Boyd was right, in his own repulsive way. From the first, there was a part of me that realized this sorry episode, as bogus as it was, could become the story that finally jump-started my career. After all those resume tapes and all those letters to news directors in other cities, here I was—at last sitting on the one story that could carry me out of WHOE and out of Festerwood and into a job at a real television station in a major market. All I had to do was ignore my conscience and fudge my journalistic integrity. But just a little bit.

"Boyd, give me a moment. I think I can pull this off, but you have to get clearance from Chief Penny and the rest of the militia."

"Don't worry about that. These guys are hungry for whatever pub they can get. I'll have Loudermilk standing by."

I hung up. I still had some time to kill before Father Mike bestowed his blessing on the Fagan household. I had an idea.

chapter thirty

"Norb, you know what we should do?"

Nutsy was leafing through a copy of *TV Guide*. He looked up. "What's Miss Kellogg's show called, anyway?"

I sat down on the couch next to him. "I'm not sure, Norb. But I have an idea. How about you and me do a quick interview—you know, kind of like practice for when Kathy Kellogg comes here tonight."

Nutsy looked confused. "But I promised Miss Kellogg that I wouldn't talk to nobody else. And I won't."

"I know, Norb, and I'm not asking you to. But this is a big interview you'll be doing. Everybody in the whole country will see it. Hell, I'll bet Marie will see it, wherever she is. So what I'm thinking is maybe you and me, we should sort of rehearse you for it. You know, kind of a dry run so you won't be surprised tomorrow."

Nutsy thought about that for a minute. "Well, I guess it won't hurt none, just as long as it's OK with Miss Kellogg."

"I'm sure she won't mind. In fact, you'll be doing her a favor. This way you'll be ready for whatever she asks you."

I reached Lowell Loudermilk on the first ring. He must have been waiting for confirmation of his pizza delivery.

"Hey, Lowell, how's it going in Camp Nutsy?"

"Not funny. It's miserable out here. Spanky can't keep the van warm and we've run out of beer. When are you going to wind up this fiasco?

"Oh, maybe as soon as you tell me that *Inside Affair* has decided not to run that tape you showed them or the information you gave them on Norma Flescher. You really screwed the pooch on this one, Lowell."

Suddenly he was very defensive. "Hey, wait a minute! You never said that tape was off-limits. I just handed it over to promotions and they took it from there. Don't blame—"

"Never mind," I interrupted. "You got all your gear with you?"

"Yeah. So far it's come in real handy for cranking out pictures of Nutsy's house. Tell him if he ever decides to sell the place, I have some great exteriors he can use."

"Well, round up your stuff and get in here. Wonder boy is clearing it for you."

"No shit? An interview with Nutsy? Wait a minute, he's not dangerous, is he? I mean—"

"Only if you shoot out of focus. Come on, Lowell, we're wasting time."

Within minutes, Lowell was in Nutsy's living room, fussing with cables and light stands.

"Damn it, Lowell, hurry up. Just set up your camera and we'll get this done."

Actually, I was a bit worried about Nutsy changing his mind at the last minute. This was no time for Lowell to be playing the artiste.

I took him aside. "Look, this is serious. I'm trying to make Boyd happy, get us an exclusive, and buy some time while we figure out a way to get Nutsy out of here alive. I don't want to make a production out of this.

But Lowell would have none of it. "Rick, I can't shoot with natural light in this dump. We won't get a picture. We gotta have lights."

I checked our host. Nutsy was squirming on the couch and looked as if he might start bouncing off the walls at any minute. This was no time for an argument. I turned back to Lowell. "OK, use your cigarette lighter for all I care, but hurry up!"

"This will just take a minute!"

I should have known better. I had worked with Lowell enough times to realize that an interview was not just an interview. It was a cinematic event. His "minute" turned into a half hour, during which he searched for a working electrical outlet. He finally found one in what passed for a downstairs bathroom, where matching brown rot in both the toilet bowl and sink dominated the decor, and several pairs of Nutsy's and Horace's underwear accented the shower curtain.

As Nutsy paced up and down like a death row inmate awaiting a call from the governor, Lowell had the gall to make not one, but two trips out to his van to retrieve extra extension cords, camera tapes, and various filters. Finally he had his lights set up. One illuminated Nutsy as he fidgeted on the couch, the other was placed behind him and aimed at the ceiling to create a haunting shadowy effect to complete the nightmare motif. As I settled into a chair opposite Nutsy, Lowell suddenly took his camera from the tripod and starting taking shots of Nutsy from all sorts of bizarre angles.

Nutsy look terrified. "What the hell's he doin'? He ain't gonna hurt me, is he?"

I wanted to strangle Lowell, but I patiently explained to Nutsy that Lowell was merely shooting cutaway shots of us that would be used later for editing purposes. Of course, there was another reason. These extra shots also gave the viewers the impression that the station had spared no expense by assigning not one, but two photographers to this gripping story. One of the tricks was to take pictures of me sitting there like a fool, nodding my head with deep concern over what my interview subject was saying, when in fact I was staring off into space.

So there we were—Lowell circling the couch and me staring at a picture on the wall as if it had just said something profoundly interesting. Nutsy just sat there with a bewildered expression that seemed to say, *And they call me Nutsy!*

Actually the interview went quite well. I guided Nutsy through the traumas of his life that had brought him to this time and place.

He talked about how he had a tendency to black out somewhere between the third and fourth beer of six-pack number five, which he only indulged in when Marie went on sabbatical. He acknowledged that he might have called the police and said some silly things about taking a hostage, but he had done that before and all the police ever did was come out to his house and let him sleep it off in jail. But this time he woke up, and there were all these policemen and reporters and big trucks with giant saucers on them. He said he thought that they were all going to kill him this time, when all he wants is for Marie to come home and for people to leave him alone.

I decided not to bring up the fact that Nutsy's deadly weapon was actually made by Mattel for fear that once the interview appeared on the air, the armed battalions on the lawn would storm the fortress. Then we would really have a problem. But I did have to put their minds at ease on one other point, that little Horace was alive and well and not in danger.

"Dammit, Horace, get your ass over here!" Nutsy finally broke through *Supertick* on television and got Horace's attention.

"Now Horace," I asked in the most reassuring manner I could. "Is it safe to say you are not being held hostage by your Uncle Norbert?"

Horace gave me his best *So what's your point?* expression and said, "Are you kidding? I'm just spending a few weeks here like I always do."

"And what about your parents? Where are they?"

Horace shrugged. "I dunno. Prob'ly out selling their corn dogs somewhere."

"Like they do every year at the carnivals and fairs?"

"I guess."

"And your uncle hasn't hurt you or threatened you in any way?"

"Yeah, right."

I turned to Nutsy. "Norbert, you would never hurt little Horace, would you? You would never hurt Marie, would you? The fact is, you are not a violent man, are you, Norbert?"

Out of the corner of my eye I could detect the rotation of the lens of the camera, as Lowell zoomed in for a tight close-up of Nutsy's face. Tears gushing from his eyes, Nutsy stammered, "No. I would never hurt them. Never!"

I led Nutsy out to the kitchen, popped a beer for him, and put my hand on his shoulder. "Good job, Norb. I think things are going to work out OK when people see this interview in a few hours. Now, just relax. I have a few things to do."

I returned to the living room to do a summarizing stand-up. Staring straight into the camera, I tried to put all this into perspective. "Norbert Fagan: a troubled man, a tormented soul caught in a web of deceit and desperation woven by an intense and unrequited love and fueled by a weakness for demon rum. I think it was Shakespeare who said that all the world's a stage. And now Norbert Fagan, a simple man—an innately decent and loving man—finds himself in the harsh spotlight of that stage: confused, frightened, and in pain, grasping for understanding, crying out for help. It would be tragic indeed if those who have surrounded his modest home and put him on the world stage for three days and nights do not reach out with compassion and understanding and give him the help he so desperately needs. What an injustice it would be if these same people left Norbert Fagan a broken man on that stage, crying out in the darkness and awaiting a bullet from an anonymous SWAT team rifle. Inside the home of Norbert Fagan, this is Rick Roberson, WHOE News."

"Great job, Rickster," enthused Lowell. "One take with just two seconds left on the tape. By the way, do you have a paper bag that I can throw up in?"

"Use your hat. OK, tear down and get the hell out of here."

Suddenly we heard a sound above us that became louder as it approached the house. It struck me that all we needed now was the theme from *M*A*S*H*. Father Michael Roarke was coming to us from above.

chapter thirty-one

THE CHARTERED HELICOPTER LANDED ON A DUSTY LOT BEHIND NUTSY'S house. Father Mike emerged garbed in jeans and a light black jacket, unzipped to reveal a blue plaid work shirt. His slightly waved light-brown hair was starting to show a little gray at the temples.

A blond reporter from the tabloid show followed him off the copter; she hunched over with him as they fought the turbulence from the copter blades. Then, as she shook hands with Father Mike, there was something positively beatific in her smile. Fortunately, Fronzman was able to short-circuit this latest challenge to Father Mike's vow of chastity, as he dashed under the copter blades and led his good friend toward a clump of dead trees to brief him on the situation.

Michael Roarke had that effect on women. In fact, he was the only member of my circle of high-school friends who got laid on command. Of course, he had everything going for him. He was ruggedly handsome, just bright enough to impress his teachers, and he was a football star. He still holds several records as a Festerwood High wide receiver. But it was his shy, quiet charm and blue eyes which oozed sincerity that got the job done.

In no time, he became the Festerwood maidens' main choice for deflowering. Not that Mike ever bragged about his conquests—far from it. But I suppose that's another thing that made him so desirable. His exploits never came up in the sex evaluation sessions at Coogie's bar near the gravel pit—our bar of choice because of Coogie McDermott's creative drinking-age limits, which were five to seven years less than the state of Indiana's.

No matter how deeply we probed, Mike would never acknowledge, let alone brag about, his sexual adventures. He gave the girls in his life genuine respect and utmost discretion and, from all accounts, what amounted to a religious experience. The only thing he withheld was commitment.

And that is why Mike's friends will always find the New Year's Eve that ushered in 1983 an evening that is forever seared into our memories. We were at Deke Halsted's house. His parents were long gone to Florida and, at that point in their lives, they couldn't care less if Deek burned down the house.

It was almost four o'clock in the morning on a bitterly cold, windswept night. Our dates were safely home, with only Mike's date feeling genuine renewal after an acrobatic, frost-free performance in Mike's Volkswagen. All the regulars were there, including Mike, soon-to-be Deputy Dennis Fronzman, and our gracious host, Deke Halsted, who was priming the keg and acting as a kind of master of ceremonies.

Our slurred conversation turned to what we were going to do with our lives. We were all in our early twenties, with either college or military service behind us, and we weren't about to take this topic seriously. Somebody said he was considering becoming a professional sperm donor. Deke, with his body-by-Budweiser physique, suggested full-figured male model. Then it was Mike's turn. Sprawled on the floor, staring through his plastic cup of beer, Mike quietly declared, "Guys, I'm going to become a priest."

"Say what?" The announcement caught Dennis in mid-burp, and everyone else started hooting, with Deek articulating the group's basest thoughts.

"Yeah, why not, Mike? You've had every broad under sixty in the county. Now it's time to start working on the nuns."

I didn't join in. One look at Mike's eyes was all I needed to know. "You're not kidding are you, Mike?"

"No, Rickster, I'm not. I'm heading to St. Stan's on Tuesday."

"Are you sure about this?" Dennis looked as if he was fighting back tears. Actually, for all his brawn, the Fronz was the most sentimental of the group. Once, we caught him getting all misty-eyed during the Jerry Lewis telethon. But he and Mike were particularly tight, and this was getting to him.

Mike propped himself on an elbow. "I've been thinking about this a long time. I just think there's something missing in my life. I know it's corny, but if there is such a thing as a calling, I have it."

"No offense, Mike," Deke said offensively, "but you are aware that this job has a vow of chastity attached to it, and it may be retroactive."

"I'm aware," said Mike with a grin. "And it's not retroactive. I checked. So what's your point?"

"My point," said Deke, "is I want your black book of easy Festerwood babes." That was met by a roar of approval, followed by the usual torrent of bad jokes that got us through the rest of the evening.

Dennis and I drove Mike to the bus on the first Tuesday of 1983, and we both agreed that we had never seen him more at peace with himself. Naturally, Deek organized a pool to guess what date Mike would bail out of St. Stanislaus seminary. Out of loyalty Dennis didn't take part, but I needed the money. I collected all four hundred dollars of it on the day that Mike was ordained as a priest.

The knock on the door was gentle and unhurried. Obviously Chief Deputy Fronzman had cleared the way for his friend, so there were no bullhorns or searchlights.

Father Michael Roarke gave me one of his bemused smiles. "Good evening, sir. I'm collecting for the St. Vincent de Paul Society's mission in Festerwood. Do you have any clothes you can spare . . . perhaps the ugly shirt off your back?"

"Sorry, Father, but I was baptized in this shirt. Perhaps I can interest you in a nine-year-old as a sacrifice to your god."

"I take it you are out of virgin maidens?"

"Yeah, thanks to you." I showed Father Mike into Nutsy's living room. "So how's Minnesota this time of year?"

"Beautiful, but bracing. I was on the verge of saving thirteen marriages when I got your call. I take it Extreme Unction won't be required here."

"Who?"

"Extreme Unction. One of the Blessed Sacraments. Page seventy-three of your Baltimore Catechism."

Another voice joined the conversation. "That's Last Rites of the Church. Right, Father?" It was Nutsy. He was just emerging from the bathroom.

"That's right, Norbert. I see you remember your lessons. Perhaps one day we can help Mr. Roberson relearn his faith. So how are you doing, Norb?" Mike effortlessly changed his tone from jovial familiarity to deep concern.

"Not too good, Father. I think they want to kill me."

Mike put his arm around Nutsy and guided him toward the couch. "I promise you, Norb, they are not going to kill you. I'm afraid you've given them as big a scare as they've given you. But I'm sure we can work this out. Now, tell me what happened."

I hate reruns, so I excused myself and headed for the kitchen to see if Nutsy had any coffee. There was a jar of instant in the cupboard, but when I finally pried the lid off, I found the only thing in there was a hard brown mass that you couldn't dent with a fork. I settled for a cold beer. Since there were no corn flakes to pour it over, I just popped the top, snapped on the tiny TV set on the counter, and sat down to watch *Festerwood at Five*.

One of those commercials showing impossibly happy people gushing over some multi-grain cereal was just fading from the screen, and up popped our own news team. Clay Bodine, looking somewhat frazzled from a workday that had actually expanded to eight hours, was droning on about Nutsy, while Melanie Farnsworth nodded with studied compassion.

Their voices drifted off as I studied the strange purple spot on Nutsy's kitchen throw rug. It was either blood or a bad jelly stain. The entire room looked as if it had been ransacked by Visigoths. I was thinking that maybe I should do a little housework while I was in here, when something on the TV caught my attention.

Clay and Melanie were doing their "around the world in thirty seconds" segment, with a stopwatch ticking in the corner of the screen for the benefit of those not keeping score at home. Clay was now talking over pictures of incredible devastation.

"It was," he said, "the worst Indonesian earthquake in recent memory, sending a tidal wave crashing into scores of islands, leaving behind a vast area of death and destruction." Then Clay and Melanie were back on camera, looking deeply troubled by what they had just seen. It was clear that Jeanette Larmer had held a crash course in "concerned anchor" expressions.

The problem was, she apparently had forgotten to tell Clay where to draw the line of anchorman angst. The result was a bit of off-the-cuff profundity that will forever be enshrined in the Festus County broadcasting hall of shame. Turning from the pictures of devastation, Bodine slowly shook his head, turned to his co-anchor and said, "Melanie, I just can't understand why a merciful God would allow such a thing to happen."

I knocked my beer over on the table and felt my jaw drop about six inches. Melanie just sat there speechless. Then she brightened, turned to the camera and said, "Turning to happier news—"

Back in the living room, Father Mike was making his pitch. "Norb, what I'm going to suggest will take some sacrifice on your part, and that might mean spending a small amount of time in the county jail—"

Nutsy responded with his predictable gopher-in-the-flashlight look, shaking his head back and forth.

Father Mike put his hands on Nutsy's shoulders. "No, Norb,

look at me. No, no, no . . . look at me. This is only going to be temporary—just a formality—and frankly, jail is the safest place you can be right now. It will only be for a few days while they decide what to do next. A lot of good people are on your side. Officer Dennis, Rick here, and, if we need him, the best lawyer in town. But Norb, we need your help on one important change you're going to have to make in your life. You're going to have to deal with what I'm afraid is a serious drinking problem."

Nutsy teared up. "Honest, Father, I only really get drunk when Marie up and leaves me like this. I get so low when she does this . . ." His voice trailed off.

"I know, I know, Norb. But she always comes back, doesn't she? Maybe it's time that you looked upon these trips she takes as vacations. She's not rejecting you. She just needs to get away now and then like we all do. But when you do drink, let's face it, you do some pretty strange things that you don't even remember doing—things that can hurt you and others. So, Norb, here's what we're going to do." Mike took a deep breath and looked at me for support.

"When we can, we're going to enroll you in the Tiedemann Clinic for Drug and Alcohol Abuse, and we're going to have you and Marie take part in some counseling sessions. I think everyone will go along with that as a way to help you deal with your problem."

Nutsy said nothing for a moment, then he turned to Father Mike. "Father, would you like to hear my confession?"

"Of course, Norb, I would, and so would The Man Upstairs."

Nutsy leaped to his feet with another surge of panic. "What man's upstairs?"

Mike grabbed him firmly by his shoulders and smiled. "I was referring to God, Norb. He's the only man upstairs right now." Father Mike sat Nutsy back on the couch. "OK, I'm going to get my white collar out of my jacket to sort of make this official. I'll be right back."

I followed Mike into the hallway. "You did good in there, Father. I think you may have a vocation."

"All in a day's work for a humble country priest. But what's next? Any bright ideas on how we're going to get Norb out of here—without him being turned into Festerwood's first official martyr?"

"I'm working on that with Dennis, and, hopefully, Nutsy's new family attorney, F. Lee."

Mike looked pleased. "That might work. F. Lee is a good supporter of St. Bonnie's."

"Really? I thought he was Jewish."

Mike slipped his collar around his neck. "Haven't you ever heard of someone covering all bets? Mr. Fenneman has turned the education and spiritual guidance of his problem child, Jason, over to us. Of course that happened after the public schools threw in the towel."

"So I take it F. Lee was impressed by Sister Mary Helena's right hook."

Sister Mary Helena was the longtime principal and eighth-grade teacher at St. Boniface Catholic School. Judging by all the firsthand accounts of those who survived her reign, she had to be ninety-seven years old by now. But she still possessed the physique and the stamina of a woman half her age. She was forever known by the nickname of Sister Mary Butkus. Dennis always speculated that she would have made a great cop with her ability to work over student suspects without leaving marks or evidence of internal bleeding.

In the interest of privacy, Father Mike set up his confessional in Nutsy's bedroom. This would give me a chance to contact Fronz to see how we should proceed now that Mike was on the job.

chapter thirty-two

IT WAS AT THIS POINT THAT I HEARD A RUCKUS COMING FROM THE FRONT of the house. There were unfamiliar voices, excited chatter, and the atonal sounds of musical instruments being tested. I opened the blinds and looked out on a carnival. Someone had erected a small raised platform about halfway up Nutsy's driveway, and there were several men scurrying about, tacking bunting to the front and sides of the flimsy structure. Others were opening folding chairs and placing them on the makeshift stage.

An electrician was repeating, "Testing . . . testing . . . One-two-three . . ." into a microphone on a metal pole in the center of the platform and getting nothing but the screech of feedback for his efforts. About a half dozen kids in bright scarlet-and-gold band uniforms were tuning up in the yard just to the right of the driveway. The huge "F" on their capes indicated they were the vanguard of the Festerwood High School marching band. Just down the street, beyond the first phalanx of police cars, a school bus was unloading the rest of the band members.

Two shiny black sedans had just arrived. They were waved through the police lines and parked just behind a paddy wagon. Out stepped the City Fathers of Festerwood, squinting into the sunset glow as they shook hands with the police chief, the sheriff and who knows how many other law enforcement officials. For all I knew, the FBI might be on the scene by now.

Just off in the distance, out of harm's way but close enough to take in the action, the citizens of Festerwood were assembling in what used to be an overgrown field adjacent to the Fagan property. The field had mysteriously been mowed and trimmed, and a bright orange snow fence—the kind that you see weaving around sand dunes along the beach—had been hastily erected to keep the crowd in check. There were several hundred people already in place, and both sides of Ralston Street were bumper-to-bumper with cars, campers, and pick-ups. And more were on the way.

As far as I could see down the street, men, women, and children were arriving on foot, some of them pushing baby carriages and carrying coolers. And there was an enticing scent in the air. Even with the doors and windows closed, I could detect the unmistakable aroma of fried food—the kind of smell that wafted from county fair midways.

Then I saw the smoke. At first I thought one of the TV satellite trucks had caught fire, but the smoke was coming from a point beyond the media area. Refreshment stands! Of course, that's where the smell was coming from. I looked back at the crowd and spotted several people chowing down on hot dogs and cups of beer. As they did so, five or six kids weaved through them, handing out hand-lettered cardboard signs on flimsy wooden sticks. It took me a moment to get one of the signs in focus. It read FESTERWOOD WELCOMES KATHY KELLOGG!

I shut the blind and flipped open my cell phone. One quick ring and a voice answered, "Hostage Central."

"Bullshit. Who is this?"

"Uh . . . Officer Wicks, sir. Who's calling?"

"This is Rick Roberson. Listen to me, Officer Wicks. I want to talk to Deputy Chief Dennis Fronzman, and I want to talk to him now! I don't care if he's taking a nap or taking a leak, I want to talk to him right now. Do you understand?"

"Sir, Deputy Chief Fronzman is in a meeting right now. Can you tell me exactly what this concerns? Perhaps I can help you."

Three days of futility and sleepless nights, warm beer, and bad pizza suddenly erupted inside of me.

"It concerns Nutsy Fagan, you moron!" I shouted. "And if you don't get Fronzman to the phone right now, I will personally drag you into this house and let this madman rip your heart out! *Now get me Fronzman!*"

A moment later, Fronz was on the line. "Jesus, Rick, you just scared the shit out of Wicks. What's up?"

"Oh, nothing much. Have you looked out the window of your command post? What the hell is going on, Fronz?"

"Oh, you mean the Kathy Kellogg business. Beats me. The chief got this call from somebody at NBS about an interview with Nutsy that you set up. How the hell did you swing that?"

I almost jumped through the phone. "I didn't set anything up! It was her idea, and Nutsy fell for it."

"Whatever. Anyway, Chief Penny figured that a national audience for his crime busters in action wouldn't hurt his election efforts, so he invited them in."

"Great, Fronz. That's just what I need right now. No telling what Nutsy might do when he looks out the window and sees that zoo in his yard. He's already paranoid and this—"

"Rick, I know that none of this makes sense. I'm as frustrated as you are. Hell, Chief Penny even asked me to lead the motorcade."

"What motorcade?"

"You'll see."

"Jesus, Fronz . . . you're not going to do it?"

"Sure, buddy. You'll recognize me immediately. I'll be the one at the point of a bayonet."

I realized that there was only so much that Fronz could do. When politics enters the picture, common sense looks for the exit.

I looked in on Horace. So far, so good. He was asleep at the kitchen table, with his head buried in the remains of a Hostess fruit pie. Nutsy was in his bedroom, reciting his sins to Father Mike. I turned on the television set and turned down the volume. There was a game show on, with a toothy host introducing a couple of contestants who obviously had just been fetched from the audience.

The man was dressed in an ill-fitting tee-shirt that barely covered his stomach, reaching just far enough to tuck into a pair of checkered Bermuda shorts. He was wearing an enormous name tag that read ERNIE. By comparison, his wife was the picture of fashion in her huge flowered dress and sandals. Her straw-colored hair fell like a kitchen mop around her face. Her name tag read CLARA.

I always wondered about people who appeared on such shows. They must have known when they left their hotel rooms that morning that they were en route to a television studio, that there was a slim chance they could be selected from the audience to appear on nationwide television, and that everyone back home might see them. If so, then wasn't there a moment when they looked into the bathroom mirror and heard a little voice inside them say, "Whoa! Look at yourself! You're not leaving this room like that!"

Apparently not. In fact, there seemed to be a kind of unwritten rule about game show contestants. Maybe that was it. The smart ones know that if they appear well-dressed and suitably groomed for the occasion, they have no chance of being chosen to compete for shiny cars and tropical vacations. So the worse you look, the better your chances. That must be it.

Anyway, the host was salivating over a dining room set when a bulletin slide appeared on the screen. Gone was the grainy, fingerprinted slide that popped on the air a few days ago. Now there were fancy, state-of-the-art graphics with bold colors and a futuristic "49" superimposed over the words BEEF WHIZ BULLETIN.

It was accompanied by an annoying burst of synthesized music and an announcer's voice trembling with urgency: "We interrupt this program for another Beef Whiz Bulletin from *WHOE Fast Attack News*. This special news report is brought to you by another 'first' for Festus County, the first all-you-can-eat breakfast buffet for under two dollars. Just drop in to the Beef Whiz Restaurant on I-70 and get your day started right. Now this hour's breaking news story."

Dirk Tubergen was on the air, standing in Nutsy's front yard with a mob of screaming kids behind him, waving and mugging for the camera. Apparently Dirk hadn't picked up on the cue, because the camera caught him shouting at the kids, "Goddammit, I told you! Keep quiet! We're on the air—"

Indeed he was, as a distant voice reminded him. Dirk turned to the camera with a sheepish grin. He looked awful, showing the effects of two sleepless nights. There was a shock of wild hair sticking wildly from the sides of his ash-colored face, and his eyes looked like two pee holes in the snow. Dirk had been wearing the same rumpled suit since the great siege on Ralston Street began. He had picked up a few accessories along the way. There was a mustard stain on the lapel and something cream-colored on his right shoulder.

But he was still the professional, recovering nicely with a crisp, "Good evening, Festerwood. I'm Dirk Tubergen, reporting once again from the home of Norbert Fagan, the Ralston Street Ra . . . uh, hostage-taking person." At least Dirk remembered that much of our conversation.

"This evening," he continued, picking up steam, "there is al-most a celebratory mood here. The tension that has gripped this city for three days has been relieved by a most unexpected source. At any moment now, the nation's most honored and trusted newswoman will arrive here to conduct an interview with our own Norbert Fagan. I see that the dignitaries have taken their places on the podium, so let's switch live to Mayor Harlan Flagler."

I raised the blinds so I could watch the spectacle from my front-row seat. Sure enough, there was the mayor, fidgeting with some notes as he rose from one of the folding chairs lined up on the plat-form. Chief Penny occupied one of the chairs; Sheriff Slope was in another; then there were several city council members and one man I couldn't identify.

The mayor tapped the microphone to make sure it worked, then he said in a booming voice, "Welcome, everyone, to this most ex-traordinary event. Who would have thought just three days ago that we would be standing here this evening about to welcome to our city one of our nation's most gifted journalists. Now, we would prefer that the circumstances were different. We'd like to welcome Kathy Kellogg to Festerwood to break ground for a new high school or to cut the ribbon on that new sewage-treatment plant we need so bad—"

Someone in the audience shouted, "You can say that again! Pee-yew!" The crowd roared as one of Festerwood's future leaders traded high-fives with his buddies.

Mayor Flagler just shook his head and continued. "But unfortunately another kind of news story brings her here. The story of one man's inner turmoil, his alienation from society that led him to a senseless, violent act. Why did our friend and neighbor Norbert Fagan finally snap after a lifetime of being an exemplary citizen? No one knows the answer to that question. But if the answer is to be found, then Festerwood is the place to find it.

"This model city in the heartland of the country—this bastion of law and order and family values—in a sense, represents every great city in this great land. That one of its citizens broke ranks with his neighbors simply means that bad things happen to good cities. No, my fellow citizens of Festerwood, now is not the time to hang our heads in shame. Now is the time to raise them proudly! What happens here could happen anywhere, and the solution we find here just could be the solution that helps other cities come to grips with its bad apples. And just let me say this: If there are demons driving the poor man who lives in this house, then I can think of no reporter better qualified to find those demons and dispose of them than—"

"Kathy Kellogg!" someone shouted from the crowd. "She's here!" All heads turned to watch as two motorcycle cops, sirens at full cry, led a huge black limousine with tinted windows to its place of honor in front of the podium. There were three sharp blasts on a whistle, and the Festerwood High School band struck up the school fight song. The crowd erupted in cheers as the limo door opened and out stepped . . . a total stranger.

A frail little man wearing a pinched smile squinted into the TV lights and gave the crowd a feeble wave. He was followed by a stocky, unsmiling woman carrying a suitcase and another woman in a tight skirt and stiletto heels, whose orange and blue striped crew cut stunned the crowd into silence. Then came a beefy man who was sweating profusely as he tugged at what looked to be a metal foot-locker, followed by a goateed young man with a ponytail, who seemed amused by the whole affair. I was guessing this was the photographer. Then came two more-serious-looking men in business suits.

Finally, as the crowd waited breathlessly, the guest of honor appeared. Kathy Kellogg, looking taller and even more beautiful than she does on camera, alighted from the limo with an enormous smile and a big wave. Her auburn hair was cut in stylish bangs that fluttered in the morning wind and her tailored suit was definitely haute couture. In fact, everything about Kathy Kellogg looked to be perfect. The crowd went nuts.

"Kathy! Over here! Kathy, look this way!" Instamatics were clicking away like katydids on a summer night. Kathy Kellogg ascended the three steps to the platform and shook hands with the Festerwood dignitaries. They all greeted her with deferential smiles, and Chief Penny even sucked in his stomach for the occasion.

The mayor said a few words about how honored his city was to host such a respected personality, then, with great ceremony, he produced a key to the city and stumbled through a proclamation that ended with this day being declared "Kathy Kellogg Day in Festerwood, Indiana." The crowd cheered, the band repeated the fight song, and Kathy Kellogg stood there, taking it all in with a gracious smile and shaking her head slowly at the great fortune that had befallen her. Finally, when the crowd settled down, she took the microphone.

"I just want to say that I have never received a warmer welcome. But then again, I shouldn't be surprised. You know, when you cover news in places like New York City and Washington, D.C., it's easy to get a little cynical about things. It's only on occasions like this that you are reminded that there is a real world out there, where real people live and work and raise their families and pay their taxes. And

I just know that when I meet the man in this house behind me, when I sit down with him, person to person, I won't just be making news—I'll be making a friend."

Jesus! *Nutsy!* I had almost forgotten all about him. I shut the blinds and dashed upstairs. I hated to walk in on someone's confession, but I figured Nutsy should be wrapping things up by now. I opened the door and heard Nutsy whisper, "And then, Father, when I was twelve—"

I knocked on the door and poked my head into the room. "Sorry, but there's a rather urgent matter we need to attend to."

Father Mike glared at me. "Rick can't you see that Norb is confessing his sins—"

"I know, Father, but the thing is—Norb, Kathy Kellogg is here for your interview!"

Mike made a quick sign of the cross over Nutsy. "Your sins are forgiven, my son. Say three Hail Marys and two Our Fathers and go and sin no more."

Nutsy was more than a bit startled. "But Father, I got lots more, like when I was—"

"Never mind, Norb, we'll finish up later." Father Mike headed for the bedroom door. "What do we need to do?"

"Just clean him up a bit. But we have to hurry."

chapter thirty-three

WHILE FATHER MIKE TOOK CARE OF NUTSY, I DASHED DOWNSTAIRS TO the kitchen, where Horace was still asleep in his dessert. It was not a pretty picture: there were pie-crust crumbs in his teeth and hair, and a ring of blueberry pie filling around his mouth, giving him an eerie *Night of the Living Dead* look. I soaked a dish rag and wiped his face, warning Horace not to utter so much as one syllable. Then I ran back upstairs to choose some appropriate clothing for Nutsy's interview. I wasn't sure exactly what was in vogue for hostage takers, but I figured a shirt and crewneck sweater would do.

I looked in on Father Mike; he was running a razor over Nutsy's stubbled face. Then I took a quick look out the window. Kathy Kellogg was still on the platform; someone was presenting her with a bouquet of carnations. Mike worked fast, and in a few minutes, we had Nutsy looking presentable. As Horace gathered up the beer cans, I sat Nutsy in an easy chair in the living room and placed his Mattel rifle under his chair. I thought some last-minute instructions were in order.

"Horace, now remember, you're a hostage. That means you just sit there and don't give your uncle—or anyone—any lip. OK?"

Horace gave me the finger. I took that as a sign of compliance, then I started to go over some talking points with Nutsy when my cell phone rang.

"Thank you for using AT&T."

"Rick, this is Chief Penny. I don't know how this happened, but I don't want you to screw this up. In a minute, Kathy Kellogg will be coming up to Nutsy's front door, and there sure as hell better not be any trouble. Understand?"

"Sure, Chief. It's a good thing you called, though. I was about to have Nutsy open fire on the first good-looking network anchor-woman who set foot on his front porch."

"You see, Roberson? That's just the kind of smart-ass crap I don't want. We've had enough of it. This lady is here to do a job, and maybe with her help we can end this thing without anyone getting hurt."

"OK, Chief, send her in. Mr. Fagan awaits in the parlor."

Suddenly, everything became very quiet out front. I looked out into a sea of faces, all of them turned toward Nutsy's house in antici-pation. The silence was refreshing but lasted only a few seconds. It was broken by an ear-splitting screech and the enraged voice of Chief Penny.

"Goddammit, how do you work this thing?" He was fumbling with the bullhorn. A couple of awkward moments followed, then the chief's amplified voice split the air.

"Fagan! Norbert Fagan! This is Chief of Police Penny. If you can hear me, give me a signal."

I figured that residents of the planet Org could hear him, let alone poor old Nutsy Fagan, but the chief needed a signal, so I lifted one of the slats in the blinds and gave him a wave.

"OK, Norb. Now listen. We have Miss Kathy Kellogg here from NBS News. She's ready for your interview. She'll be coming up the walk in a second and I don't want any funny business. Now, Norb, I'm warning you: Miss Kellogg will be escorted by police officers, so if you make one false move, they will respond."

There was a pause. Then the chief's voice again: "Goddammit, Slope, I told him that. I got this covered." Another pause. "OK, Norb, she's comin' in."

I turned to Nutsy for some final instructions. "Now Norb, try to relax. Just pretend that Kathy Kellogg is a neighbor who's dropping by for a chat. This is no big deal."

Nutsy shifted in his chair. "I know, Rick, but I gotta take a leak."

"Oh, Norb, not now!" I looked out the window. Kathy Kellogg and her entourage were coming up the front walk.

"But I really gotta go!" Nutsy had his legs crossed like a four-year-old in a church pew.

"OK, Norb, go ahead. I'll make sure everybody's comfortable."

Just then, a tremendous thudding noise shook the house, knocking ashtrays from the coffee table and rearranging Marie's collection of Starving Artists paintings on the living room wall.

I ran to the door and yanked it open. "For Christ's sake, what the hell's—?"

I was immediately shouldered out of the way by two of Festerwood's finest, dressed in flak jackets and goofy looking helmets.

I peered under one of the visors. "Clyde, is that you? Well I'll be damned, I didn't recognize—"

"Secure?" He shouted to his partner.

"Secure."

The first cop—who I'm pretty sure was Clyde Furrows, an old CYO buddy—turned toward the door. "Bring her in." It sure sounded like Clyde.

I turned back to the door as a parade of unsmiling people entered Nutsy's house. I recognized most of them from Kathy Kellogg's limousine: the big woman with the suitcase led the way, heading straight for the living room as if she owned the place. The lady with the strange hair followed, her disapproving eyes darting about the house. Then there was the beefy man dragging an equipment box; the photographer who looked distracted, as if he was sizing up his first shot; and the suits, who stayed pretty much in the background. Then Kathy Kellogg breezed in, smiling radiantly and extending her hand.

"Hello, I'm Kathy Kellogg. You must be Mr. Fagan."

I shook her hand. "Well, actually, no, I'm not. I'm Rick Roberson. We talked on the phone."

A cloud of contempt passed over her sunny features. "Oh, yes,

Mr. Roberson. Well where's Mr. Fagan? I have something for him."

At that moment, I heard the downstairs toilet flush and Nutsy walked out, zipping up his fly. Father Mike was right alongside.

"And here," I announced, "is the man of the hour, accompanied by his spiritual advisor, Father Michael Roarke!"

The famous network anchorwoman reacted the same way every sixteen-year-old cheerleader did when they first saw young Michael Roarke. She ignored Nutsy completely and walked straight up to Father Mike.

"Well, hello, Father. I'm Kathy Kellogg. It's good of you to agree to be at Mr. Fagan's side for our interview."

"Oh, it's no problem, Miss Kellogg. After all, what are we here for if not to help those in need?" Mike sounded very clerical, but his face was turning beet red. I could tell that even he was a bit unnerved by our celebrity guest.

Kathy took Father Mike's arm and led him to the couch. "You know, Father, I've always been fascinated by the priesthood. I did a story once on a man who renounced his vows and married a former nun. He was named "Father of the Year" in his hometown, which I thought was a bit ironic. But I know he was the exception to the rule. How you obey your vow of chastity and resist the temptations of the world is beyond me."

Father Mike took a seat. "Well, Miss Kellogg, we are only human, after all, but I'd be lying to you if I didn't say that occasionally the secular world does have its attractions. For example—"

I hated to interrupt this fascinating discussion, but there was work to do. "Excuse me, Miss Kellogg, but Norbert here has been dying to meet you."

She looked up with just a hint of embarrassment. "Of course. Mr. Fagan. I'm so sorry. Perhaps, Father, we can continue our discussion when we have some time to ourselves."

Father Mike smiled sheepishly. "Certainly, Miss Kellogg. I look forward to it."

"Mr. Fagan, we meet at last!" Kathy Kellogg embraced Nutsy

and pecked his cheek with one of those phony show-business kisses. Nutsy just stared at her and said nothing. I was afraid he was going to pass out.

"Norb, why don't you take a seat over here in your favorite chair?" I guided Nutsy into the living room and sat him down.

Kathy Kellogg turned to one of the men lurking by the door and nodded. Then they nodded, and a moment later two men appeared carrying heavy cardboard boxes. They placed them on the floor directly in front of Nutsy's chair. Kathy Kellogg waited a beat for dramatic effect, then said, "Norb, do you know what these are?"

Nutsy bent down to inspect the boxes. Nutsy knew a case of beer when he saw it. "Beer," he said. He looked up for approval.

"Exactly, Norb. Two cases of beer and no green bottles!" Kathy Kellogg laughed nervously, and everyone in the room did the same.

"But not just any kind of beer, Norb." Kathy signaled to one of the suits, who then dashed over and pried open a case. He removed a dark brown bottle; it had some kind of intricate metal lever at the top that looked like a pump handle.

"This," Kathy Kellogg proudly announced, "is a bottle of Grolsch!"

You could have cut the silence with a bread knife. Everyone just stared at the bottle as if it had been lifted from a pharaoh's tomb. Finally, Nutsy said what was on everyone's mind.

"What's that?"

Kathy Kellogg looked perplexed. "Why, Norb, it's a bottle of Grolsch, one of the finest imported beers in the world. And you now are the owner of not one, but two cases."

Nutsy looked up at her. "Did you say imported? Like Coors? I had one of them once."

Kathy knew this was going nowhere. "Well I hope you enjoy it, Norb. Now let's get ready to chat."

As if on cue, the woman with the suitcase and the woman with the hair were swarming over Nutsy—brushes and makeup sponges flying.

"This will never do!" sighed the woman with the hair as she tortured poor Nutsy's scalp with a comb.

"I'll need number-eight foundation and lots of it," the woman with the suitcase said as she rummaged through a tray filled with jars and compacts.

Nutsy sat there in sheer terror, looking for all the world like a man who had just been mugged.

"Rick! What's goin' on?"

"It's OK, Norb. They're just getting you ready for your interview."

Nutsy shook his head. "Yeah, but you didn't do this when we—"

"It's OK, Norb. Trust me."

The photographer was setting up his tripod, while the big guy—sweating up a storm—pulled an endless supply of lights out of his metal case and placed them around the room. Kathy Kellogg spent the time arguing vehemently with the suits in the doorway. I couldn't make out exactly what she was saying, but it was obvious that one guy was taking most of the heat. I figured he was her agent, and I think their conversation had something to do with her network contract. "Crock of shit" was about the only thing I distinctly heard.

"Ready, Kathy!" The frail little man in the turtleneck uttered his first words. He was agitated, nervous, and constantly talking into a cell phone. Obviously he was the field producer for this piece of hall-of-fame journalism.

I turned to look at Nutsy, and I couldn't believe my eyes. Sitting there, in the same chair where I had deposited one Nutsy Fagan just minutes ago, was a tanned, well-groomed stranger, whose pale, puffy face had been magically transformed into the picture of health. Even his wild-man hair had been tamed. It was amazing. Nutsy Fagan looked like the poster child for A Drug Free America.

Kathy Kellogg took her seat opposite Nutsy and made one last check of her notes. I thought I might offer a last-minute suggestion, so I leaned over and whispered, "Miss Kellogg, far be it from me to offer you any advice, but I think you should know that Norb has been through quite an ordeal here. You can see he's not the brightest guy around, but he has a good heart. And right now he's confused, disoriented, and frightened by all this attention. I would only ask that you try to be as sensitive—"

She cut me off. "Mr. Roberson, I know my job." With that, she nodded to the photographer, turned to her prime-time interview subject, and asked, "First of all, Mr. Fagan, just between you and me, can you tell me how is it that everyone calls you 'Nutsy'?"

Before Nutsy could answer, a booming voice filled the room. "Tonight, another *Inside Affair* exclusive! For the first time, we take you inside the home of the man whose story has captured the imagination of the entire country! Tonight, in his own words, a deeply troubled man tells us how a life of failure led to an act of violence. Tonight, *Inside Affair* goes one-on-one with Norbert Fagan of Festerwood, Indiana!"

And sure enough, there on the screen of Nutsy's living room TV set was Nutsy *au naturel*—unshaven, uncombed, but not unplugged. He looked, in fact, a lot like the same Nutsy Fagan I had interviewed just a few hours earlier.

"What the fuck is this?" sputtered the famous anchor lady as she tore off her microphone and charged across the room toward the television set with such ferocity that Horace, the hostage, who had turned it on, was now in full retreat.

She glared at the set for a moment then wheeled on Nutsy. "Mr. Fagan . . . where did that come from?" Nutsy looked startled and confused.

She stormed across the room and loomed over him. "How dare you? How dare you double-cross me that way, you little pipsqueak! Do you know who I am? Do you have any idea who you are talking to? Prime ministers beg to be interviewed by me, but I chose to come all the way out to East Jesus, Indiana, or wherever we are, because I thought that maybe this one time somebody in this Godforsaken part of the country might have something to say! But no! Instead I get some pathetic town drunk who decides to sell his soul to a half-ass tabloid show! But you know what, Nutsy?" Now she was really in his face, and Nutsy looked absolutely terrified.

"You know what? I'm not surprised. Because people in hell-hole towns like this get their kicks watching shit like *Inside Affair* when legitimate news shows like mine get stiffed right and left. Well you can take your story and your miserable life and shove 'em. You're not worth my time, Nutsy Fagan!"

I was certain that Nutsy was going to burst into tears, but then something seized him. Five days of trauma, of watching his simple life being turned into a televised nightmare, and then this final insult from a celebrity he loved and trusted—it all erupted in one heroic moment.

Nutsy leaped to his feet and shouted, "My name isn't Nutsy! My name is Norbert Fagan! And I'm tired of everyone messin' with me! I just want Marie to come back and everybody else to leave me alone! Now, goddammit, I'm givin' all you people thirty seconds to get the hell out of my house!" And with that, Nutsy reached under his chair, picked up his toy rifle, and started waving it at his guests.

Kathy Kellogg jumped about a foot off the floor. "Jesus! He has a gun! *He has a gun!*"

Absolute panic set in. There weren't many places to hide in Nutsy's sparsely furnished living room, but every member of the crew found some sort of cover. The photographer abandoned his camera and dove behind the couch. The makeup lady scooted under an end table. Kathy Kellogg just stood there flailing her arms in the air.

"He has a gun! Oh, God help me! We're all going to die!" She was turning circles in the middle of the room, screaming at the top of her lungs. It wasn't quite the measured, confident voice that NBS viewers were accustomed to hearing. "Please don't shoot me! Oh God, don't let me die like this!"

At last, Father Mike intervened. He walked over to Nutsy, lowered the gun barrel with his finger, and put his arm around him. "It's OK, Norb. It's OK. We're going to get you some help. Trust me."

Calming Kathy Kellogg would take a bit more doing. Calling

on the skills he learned as wide receiver for Festerwood High, Iron Mike stopped her spinning with a nifty waist-high tackle and lifted her off her feet.

"That's enough, Miss Kellogg," he said in his most solemn voice. "No one's going to hurt you. Just calm down." With that, he dropped her onto the couch and pinned her shoulders to the cushions. "Now take a deep breath. That's it. Listen to me. Mr. Fagan's gun is not real. You are in no danger. There is no need to be afraid."

Kathy Kellogg just lay there, staring at him with wide, terrified eyes. Her face was shiny with tears, and her hair was a tangled mess. Then, in one sudden movement, she reached up with one arm, clasped her hand behind Father Mike's collar and pulled his face into hers to receive a big, wet, passionate kiss. If Mike Roarke was ever going to have second thoughts about his vocation, that would have been the moment. Instead, he reached back and loosened her grip, raised his head, knuckled away a big smear of lipstick, and continued as if nothing had happened.

"That's better. Just relax."

Amidst all the hysteria, I felt a firm tugging at my jacket. It was young Horace, looking more annoyed than concerned by all the mayhem around him.

"It's for you," he said.

chapter thirty-four

"WHAT'S FOR ME?" I TRIED TO MAKE MYSELF HEARD OVER THE CLATTER of the network crew as they emerged from their hiding places and frantically started packing their gear.

"The telephone, stupid. It's been ringing for an hour." Horace pointed to my cell phone on top of the TV set. I assumed that's where I had left it, although for all I knew Horace may have been using it to call 1-900 numbers for psychics and phone sex.

The voice on the other end was clipped, urgent. "May I speak to Mr. Norbert Fagan, please." The *please* threw me off for a moment, but there was no doubt that the city's most colorful barrister, F. Lee Fenneman, was on the line.

"I'm afraid that this is not a good time to talk with Mr. Fagan. May I ask who's calling?"

"Who is this?"

"Sorry, but I asked first."

"Look, Roberson, you would be doing all of us a big favor if you suppressed your desire to be a twenty-four-hour-a-day wise ass. We have a dangerous and tragic situation here."

"Howard Fenneman, is that you? How nice of you to call."

Fenneman's voice now took on a tone of official, less spontaneous anger. "Roberson, I demand you cease and desist any further interviews and conversations with my client. And who the hell is that carrying on in the background?"

"Well, counselor, that all depends. The sobbing you hear is provided by one of this country's most beloved and trusted news anchors, who, I am sure, wishes you had called a bit earlier to demand a gag rule on your client. The crashing noises you hear are courtesy of her crew, scrambling to get out of harm's way, and the other voices are coming from Mr. Fagan's television set, which has been a constant source of entertainment for all of us."

"What about Fagan? Where's he?"

"Right here. Does he know that he's your client, and should I tell him to start saving his money?"

Fenneman actually sounded offended. "My services on his behalf have been arranged by concerned members of the community, including your saintly mother, as I suspect you know. And of course I'm doing this *pro bono* in the interest of bringing justice to this unfortunate and defenseless man. So put him on the phone. I want to talk to him now."

I took the phone to a corner of the room, away from the noise. "Look, Howard, I'm just as anxious to extricate Nutsy from this madhouse as you are, but we have to get him out of here and down to the police station as quietly as we can, without the media hounds and the squirrel hunters from the sheriff's department noticing. Nutsy is scared to death that they're going to kill him, and nothing we can say right now is going to convince him otherwise."

"That's why I need to talk with him, to—"

"No, Howard, there will be plenty of time for talk later. Right now we just need—"

Then it hit me: an actual, honest-to-God idea. "Wait a minute, Howard, you can help after all. Listen, I have an idea." My mind was racing. "If we could just create some sort of diversion, some way to get Nutsy to safety without anyone noticing—"

Fenneman was getting irritable. "What do you mean? Have you looked out your window? They could be selling tickets to this sideshow. You'll never get him out of the house without—"

"But we can! Listen, you can do it. Is Fronzman right there?"

"Yeah, right alongside me. I'm using the phone in his squad car."

"Perfect." I waved Father Mike over to join me. He whispered some reassuring words to both Kathy Kellogg and Nutsy, then he walked over.

"What's up?"

"This is Fenneman on here. He's using the Fronz's phone. Howard, I have Father Mike here now. Get Fronzman on the line. OK, here's the plan. Howard, you call a news conference—"

Fronz laughed. "Great. Another lawyer meets the press. Just what we need—"

"No, Fronz, listen. This may work. Howard announces to the multitude out there that he is now representing Nutsy and will make a few comments on his behalf. Hell, this will be the first real news these guys have had in five days. Believe me, Johnnie Cochran wouldn't get this kind of attention. Just make sure that you impress them with how important this is. Give 'em a lot of umbrage. The media loves umbrage. This has to be on live television for me to get my cue."

"It might work," said Fenneman. "But what about the cops?"

"That part's really up to you, Howard. You need to push a few buttons. Get into a shouting match with the chief and the sheriff. You're good at that sort of thing. Then, just when things are really chaotic, Fronz'll bring his cruiser around to the back door and we'll quietly whisk Nutsy out of here."

Now Fronz was on the phone. "I think it can be done, Rick. The guys guarding the back of the house all belong to our department. But what about that network crew in there with you?"

"Well, I think we can get them out of here with no trouble, although they may need a change of underwear. Give us about five minutes. Everybody OK with this?"

There was a nervous pause, then Fronz and Fenneman said in unison, "Yeah, guess so."

"Great. See you on the next newsbreak."

I hung up and turned to Father Mike. "Do you think you can convince your girlfriend and her crew to clear out of here?"

"No problem. And look, when this is over, I don't want to hear any stories about this. *She* kissed *me*, you know."

"Right. I'll hear your confession later, Padre. Right now, shepherd your flock out the door."

Mike made short work of that assignment. Kathy Kellogg and her entourage were only too happy to leave the scene of the crime. He promised to be back in seven minutes. And he was; I timed it.

chapter thirty-five

ACTUALLY I USED THIS QUALITY TIME TO WRESTLE FOR CONTROL OF THE television set from Horace, who sat cross-legged on the floor, oblivious to the chaos around him. Horace was watching the *Monty Spaulding Show*—the "Stockbroker by Day, Bondage by Night" episode.

On the dais were three clean-cut, well-groomed young men with conservatively short haircuts and carefully trimmed mustaches. They appeared to be the very essence of their stockbroker calling, except perhaps for their studded leather ensembles, complete with dog collars and nipple rings, suggesting Merrill Lynch's new motto might be "No Pain, No Gain."

"Sorry, Horace," I said when I finally figured out how to change the channel manually. "We have to get ready to be rescued from his madhouse."

I no sooner walked away from the set, than I heard the commanding voice of Dominatrex Donna; she was explaining how her whips and handcuffs actually improve her clients' ability to select a profitable portfolio for the cautious investor. I stalked back to the set. As Horace sensed my disapproval, he punched up Channel 49, just in time to catch Dirk Tubergen declare, "WHOE has learned that famed defense attorney Howard Fenneman has been hired to represent Norbert Fagan on any criminal charges that may result from this hostage crisis. Mr. Fenneman has called a news conference that should get underway at any moment here on the front lawn of the Fagan home, and as we understand it—"

"Oh yes, Monty, at first I was nervous about what my supervisors at Merrill Lynch would think of my interest in bondage, but since meeting Donna, I have been able to get in touch with my sexual selfhood. As a result, our third quarter earnings were up twenty percent—"

"Goddam it, Horace, give me that remote!" I yelled, snatching it out of his hands and grabbing his shirt collar in one motion. I pushed him into his room with a final warning: "Don't leave this room until I tell you. You got that?"

"I see Sister Anastasia taught you well." It was Father Mike, calling from downstairs.

"I got news for you, Mike. If Sister Anastasia was dealing with this case, young Horace would be undergoing an autopsy."

I hurried downstairs. "OK, we have work to do. Dennis is about to come by in his limo to squire us to the lockup. Get Nutsy ready, and I'll stand by the TV for Counselor Fenneman's news conference."

Come to think of it, Nutsy was strangely silent during my confrontation with his nephew. Mike soon discovered why. Apparently the excitement, or the beer, got to him. Nutsy was passed out on the floor, surrounded by empty brown bottles of Grolsch beer. Kathy Kellogg's little gift had come in handy. Father Mike got to work awakening Nutsy, and I pulled up a chair in front of the TV.

There was the freshly laundered F. Lee Fenneman—his jet black toupee firmly in place—standing majestically before a battery of microphones. Every television station in the Midwest must have been there, plus CNN, and of course the tabloid shows. Even so, that didn't stop our director from flashing the words WHOE EXCLUSIVE! in the lower right hand corner of the screen during the entire news conference. It was the same spot where the terminally annoying THUNDERSTORM WATCH had become an almost permanent fixture every time a stray cumulonimbus cloud entered the Festerwood airspace.

Fenneman rose to the occasion. "Ladies and gentlemen, my name is Howard Fenneman, chief partner in the law firm Fenneman, Barker, Lemuel and Fenneman. I am here to announce that I have been retained by concerned citizens of Festerwood to represent one Norbert W. Fagan, and to deliver him from this monstrous outrage perpetrated by a grotesque, inept, and corrupt law enforcement establishment and from the news media, which has totally lost its moral focus and is rabidly out of control.

"We will use every legal weapon in our arsenal to see that this poor, unfortunate man is not only cleared of any wrongdoing, but also that his dignity and reputation are restored, although I suspect the latter may be an impossible task in light of the unconscionable assault that has been waged on his fragile psyche. I want you to know that I am foregoing my normal fee; such is the state of my personal horror and sadness at what this oppressive system has done to this man."

Fortunately, Dennis arrived just in time to bring me out of my fascinated stupor. "I see F. Lee is in fine form. Now let's get the hell out of here. I got the family station wagon out back."

"How about the snipers?"

"There're only four of them, and they're all ours."

"Which means they can't hit the ocean with a howitzer?"

"Which means they'll be launching scud missiles if we aren't out of here in two minutes. Let's go!"

Nutsy was shaking as Mike led him groggily toward the kitchen door. "They're not gonna kill us, are they, Father?"

"No, Norbert, they won't kill us. God is with us."

And with that, we headed out into the pitch blackness of Nutsy's backyard, a quartet of hunchbacks running toward Fronz's Ford station wagon. None of us had paid much attention to the terrain of Nutsy's backyard, so when Fronz pulled away, careful not to turn on the headlights to draw attention, he drove straight into a spruce—a rather large one at that. Dennis hit his head squarely on the sun shade that was sticking straight out, opening a pretty good-sized gash in his forehead. I had to do all I could to keep from flying out the passenger side as the door flew open. Mike and Nutsy catapulted forward, nearly landing in our laps.

It was at precisely that moment that we heard the first round of artillery fire crashing into the Fagan homestead.

Fronz jumped out of the car and almost into the arms of Officer Luther Dorien, Festerwood's most prolific parking meter enforcer. "Jesus, Luther, what's going on?"

"Sheriff Slope ordered 'em to open fire. Says there were shots coming from the house. You better let me drive, Denny. That cut's lookin' kind of nasty."

Speaking of nasty, Nutsy had a pertinent question. "Uh, has anyone seen Horace?"

"Oh shit!" I ran for the house. "Keep the engine running! I'll be right back!"

Frankly, I didn't think I was capable of this, but there I was, making like John Wayne, dashing through the back door, crawling on my hands and knees through the kitchen, the living room, and up the stairs with bullets ricocheting all over the place, shattering glass and tearing into the walls and banister. Smoke was starting to billow from the drapes on the front picture window as I reached the top of the staircase.

"Horace! Where are you?"

I opened the bedroom door and there was Horace, kneeling at the foot of the bed with a look of total fascination on his face as fireworks exploded all around him. They were coming from outside the house, but, I was intrigued to learn, from inside as well. It turns out Horace had set off a long string of firecrackers, cherry bombs, and other explosives he had purchased at the Boom Works firecracker outlet, part of his parents' bribe to get him to summer at his uncle's house. That was what Sheriff Slope had mistaken for gunfire, and it had given him the excuse he needed to turn Nutsy's house into a police firing range.

I picked Horace up. Slinging my right arm over his rib cage and resisting the urge to use him as a human shield, I dashed down the stairs, through the first wall of flames, out the door, and into the waiting car. The crash had only crumpled the front fender and hood.

Officer Dorien was at the wheel, looking rather sour that his superior was bleeding all over the upholstery. I literally tossed Horace on his uncle's lap and hopped in. We took off, our path illuminated by the inferno engulfing Nutsy's house. Nutsy was simply dazed, as was Father Mike. Dennis continued to bleed, and Dorien took us to the police station using only alleys.

chapter thirty-six

WE ALL PILED OUT OF THE SQUAD CAR, LOOKING LIKE WE HAD JUST RE-
turned from a fact-finding trip to a toxic waste dump. We could see
the orange glow lighting up the sky over Nutsy's house.

I looked at Father Mike. "Is that what Hell looks like?"

"According to my source, Sister Ignace, it's a reasonable fac-
simile. The way we're going, we'll know soon enough."

We hustled the dazed Nutsy and his brooding nephew into the
city lockup, presided over in totality by lockup legend Theda Jenkins.
She was hovering over the front desk with her ever-present Marlboro
in hand. She held it in a way that made it clear that as long as she was
matron, the Festerwood City Jail would never tolerate a smoke-free
environment. She was reading a magazine, which I suspect promi-
nently featured grisly Midwest murder cases.

Theda was a buxom lass of fifty-four with the body of a nose
tackle. She did her job of processing her guests with great aplomb,
unfazed by the rowdiest drunks and the most belligerent barroom
headcrackers. She got them all fingerprinted, photographed, and deposited on their bunks with dispatch, amidst a constant flow of
motherly wisecracks and good-natured insults. And through it all,
she made it clear that she was taking zero crap from anyone on either
side of the law, including practicing wise asses from the media.

She greeted our untidy arrival with, "Well, if it ain't the Four
Horsemen of Festerwood. Jesus, Dennis, you're bleeding like ground

chuck. You didn't accidentally stab yourself in the forehead with your ballpoint again?"

The Fronz sank into the nearest folding chair. "Theda, I'm in no mood for your soothing words of comfort."

She looked him over. "Well, if it's any consolation to you, Dennis, you look pretty good considering the rest of the world thinks you and your friends are toast." She pointed at the vintage, seventeen-inch, black-and-white TV perched on a locker with rabbit ears twisted in the form of a swastika. Theda did see fit to have the channel on WHOE to monitor the events on Ralston Street, just in case she needed to change the sheets on the jail cell bunks. The television, even in black and white, showed eerily dramatic scenes of Nutsy's home engulfed in flames. I turned up the volume.

Dirk Tubergen, or what remained of him, was looking into the camera with dark, bleary eyes, and his voice sounded like he had been gargling with razor blades. ". . . a house now reduced to smoking rubble, where search parties are hoping against hope to find anyone alive. In that house: a gutsy, courageous reporter; a saintly, charismatic man of the cloth; an innocent nine-year-old boy who delighted in cruising the streets of Festerwood on his treasured skateboard; and a naive, troubled man who asked only that he be left alone, as we saw in Rick Roberson's final report just minutes ago. Three brave men and a veritable baby trapped and presumably consumed in a holocaust of flames, sparked by the tensions of a four-day standoff that exhausted the resolve and patience of police."

"Gee," said Theda, "were there other people in there with you? Turbie surely isn't talking about you birds."

"No offense, Theda," I replied, "but I was hoping you would show a little more compassion and distress at our obvious demise. I was going to make you my only pallbearer."

"I'm deeply touched, Roberson. But I know the cops in this town couldn't hit a pumpkin with an AK-47." She strolled over to the bemused Father Mike, who was standing next to a confused Nutsy in his capacity as spiritual adviser. "And, besides, you had this gorgeous angel of mercy to guide you through. Give me a big hug, Padre." She flung her beefy arms around Mike, and he responded with genuine affection.

"Always a joy to see you, Theda. Did you miss me?"

"Miss you? I want you to know that I've been celibate ever since you went into that goddam seminary. You broke the hearts of a lot of girls, Michael."

Mike gave a mock sigh. "I should have become a television evangelist, then I could have had both."

Now Dirk was launching into a little speech about what a worthwhile human being I had become since my death and the station's unilateral decision to waive all of the Catholic Church's canonization procedures to declare Father Michael Roarke a saint—right there before weather and sports.

Tubergen continued to ramble on about what he could remember of my career, while some fascinating pictures appeared on the screen. TV stations—especially my TV station—never keep their picture files up to date when it comes to reporters, so as Dirk reminisced about me, viewers were treated to pictures of a really ugly, young guy with long and unruly hair, five-inch sideburns, a paisley tie, and a dog-shit brown leisure jacket that made me look like a rhythm guitarist for Freddy and the Dreamers.

"Let me see," said Fronz. "Was that during your Elvis period or was it at Purvis' Halloween party, where he asked you to dress up as your favorite Monkee?"

"I remember that party," I said. "You dressed up as one of the guys on *Adam 12*. My God, you were a fascist even then."

Theda turned to Nutsy. "So, Mr. Fagan, in for your annual checkup, I see. You've had a lot of people in this town wetting their pants. Let's get you cleaned up and get a hot meal in you. And it might be a good idea, Dennis, to let the chief know what the hell you've been doing. He's beside himself."

"I can't believe he opened fire like that," said Fronz, holding a wet towel to his forehead.

I looked up at the set. "Wait a minute; turn the volume up some more. Old Dirk has a guest."

Dirk's voice reached us through a wall of static. "With me now is Sheriff Slope, who was in charge of this operation, and who directed the assault on Norbert Fagan's house. Sheriff—"

Slope yanked the microphone out of Dirk's hands before he could ask his question. "Let me make one thing clear: this was a joint operation. Chief Penny was responsible for many of the decisions we made here today—"

Dirk grabbed the microphone and pulled it toward him. "But, Sheriff, you told reporters on several occasions that you were in charge, and that—"

Now Slope took what was left of the microphone with his other hand. They looked like two Pony League kids fighting for the last space on a bat handle. "You are mistaken, my friend. I am not about to take the blame for this tragic episode. Let me just say that I only wish I had demanded more authority; then, perhaps, we could have avoided the drastic measures that were taken."

Dirk seized the microphone with such force that the sheriff looked a bit startled. "So, Sheriff Slope, you are saying that when the voters go to the polls to cast their ballots, they have a choice between a forceful law officer who makes on-the-spot decisions—even if they are wrong—and a vacillating, buck-passing politician who is a bit too eager to blame someone else for his own mistakes."

I jumped to my feet and shouted, "Attaboy, Dirk! I didn't know you had it in you!" I figured three days of no sleep and bad food had taken their toll on Tubergen, but sometimes that's what it takes to clear the mind.

Sheriff Slope looked dumbfounded for a moment, then he lost it—right there on camera. "How dare you! How dare you! You and your pampered, self-important friends in the news media who think you're so high and mighty that you can stand there and second-guess every decision made by honest, God-fearing officers of the law!"

Now he was jabbing a stubby finger into Dirk's chest, almost backing him out of the picture. "I thought you were different, Tubergen. I thought you were fair. Not like that smart-ass Roberson who went in there just to grandstand for a few days and take all the credit—"

Dirk politely reminded the good sheriff, "You mean the late Rick Roberson, don't you, Sheriff?"

"Uh . . . well, yeah, I guess so. But he can't say I didn't warn him. This was a dangerous situation, no place for a cocky, half-ass reporter to make a name for himself."

Slope paused for a moment and took a deep breath. "Listen, Tubergen, this is bullshit. Do me a favor and don't run that part tonight, OK? I got a little out of control there. Just be a good guy and edit that part out, 'cause if Roberson is dead I'll look like shit to the voters."

There was a faint smile on Dirk's face. He looked at the camera and said, "Sheriff, that is going to be difficult, since we are on live television right now."

Slope looked at the camera, looked back at Dirk, and silently mouthed, "This is live?"

Dirk nodded, and the sheriff of Festus County—his face drained of color—slumped out of camera range and out of the political picture. It was Dirk's finest hour, and I had to tell him so.

I found Fronz bent over some paperwork in an adjoining office. "Deputy Chief Fronzman, this is none of my business, but don't you think it's time we informed the public that Nutsy and his entire supporting cast survived this little melodrama?"

Fronz looked up and smiled. "Yeah, I was just thinking that. I'll knock out a statement for the chief and call a news conference."

"Before you do, can you run me over to Nutsy's place? I want to personally deliver a message to Dirk Tubergen."

Fronz dropped his pen and stood up. "Wait a minute—that's a hell of an idea. Why don't you make the announcement, live, on your own station? You're the guy who got Nutsy through this insanity. I'll have the chief meet us there."

"I don't know, Fronz. I'm supposed to report the news, not make it."

Fronz raised an eyebrow and just stared at me as if to say, *What the hell do you think you've been doing for the past week?*

The thing is, old Fronz had a point. After all, I was responsible for Nutsy's health and safety. And, besides, there was still this nagging voice in my head telling me that I might never get a chance like this again to impress every TV news director in the country.

"Fronz, as unaccustomed as I am to public speaking, I will defer to your good judgment. Let's go."

chapter thirty-seven

THE TIMING COULDN'T HAVE BEEN BETTER. AS FRONZ PULLED HIS SQUAD car up behind Nutsy's bullet-riddled house, Lowell was turning on the cine light on his camera, casting Dirk in an eerie, surrealistic glow on the smoky front lawn.

I got out of the car and crept around the side of the house just in time to hear Dirk say, "If you will indulge me, Clay, I'd like to take just a moment for a personal comment. They say a reporter should keep some distance between himself and the story he is covering, and I have tried to do that in my five years in television news. But what happened here in this house this past week was more than a news story—it was a personal tragedy. Because somewhere in the devastation of that house is the body of a colleague, a man I learned to respect as a fellow reporter; a man whose integrity and dedication were a beacon to us all; a man whose work will live on as an example of broadcast journalism at its best."

Then, dropping his head and casting his eyes downward in one of those dramatic pauses that news consultants love, Dirk took a beat, squared himself, and looked intensely into the camera's eye. "But more than that, on this day, in this week, Rick Roberson was . . . a hero."

That did it. I cleared my throat and hollered from the bushes, "Bullshit!"

The next pause was definitely not rehearsed. Dirk spun around, squinted into the darkness, and, in a shaky voice, asked, "Who's there? Who is that?"

"It's me, for Chrissake. Don't you know a hero when you hear one?"

Dirk recovered just in time to look at the camera and say, "Clay, it appears there is some new information that's about to be released by the crews searching the Fagan house. So I'll send it back to you for now, and I'll be back with the latest in just a moment. This is Dirk Tubergen, live for *Fast Attack News*."

He dropped his mike at about the same time Lowell dropped his camera. I walked out of the shadows. "Nice job, Dirk. A little heavy on the hero stuff, but I can't argue with the rest."

"Christ Almighty, Rick, what happened?"

"Well, first of all, thanks for caring. Yes, I'm glad to see me alive, too. As for your question: Fronz, Father Mike, and I sneaked Nutsy and little Horace out the back door just before the first artillery barrage. They did a nice job of remodeling Nutsy's house, though. It needed it."

Lowell just stood there speechless, as Dirk stammered, "But . . . but, you mean . . . I mean . . . you were gone the whole time?"

"You got it. In fact, the only living thing in that house was green and brown and sitting on the third shelf in Nutsy's refrigerator."

Dirk just sank to the grass. "Well, I'll be damned. Hey, wait! We've got to get this story out! Everybody thinks you're dead." Dirk fumbled with his cell phone. "Lowell, get set up. And use the tripod this time. Christ, Rick, I don't believe this!"

I waved Fronz out of the shadows to join us. "Dirk, you know Deputy Chief Fronzman. He was a key player in this great escape."

Dirk nodded as he punched the last button on his cell phone. "Newsroom? Karen? This is Dirk. Listen, you are not going to believe this. Guess who's alive and well and standing not three feet from me?" He paused. "How in the hell did you know? What do you mean? What desk sergeant?" Dirk capped his hand over the mouthpiece. "She says some woman at police headquarters phoned to say she was making a report on survivors and needed the spelling on Rick's name."

That was about all Fronz and I could take. We both collapsed on the lawn in spasms of life-threatening laughter. I had this tremendous cramp in my side, and Fronz was on his hands and knees gasping for breath.

It took us some time to recover, and, until we did, Dirk ran a breathless bulletin that reports of our deaths were greatly exaggerated. As he did so, all the principle characters of the Nutsy Fagan story were alerted and began assembling in the front yard.

Chief Penny arrived wearing his immaculate dress blues. Grumbling network reporters reset their cameras and lights—chagrined that they were scooped by some nowhere local TV station. F. Lee Fenneman reappeared, having somehow had time to change into another dark pin-striped suit, complete with a red silk pocket handkerchief. And, there on the lawn in front of Nutsy Fagan's smoldering ruin of a house, Fronz, Father Mike, F. Lee, Chief Penny, and I recalled the historic events that led to this triumphant moment.

There weren't many questions, since everyone had gotten pretty tired of the whole affair and was ready to move on to the next moment of high drama that would cause Americans everywhere to drop their coffee cups and say, "Honey, look at the TV. You won't believe this!"

Chief Penny was asked about the fusillade that had obliterated Nutsy's house, but he referred all questions to Sheriff Slope, who was off somewhere rethinking his career path.

And Fenneman was his usual belligerent self, claiming that once he cleared Nutsy of whatever charges might result from this episode, he would sue the Police Department; the City of Festerwood; and the Bureau of Alcohol, Tobacco and Firearms. Of course, the ATF wasn't involved, but Fenneman had always been convinced that the organization got off way too easy after Waco and should have to pay for something.

Unfortunately, Larry the Loon also showed up at the last moment, putting his arm around me and gushing into the cameras, "I couldn't be prouder of what this man has accomplished." Then, with a wink, he added, "I just hope that he doesn't ask for a raise!"

Everyone had a big laugh, and then it was over. Within minutes, the police cars and satellite trucks were gone, leaving behind a street littered with spent shells and empty tape boxes. Ralston Street, the center of the media universe just two hours earlier, was just like it had been before and would be in the future: a quiet, dead-end street in a remote corner of a little town in western Indiana.

chapter thirty-eight

I HAD SEVERAL CALLS WAITING WHEN I GOT BACK TO MY APARTMENT. THE most recent was from my mother. "Rick, dear, thank God you're all right. I watched on television. Call me."

I reached into the refrigerator for a can of Old Style with one hand and punched up my mother's phone number with the other. There was just a burp of a ring. "Hello? Rick, is that you?" Mother was blessed with a woman's psychic sense of when the phone would ring and who would be on the other end.

"It's me, Mom. Alive and well, no matter what you heard."

"Well, you had us all worried sick. I tried to find you, but I got lost, and by the time I arrived at Mr. Fagan's house, no one was there." My mother, no matter what her achievements in her public life, still had trouble navigating the labyrinthine streets of Festerwood.

"That's OK, Mom. If you were watching, then I suppose you saw your friend Fenneman's little performance."

There was a small sigh of disapproval. "Yes, but you must remember, dear, that Howard is a first-rate lawyer despite his pomposity. Besides, he's one of the few Democrats in town."

"I'm sure he'll be terrific, Mom. Listen, I need to get cleaned up. I promise I'll stop by tomorrow."

"Wait, dear, before you go . . . is there anything you need?"

For some reason, I knew that I was about to receive some intestinal advice. Mother might at times be a radical politician, but she was a traditionalist when it came to matters concerning the colon.

"I'm worried about you. I know you didn't eat well this week, and I think you probably could use a stool softener about now. I happen to have—"

"That's OK, Mom. I'm fine." Actually, a laxative was definitely one thing I did not need. Several days of pizza and beer had me shitting like a goose.

There was a message from the bank about an overdue car payment, and one of those recorded telemarketing pitches for a free vacation in the Bahamas. I was pretty sure that my recorded message didn't fall for it, but you never know. It hadn't been out of my apartment for months.

Then there was a familiar voice, husky and seductive. "Hi, Rick. It's Jeanette. I'm just calling to say how proud we all are of what you did. And to tell you I've missed you. If you're not too tired, drop by the hotel. I think you know the room number."

Actually, I figured I could use a little R and R. I peeled off the grubby shirt and slacks I had worn for three days and dumped them in a stiff, fetid heap on the floor. Then I showered, shaved, and searched through the meat drawer of the refrigerator to find something to eat that was still a reasonable shade of brown.

An hour later, I was sitting at the bar of the Ramada Inn, enduring Dex's insults, as usual. It was reassuring in a way, almost as if nothing had changed.

"Son of a bitch! If it isn't Lazarus back from the grave!"

"Yeah, I'm sorry about that. I know you were all set to name a drink after me."

Dex filled a shot glass with scotch and slid it across the bar. "Damn, Roberson. You look like shit. Not bad for a dead man, but shit all the same."

"Well, it's not something I recommend. Look, let me have a bottle of wine, will you? I have some unfinished business upstairs."

"You're a regular iron man, aren't you?" Dex leered. "Save a life, dodge a bullet, escape a fire, and screw your brains out—all in one week. You really are gonna kill yourself, Roberson."

"With any luck, Dex. With any luck."

I trusted Dex's wine selection—something white and fruity from California—and headed for my assignation with the WHOE news consultant.

Minutes later, we lay exhausted in a tangle of damp sheets, the bottle of wine still unopened on the bed stand. I lifted a strand of hair from Jeanette's forehead. "Now, where were we?"

She raised up on one elbow and laughed, reaching for a cigarette. "As I recall, this was about the time we looked up at the television and heard Mr. Fagan invite you over for a snack."

"Right. I said no way I was going to get involved, and that's when you questioned my masculinity and said I was a half-ass, small-town reporter who was going nowhere, and I said that's what you think, and next thing I knew I was sitting in Nutsy's living room with every gun in Festus County trained on me. Is that about the way it was?"

Jeanette leaned over and kissed me on the shoulder. "Not quite. Fact is, you did a hell of a job over there. And the best part is, everybody came out a winner. Festerwood is on the map, WHOE is on the move, and you're probably on your way out of here."

The television set was turned on, of course—to one of those "Movies of the Week" that are made for network television. Just spicy enough to arouse some interest at ratings time, but pretty tepid by cable standards. Jeanette pushed the volume button on the remote control.

"I saw the promos for this movie. Looked pretty good. Something about a phone-sex girl who hooks up with one of her regular callers and winds up as his victim."

I nodded. "Hmmm, a nineties story with something for everyone. Murder, sex, and telecommunications. A little short on family values though, wouldn't you say?"

Jeanette just shrugged. "I don't know. Makes sense to me. The world is upside down, and we're just telling stories about it. That's all we do, Rick—"

"Hold it," I said. "I think we had this conversation before. Anyway, I was kidding. To be honest with you, I really don't care what the networks are up to these days. Just as long as they don't bring Buddy Ebsen back as a cross-dresser."

Just then, the screen filled with a silhouetted figure and the urgent voice of an obviously overwrought announcer. "You're watching the network premier of *1-900-DEATH*. How a phone-sex relationship leads to murder. But could it happen here? Tonight on *WHOE Fast Attack News*, this woman says, 'Yes.' You'll hear her own harrowing story of how her teenage son's phone-sex calls led to bills so enormous that they almost caused her to take her own life. Coming up on *Fast Attack News*, right after the movie: the story of phone sex in Festerwood—just one call away from *Death on the Line*."

I shook my head. "Now I'm impressed. You and Teri have been working overtime."

Jeanette looked at me like a parent trying to explain phonics to a three-year-old. "It's called a vertical promotion, Rick. TV stations in all the bigger markets do it. You try to find a news story that relates to the show that just ran on the network."

I nodded and reached for the wine bottle. "I get it. Phone sex in Los Angeles. Phone bills in Festerwood. Cute."

Jeanette slowly shook her head. "You're hopeless, I'm afraid. But what really bothers me is that you don't seem to care. I thought maybe you learned something this week. Like it or not, Rick, sometimes the news is what we say it is. That's just the way it happens."

I opened the wine bottle. "Great. It's a twist-off cap. Good old Dex. None of that messy cork stuff."

"Seriously, Rick," Jeanette said, looking very serious indeed. "What happens now?"

I filled two plastic motel glasses with wine. "Well, I imagine that what happens now is I go back to work tomorrow in my dead-end job to report bridge repair stories; you stick around long enough to jazz up the rest of the rating period, maybe with a follow-up series called, *Nutsy, We Hardly Knew Ye*; and life goes on—oobladee, oobladah."

"And we pretend that none of this ever happened?"

I sampled the grape from Dex's collection. It was a crisp, sassy wine with a pleasant, slightly mischievous bite. Good for gulping. "None of what ever happened?"

"You know what I mean. Not this, not the sex part. We'll both forget this soon enough. I mean . . ." Jeanette took a swig from her glass. "I just mean that I hate to see a talent like yours wasted. The fact is, Rick, we need you. I don't mean just WHOE. I mean the television news business as a whole. Soon enough we're going to take over, you know. The consultants, the marketing people, the promotion types—we'll all be in charge. We have to be. Just churning out solid newscasts won't be enough anymore. It isn't enough now!

"Those people out there have about a zillion channels to choose from. Pretty soon they'll have even more. That guy sitting at home at night holding his remote in one hand and a can of beer in the other, grazing through fifty channels offering everything from sports to knitting—how are you going to convince him to stop at Channel 49 when it's time for the news? What do you think would do it? Phone sex or bridge repairs?"

I know a rhetorical question when I hear one. "OK, but maybe that's the bridge he has to drive over on his way to work in the morning."

Jeanette sniffed back a laugh. "Rick, this town isn't that dull. Look, the stuff I do—packaging, promoting, merchandising the news—I know it's all very repulsive to you, but it's become more important than ever. All I'm saying is, when we're really running your newsrooms for good, we are going to need some rock-solid people like you to work with. I really believe that.

"I'm still enough of a journalist to know that the Boyd Nelsons and Jeanette Larmers of this world would run amok without someone standing in the doorway to tell us that there still are boundaries, places we cannot go. Someone to remind us that this is still news we are reporting, and that there are limits of good taste and good judgment." She set her glass on the table. "Someone like you, Rick."

I was impressed. "Very nice," I said. "Very convincing. But let me see if I have this straight. If—I'm sorry, I mean *when*—when you and your friends take over all the local news operations in the country—rather than simply advising us about how to dress and talk and what makeup to wear—you will, in fact, be dictating what kinds of stories we should be reporting.

"But even after you have seized ultimate power, you realize that to put a good face on things, you need a couple of so-called serious journalists around—a couple of flunkies—to give you legitimacy. And that's where I come in. Kind of the Marshal Petain of the newsroom."

Jeanette was surprisingly calm. "Forget it, Rick. You'll never understand. Or maybe you just pretend not to. It doesn't matter. I think you should go."

I set my glass on the table and looked under the sheet. "Don't think so. Looks like I have a vertical promotion that you may want to start working on."

She laughed and threw her glass against the wall. "You are a bastard, Roberson. But at least you're good for something."

chapter thirty-nine

THE WHOE NEWSROOM WAS ABOUT THE LAST PLACE ON EARTH YOU'D expect to find a party, but I sure walked into one the next morning. Someone had strung a banner over the newsroom door that read NUMBER ONE NEWS! I ducked under it, only to collide head-on with Leon, the producer. Not a good sign. That was exactly how my week had begun.

"Rick! Rick, ol' buddy, how are you?" Leon slurred as he spilled the contents of his plastic glass all over my suit.

"Isn't it a bit early for Happy Hour?" I asked, brushing what smelled like cheap champagne from my jacket.

"Not on your life, Rick, ol' man!" Leon was obviously well beyond his two drink limit, and it was still early morning.

"Hey, everybody! Look who's here!"

Within seconds, my co-workers were all over me like a dollar mop, shaking my hand and slopping me with wet kisses. Even Karen Armstrong threw her arms around my neck and about choked the life out of me. "Great job, Rick! I mean it. You made us all proud."

"Stand back, everyone! Give the poor guy some air!"

It was Boyd Nelson, pushing his way through the pack with one hand and waving a computer printout sheet with the other. "Hell of a job, Roberson, just look at these numbers." With that, he thrust a paper into my hands that made absolutely no sense to me.

"Sorry, Boyd, I never could read these."

"Well let me give you the bottom line, Rick." Young Boyd was really in his element now. With a flourish, he took the sheet from me, turned to the newsroom, and announced, "As of last night's five o'clock show, WHOE is now the highest-rated newscast in the entire viewing area! And that includes those foreigners in Champaign and Decatur!"

The newsroom erupted in cheers, with Dirk Tubergen leading the chant, "We're Number One! We're Number One! We're Number One!" The place looked like an Amway convention.

"Anybody got any of that champagne left?"

"Sure, my friend, drink up." It was Morris Chiles, pouring my plastic cup to the brim. "Actually, I'm glad to see you, Rick. I'm tired of taking all these goddam phone calls for you."

I started for my desk. "What calls?"

"Oh, the usual. Job offer here, job offer there. You know the drill."

I stopped in my tracks. "You're kidding, right?"

"Wish I was, my friend. But the fact is, this Nutsy Fagan business has made you just about the hottest commodity since computer sex. I put all the messages on your desk."

He wasn't kidding. There was a stack of "while you were out" slips next to my phone. I started to flip through them. There were calls from Minneapolis, Detroit, even one from a station in Chicago. Christ almighty, it had worked! Nutsy Fagan turned out to be my ticket out of Festerwood! I looked around the room, but everyone was having too good a time to notice. Producers were hugging reporters, photographers were hugging each other, so why wasn't I feeling anything?

Here I was, a hero in my own hometown, holding in my hand a stack of offers to any big city reporting job I wanted. And yet, I couldn't feel a thing. Nothing. Just empty.

I sat down and stared at the slip of paper at the top of the pile. *WCCO, Minneapolis. Called Thursday. Urgent. Call Ted Lindsey, News*

Director. And then the number. WCCO! I would have had to perform an unnatural act to get a call from WCCO just a week ago. But here I was, just a phone call away from working there, and I couldn't care less.

I stood up and took a deep breath. I needed to get hold of myself. What the hell had happened? There was a folded copy of the *Festus County Fanfare* on the desk next to mine. I opened it to the front page. There was a headline in bold print: HOSTAGE CRISIS ENDS! And beneath that, in slightly smaller print, "Fagan surrenders to end three-day siege."

I smiled to myself. Is that what it was? A siege? A three-day siege at the home of a poor, lonely, confused man who had been turned into a national phenomenon and now would be discarded with the rest of the day's news? I told myself I was being just a bit too high-minded, but I couldn't help it. Everyone had gotten a piece of Nutsy, and now we were all cashing in and moving on.

The phone rang. "Roberson, news."

"Rick! I didn't think you'd be answering. This is Tim."

Tim Facenda. I hadn't talked to him since I began checking out the Norma Flescher story about an ice age ago.

"Tim! You should be here. It's your kind of party. Lots of drinking and groping going on. You left this place too soon."

"Yeah, I saw your 'We're Number One' promo this morning. Bet you never thought old Nutsy Fagan would be the guy who turned things around for you. Hell, I remember when—"

"I know, I know. Listen, Tim, what the hell happened with that Norma Flescher business?"

"What do you mean? You mean you don't know?"

I was getting a bit irritated. "I know that you were only too happy to tell everything you knew when the station called you."

"Wait a minute, Rick. Don't hang that on me. I knew you had your hands full with Nutsy, so I figured you told your buddies down there to call me for the Flescher stuff. Anyway, does it matter after what's happened?"

"What are you talking about? What's happened?"

"You didn't see the story? The one on *Inside Affair* last night?"

I had this sinking feeling in my stomach. "OK, Tim. Let me have it."

"I thought you knew, Rick. I really did. *Inside Affair* went ahead and ran the Flescher story. Only you won't believe how badly they screwed it up. Instead of Norma Flescher, they ran video of—"

I finished the sentence for him. "Dawn Rae Hargis, daughter of the minister of Festus Friends in Faith Church."

"Right, but how did you know?"

"Tim, old buddy, you wouldn't happen to have a copy of that show, would you?" I knew that Tim taped everything on television. His collection of *F Troop* shows was legendary.

"Sure, I taped it. But how did you—"

I looked at the newsroom clock. It was still early. There was time for damage control. "Do me a favor, Tim, and bring that tape down here right away, will you?"

There was a slight pause. "Well, I guess so. I was expecting company, though."

"Right. It's too early for taxes or sex. Just get that tape down here. Thanks."

I hung up and sank into my chair. All I could figure is that *Inside Affair* got pissed that Nutsy turned them down for a one-on-one interview and decided to run the Norma Flescher story as is, even though the bastards ran part of my interview with him. But wait, how the hell . . . ?

At that moment I felt a warm hand on the back of my neck. I knew that hand. It moved slowly and sensually, as it stroked the fine hairs at the nape of my neck; the fingers moved up to the base of my skull, making tiny rhythmic circles that released a flood of well-being directly into my groin.

"Hi. Remember me?" The voice that went with the hands was just as familiar.

"Hi, Teri. Miss me?"

"More than you'll know. Rick, you were great. We're all so proud—"

I swiveled around in my chair. Teri looked stunning, as usual. "I know. I know. The ratings are up; the champagne is flowing; life is good."

Teri leaned back against the desk and folded her arms. "Really, Rick, this is all anyone is talking about. All the networks—"

"And *Inside Affair*, of course. Only, as I understand it, Nutsy had to share his moment of fame with Norma Flescher. Or is it Dawn Rae Hargis? I get so confused."

Teri looked down and smoothed an imaginary wrinkle from her skirt. "I was going to mention that. I have no idea how that happened, believe me. We thought we had a deal. We let them have your interview with Fagan, just so we could get some promotion value from it. But this other story—"

"You were expecting honor among thieves? Ms. Tremont, you do have a lot to learn about this business."

Teri shook her head. "It gets worse, Rick. They haven't heard about this yet." She nodded to the newsroom staffers who had started a conga line around the assignment desk. "But the word is, there's talk that Pastor Hargis might sue the station for libel, since we were the source of the story."

I drained my plastic champagne glass. "Well, look at it this way, Teri. You have one hell of a promotion in the making here. WHOE: the only station to create a hostage drama, solve it, and get sued all in one week's time. Oh, I almost forgot the lead: We also climbed to number one in the ratings. Now *that's* television!"

chapter forty

TIM FACENDA SQUEEZED INTO THE EDITING BOOTH AND SHUT THE DOOR behind him. I slipped the video cassette into the machine, punched the PLAY button and fiddled with the volume. There was a blast of static over a screen full of snow, then the picture tumbled into focus.

"Is this what you want me to do, Master?" A statuesque blonde purred into the camera, slowly removing a black lace brassiere.

Tim lunged for the FAST FORWARD button. "Uh, that's not it. I guess I forgot to cue it up."

"I don't know, Timmy, you might have something here. I heard that the Spice Channel is looking for new talent."

"Very funny. Here—here we go."

"And so as one man's personal crisis ends in Festerwood, Indiana, townspeople are talking about another scandal in the most unlikely setting—a local church."

The *Inside Affair* anchorwoman looked severely beautiful and shook her head slowly to convey just the proper amount of disapproval. "For the story, here is Nigel Dunston in Festerwood."

Nigel Dunston was a dapper Englishman whose accent and demeanor invested the show with a kind of counterfeit authority. He was standing in front of city hall.

"The good people of Festerwood, Indiana, must be asking, 'What more can happen here?' The answer is, plenty more. Consider the irony. Even as Norbert Fagan is confined to a cell in this building behind me, on another floor of this same building a scandal is brewing over how a city department is spending taxpayers' money. But don't look for the story here. Look instead to, of all places, a church just across town."

Sure enough, the next shot was of the Festus Friends in Faith Church, just as Wednesday night services were ending. The church doors were open, and people were chatting on the front steps. But the camera knew exactly where it was going; it zoomed in with a series of choppy shots that were meant to convey a sense of urgency. Finally, it focused on an angelic figure standing in the doorway, warmly clasping the hands of each parting worshiper. Dawn Rae Hargis never looked lovelier, and Nigel Dunston never sounded more solemn or more disapproving.

"She is the beautiful daughter of a church minister, and on this weekday night, she is positively beatific as she greets the members of her father's spiritual flock. But that serene smile hides an ugly secret."

The camera cut to a shot of one of Festerwood's scenic downtown streets, where a snowplow was piling yellow mounds of slush along the curbs. Nigel continued talking. "Nothing extraordinary here. Just another wintry day in the town of Festerwood, Indiana. But as this snowplow clears a street for rush-hour traffic, little do the taxpayers of this community know that the chemicals that soon will be spread on this street are at the core of a city hall scandal. Or that the woman who blew the whistle on that scandal is none other than . . ."

The shot changed abruptly, to an extreme close-up of Dawn Rae, her face frozen on the screen in a kind of fetching pout. "The minister's daughter. Just how did this woman of God become a party to this sordid affair? That's something *Inside Affair* wanted to find out, so we asked the man in charge. His name is Tad Tyler, head of the powerful purchasing department of Festerwood city government."

Now poor old Tad Tyler was on the screen, leisurely strolling across the main walk of Festerwood city hall, probably on his way to

grab a sandwich at Larry and Loretta's and totally unaware of the am-
bush that awaited him. As he walked, Nigel talked. "*Inside Affair*
sources say that it was Tyler's long-running affair with the minister's
daughter, and his abrupt ending of that affair, that led to the revela-
tion of rigged prices and kickbacks that revealed this sedate city hall
as the viper's nest of greed and corruption it has become."

Suddenly Nigel attacked, looming into the picture alongside
Tyler, jamming a microphone into his face and shouting at the top of
his lungs, "Mr. Tyler! What can you tell us about your affair with
Miss Hargis?"

Tyler looked absolutely bewildered. "Who? What are you talking about? Who are you, anyway?"

Perfect stuff for *Inside Affair*. The cameraman was bouncing
alongside as Tyler walked faster; Nigel continued his breathless pursuit. "You know perfectly well who we mean, Mr. Tyler. Dawn Rae
Hargis, the minister's daughter. Are you saying you didn't have an affair with her?"

Tyler was walking faster now, holding a newspaper over his face,
still asking, "What do you mean? I don't know anyone named Dawn
Rae . . . what's-her-name."

Then, back outside the church. Nigel was there, no longer the
abrasive, pushy reporter; it was the courtly Nigel, nodding sympa-
thetically as members of Billy Joe Hargis's church talked about the
minister's daughter.

"I didn't like her the minute I set eyes on her," said one elderly
woman, who was wearing a plastic bonnet to protect her blue-gray
hair. "She just wasn't one of us. Kind of standoffish, you know. But
Lord help us. How she could do such a thing is beyond me. I just feel
for poor Pastor Hargis."

I couldn't watch any more. I punched the STOP button and
turned to Tim.

"I take it there's more."

"Lots more. This is only part one. Part two runs tomorrow."

"Shit, Tim. Now I can see why we're being sued."

"I don't suppose it would help if we tried to set the record straight."

I hit the EJECT button on the machine. "We're going to have to try. But I doubt it will do much good. We could maybe restore a few reputations, but this place just may become the world's largest Dairy Queen when this is over."

"It's funny in a way," Tim said. "Your notes, my research, Lowell's pictures—put 'em together in just the wrong way, and this can happen. The thing is, how the hell did *Inside Affair* wind up with this?"

"Oh, that part's easy. In case you haven't noticed, there's a new crowd in charge of this place; they probably figured they'd score a few points with a national tabloid show and get the station some notice at the same time. With that kind of incentive, you can justify being a little reckless with the facts."

Suddenly there was a tremendous commotion in the hallway.

"Who's in charge here?" a booming voice demanded. "I want to talk to somebody in charge!"

I wheeled my chair out of the editing bay just as the Reverend Billy Joe Hargis stormed into the newsroom with his lovely daughter several strides behind, looking somewhat embarrassed.

They say timing is everything, and, in this case, the good Reverend's timing couldn't have been worse for the denizens of the WHOE newsroom, most of whom were absolutely shit-faced from the morning celebration. Spanky, the photographer, was spread-eagled in one corner of the room, trying in vain to shake a drop of champagne out of a very empty bottle, which he held over his mouth in anticipation. Morris Chiles sat bleary-eyed at his work station, trying to focus on something in front of him. A couple of the younger kids had already ralphed their breakfasts in the men's room and just sat on the floor, rocking back and forth and moaning.

I figured that as the senior-most sober person in the newsroom, it was time for me to make a command decision. "Reverend Hargis, welcome to WHOE News. I'm Rick—"

That's about as far as I got. The Reverend Billy Joe Hargis, who is a lot bigger in person than he looks on television, loomed over me, his beet-red face shining with perspiration.

"You're in charge here?"

I looked around the room. "Well, not officially, but I can assist you with any—"

"Assist me? *Assist me?*" The Reverend was shaking now, his voice tumbling out of his immense body with volcanic force. "You can assist me by explaining just how I am supposed to continue my ministry in this town after what you nincompoops did! Do you realize . . ." His voice was even louder now, thundering against the walls. I had a feeling that this must be what they mean by fire and brimstone. "Do you realize what you have done to the reputation of my church, not to mention my daughter?"

Dawn Rae stood off to the side with a sad, wounded expression on her face. But just at that moment she looked up, and I swear she winked at me.

Her father saw my attention wander. He resumed bellowing into my face. "You can tell your bosses that they haven't heard the last of Billy Joe Hargis or the Festus Friends in Faith Church. I'll see you in court, young man!" With that, Reverend Hargis spun on his heel and barked, "Come on, Dawn Rae, we have no further business here."

"I'll be right there, Daddy." Dawn Rae obviously did have further business, and it appeared to be with me. As her father stormed out of the newsroom, she took my arm and led me back into the editing booth.

"I know this isn't your fault, Mr. Roberson. You're a decent man, and I know you were distracted by that poor man who took the hostage."

This was odd. I expected Dawn Rae to be furious. After all, her face had just been beamed all across the country, connecting her to a scandal that she had absolutely no knowledge of.

"Well, yes. I was, of course," I stammered. "Still, Miss Hargis, that was a gross error and I don't blame your father—"

"Oh, Daddy is beside himself. Not much I can do about that. But that nice Mr. Grossbaum told me that I should make the best of this, and that's what I want to do."

"Mr. Grossbaum? I don't think I know him."

She giggled. "Oh, of course you don't. He is the nicest man. He called me just minutes after that story ran on *Inside Affair* and said I should start thinking about my future. Well, you know, I never looked at it that way, but—"

I slowly eased the door shut. "Miss Hargis, exactly who is this Mr. Grossbaum?"

"Well, his first name is Ira, and he's a talent agent in New York City. He says I have great potential, and that he can represent me!"

Suddenly the picture was clearing up. "A talent agent? I didn't know you were a performer."

She shrugged. "Well, I'm not. But I think he has something else in mind—maybe some TV talk shows and maybe even a book deal. Can you imagine that?"

The thing is, I could imagine that. In today's media climate, a person could stretch his or her fifteen minutes of fame into a year's worth of profit in no time.

"I'm not sure this is a good idea," I cautioned. "For one thing, you have no story to tell. You had nothing to do with that city hall scandal, and once Irving finds out—"

"It's Ira."

"Right. Ira. Whatever. Once he finds out that you weren't in-volved, that the whole thing was a mistake, it pretty much takes you out of the spotlight, doesn't it?"

Dawn Rae apparently had thought this through. "Oh, I know that. The thing is, once Mr. Grossbaum sees me on camera, I'm sure he'll find something for me to do." Suddenly she was very excited again. "I could tell the real story! You know, how I got mixed up with somebody else and how my father is suing your station. That would be a good story, don't you think?"

Dawn Rae Hargis, as it turned out, was not as naive as first appearances would indicate. Or maybe it's just that everybody is media-savvy these days. The trouble is, she was probably right. I could just see the talk shows salivating over Dawn Rae, the gorgeous blonde church lady from the Midwest who was done wrong by the thoughtless, insensitive media, who was now telling her wrenching story to an adoring, sympathetic nation.

Dawn Rae moved closer toward me, and I caught a trace of her perfume. "Anyway, Mr. Roberson—Rick—I sure could use your help."

My hormones began their familiar surge, but the tiny voice of experience told me to watch my back. "Uh, Miss Hargis—Dawn Rae—I'm not sure how I could possibly be of any help. After all we've put you through—"

"But you're the best, Rick. I know you are. Everybody says so." Sex followed by flattery. That usually works for me.

"So I thought maybe you could arrange some time for me to make a tape here at your studio, so I could show Mr. Grossbaum what I can do." She was practically on top of me. It was the second time that morning that a member of the Hargis family had been in my face.

I squirmed through the small space she had given me and walked back into the newsroom. "Well, I suppose it wouldn't do much harm. Call me tomorrow and I'll set something up."

"You won't be sorry," she cooed, then she glided from the room.

"Rick, if you're not too busy seducing the minister's daughter, could you pick up on line three?" It was Karen Armstrong, wearing her perpetual look of disapproval.

"Roberson, news."

"Tad Tyler here. I'm surprised you have the nerve to take my call, Roberson."

Great. Another satisfied viewer. "Mr. Tyler, look—I'm terribly sorry about what happened. We had no intention—"

"Looks to me like you had every intention in the world of making me look like a common criminal."

I paused for a moment. "Well, the fact is, the names and faces may be wrong, but we still have the story right."

"You have no story. That's my point. You've dragged my office and my reputation through the mud, and I have a good mind to take you to court."

Evidently, suing had become a popular pastime in Festerwood.

"Now wait a minute, Tyler. We have enough dirt on you and your little salt scam to put you away for years. That's a fact. We have an ex-employee's story and independent corroboration. If I were you, I'd be a little careful about taking any of this to court."

Now he was sputtering. "Is that . . . is that a threat, Roberson?"

"Sure sounded like one to me."

Tyler's pinched, nasal voice now screeched over the phone like bad feedback. "That's the trouble with you media types! You think you run the world, that you can go on television with some half-assed story and destroy all the good a man has done in his community! Well, two can play your game. I have some powerful friends in this city, and we'll just see who winds up with egg on his face!"

"I'm sure you do have powerful friends, Tyler, and I'm sure that prosecutor Tibbert is one of them. He'd better be, 'cause that's who will be investigating you and your friends." I hung up. I was guessing that one lawsuit had been averted.

chapter forty-one

THE NOON NEWS WAS JUST COMING ON, SO I PICKED UP A HALF-FILLED glass of champagne and cleared away a seat on the assignment desk. Morris Chiles, who obviously was not accustomed to a champagne breakfast, looked like he had been mugged on his way to work. By contrast, Peggy Carnowski was the picture of perkiness.

They brought the audience up to date on the aftermath of the Nutsy Fagan story—how he spent the night in jail, or protective custody as they called it. There was a quick sound bite from F. Lee about how the charges against his client were bogus and how he was already lining up targets for his lawsuit. Then there was a picture of the charred remains of Nutsy and Marie's house with Morris saying, "Today, as she assessed the damage to her home, Marie Horsley, the common-law wife of Norbert Fagan, could barely hold back her tears."

Now Marie was on screen, looking like she wanted to disembowel somebody. "Just look at what has happened to my beautiful home! Someone is going to have to pay for this!" Another lawsuit! Mother was right. I should have become a lawyer.

"Jesus, Rick, you're not going to believe this!" It was Jerry, the producer, looking as if a two-minute interview had just run two-forty. "They're gonna shit-can Hargis!"

I looked up from the television. "What do you mean? Who says?"

Jerry handed a piece of paper to me. It was a mimeographed news release under the heading FESTUS FRIENDS IN FAITH and right under that, the headline, "Church elders vote to defrock Pastor."

"Great, this is all we need. Does the old man know about this? Or the Loon?"

Jerry nodded. "I hear the old man is so pissed he's actually cut a golf game short to get back here. I'm sure that Junior knows. Man, this is trouble. If Hargis loses his church—"

I finished for him. "He'll take us for everything we've got. We may wind up actually working for a living, Jer."

I cleared up some paperwork, made a few calls, and grabbed a quick bite to eat at Larry and Loretta's. It took longer than usual, because I was stopped several times to sign autographs. Ten years of reporting the news every night on television, and the only time anyone demanded my autograph was when it came time to sign the divorce papers. I shack up with Nutsy for a few days and I'm a celebrity. Cinq even named a sandwich after me. It was scribbled on the chalkboard in the window—NEW! RICK'S ROBO BURGER!

There was another phone message waiting for me back at my desk telling me to call Sid Klein at the *Fanfare*. I wondered how long it would take the newspaper to sic someone on me. The newspaper guys hated television people for a lot of reasons. They thought we were ersatz journalists, at best, with our hit-and-run tactics and our tendency to reduce complicated stories to thirty seconds of tape and a talking head. But more than that, they hated the fact that people actually watched television and got their news that way. I couldn't blame them much. No one ever likes the new, slicker kid on the block—the one who gets all the girls. To make matters worse, they also thought that we all made the big bucks and got all the glory. Obviously they hadn't seen my apartment.

I figured that Klein would be the one to call me. Of all the newspaper people in town, Sid had the lowest opinion of television news. If we were arriving to cover the same story, he would shout at the top of his lungs, "Hey, Roberson! Time to get out there and scratch the surface!" Then he would start laughing hysterically as if he couldn't believe the genius of his own humor. He was an asshole.

Still, I had to call him back. Television people won't admit this openly, but most of them still feel a sense of inadequacy in this news business, a gnawing suspicion that they really don't measure up to the print journalists, who, after all, were here first. Maybe it's because a newspaper story is preserved forever in print, while the stuff we do is headed for Mars before the viewer can give it a second thought. As a result, a lot of us go around with a chip on our shoulder, convinced that we are the redheaded stepchildren of journalism. Whatever the reason, there is a lot of insecurity in a local television newsroom and a lot of phony bravado to go with it. So, naturally, I called Sid Klein.

"City desk, Klein."

"Hi, Sid. Time to get out there and scratch the surface."

"Roberson! You called me back! I bet Pappy you'd chicken out."

Pappy Tolliver was the city editor of the *Fanfare*. He'd been there since the invention of the printing press. He obviously knew far better than Klein just how paranoid we TV people can be.

"No, Sid, I know how you love to get sloppy seconds on any story you can. So what can I do for you?"

Klein suddenly became very defensive. "Listen, Roberson, I've been on top of this Fagan thing since day one. I don't need you to make this story work. I got all the facts I need. I'm just calling—"

"To talk to someone who was really there?"

Now he was shouting. "No! Because Pappy ordered me to! I need a quote or two to round out the story, and of all the people involved, you're the only one who doesn't qualify as a saint or a madman."

"Well, thank you, Sid. Although I think it's a bit early to canonize Father Mike."

"So give me something, OK?"

I waited a moment then said, "How about this, Sid? This should convince both of your readers that you gave this careful thought. You can quote me as saying, 'Sometimes a journalist must decide: is a

story more important than a human life? If I can make a difference—
no matter how small—in a man's life, then isn't that my duty? In this
case, the answer was clear. I chose to be of service to my fellow man
instead of to my job.' "

"That's a crock, Roberson. I'm not going to print that."

"Have it your way. You wanted a quote, and, as quotes go, that
one wasn't bad."

"C'mon, give me something I can use—"

I felt a tugging at my sleeve. It was Karen, looking as if something had just sobered her up very quickly.

"Gotta go, Sid. If I get any more exclusives, you'll be second to
know."

I hung up. "What is it?"

"Big rumor making the rounds. The old man is back in town
and he's calling a station meeting at any moment. Word is, he's about
to cave in on this Hargis thing."

"Cave in? What the hell does that mean?"

Karen sank into the chair next to mine. "Beats me. But I guess
we'll know soon enough."

The phone again. I picked up on the first ring. "Tell them that
Nutsy and I were separated at birth, and I went in there to bond with
the brother I never knew."

"No shit? You and Nutsy? Identical or fraternal?"

It was Morris Chiles.

"What is it, Morris?"

Big meeting up here in the news studio. I am your wake-up
call."

Old Thumbtack didn't waste any time. I drained the last drop of
warm champagne from my cup and followed Karen out the door.

chapter forty-two

I HAD A SINKING FEELING OF DÉJÀ VU AS I WALKED INTO THE NEWS STUDIO; the entire staff was assembled on folding chairs. The last time we gathered here, the Loon was introducing the storm troopers of Larry's Legionnaires. I took a seat in the back row, just as Thumbtack approached the microphone. He was sporting a dark tan and wearing a yellow golf shirt stretched over his substantial belly. Obviously, C. T. had not been planning to return to the land of frostbite and wind chills quite so early.

"Folks, we're in trouble," he began. "As most of you know, these last few days have been, well, unusual. I followed the Norb Fagan story on TV down in Florida, and I was proud of all of you. I was especially proud of Pat Robertson's report from right there inside Fagan's home. Is Pat here? If so, take a bow, young man."

Obviously, C. T. had no idea who I was, even though I was the senior reporter on his TV station, but I managed a weak smile anyway, acknowledging a smattering of applause and giggles from my colleagues.

Thumbtack sighed. "That was the good news. The bad news is, it looks like we got ourselves in a heap of trouble with the Friends in Faith Church. I'm not sure what this is all about—I just got back into town—but I know enough to tell you that the Reverend Billy Joe

Hargis is plenty mad and wants to take this station to court. He says we are guilty of libel and he wants satisfaction."

Now C. T. straightened his shoulders and grabbed the microphone. "Well, I'm here to tell you today that he won't get away with it! No sir! WHOE stands by its story—whatever it was—and nobody, not even a minister, is gonna come in here and threaten us!"

There was a small pause while the somewhat bewildered members of the WHOE staff pondered just what the hell old Thumbtack was talking about. Most of the employees were involved in their own departments, such as sales and engineering, and were almost totally out of touch with what the station was actually broadcasting. The silence was becoming a bit embarrassing, so Larry the Loon broke it by jumping to his feet and wildly applauding. A few others chimed in, but it was obvious that most of them were clueless.

"No sir," C. T. continued, swiping his forehead with his handkerchief. "No one is going to come in here and tell us how to run this TV station. However . . ."

Uh-oh.

"However, we are in a tight spot, my friends. From what I've been told so far, the Reverend Hargis may have a strong case against us. I'm not saying that he does, mind you—and no one values the First Amendment like I do—but I've been given to understand that we may have wronged this man and his church in a grievous way. If so, then we should face up to our responsibilities."

Suddenly, old C. T. was sweating like a short-order cook. "You know, my friends, I'm not getting any younger. Pretty soon I'll be the same age as my golf score . . ." He paused for laughter, and got a titter from the sales section. C. T. cleared his throat. "I've loved this TV station ever since we signed on the air with *Rosie's Rumpus Room.* Remember that, Virgil?"

He turned to Virgil Addison, chief engineer and the oldest person on the staff, who should have retired years ago, but . . . he was an engineer, and nobody was exactly sure how to replace him.

Now C. T. was in a nostalgic mood. "Yes sir, those were the days.

Live television. No tape—everything live. Even the commercials. Most of you are too young to remember, but way back in the beginning . . .”

Thumbtack perched on the news anchor’s desk and looked off into the lights. “Way back in the fifties, we did live commercials, and . . . and . . .” He was chuckling to himself and shaking his head. “And Robin Peters—that’s right, Robin Peters was doing that spot for some home appliance company. Remember, Virgil?”

Virgil nodded.

“And he was saying into the camera, ‘And ladies, this window air conditioner is so compact . . .’ Now remember—this was live. Then old Robin said, ‘Ladies, this air conditioner is so compact that it only sticks six inches into your womb!’”

Again, deafening silence. C. T.’s eyes pleaded with his audience. “Get it? Six inches into your *womb*! He meant *room*! Six inches into your *room*! But he said *womb*! And it was *live*!”

Larry started laughing like a hyena, and everyone else did, too, even though C. T. had told this story maybe a dozen times over the years at company Christmas parties.

C. T. got up off the desk and continued. “Well those were the days, my friends.” Suddenly, he was no longer back in the fifties; he started sounding more weary than wistful. “But that was long ago and things change. Sometimes things happen that you just can’t control, and I’m afraid this is one of those times. So, I’ve made a deal with Reverend Hargis.”

You could hear the room holding its breath.

“It makes sense in a way. One of the first programs on WHOE radio was *Chapel Door*, and it was sponsored by the Friends in Faith Church. Now . . . ,” C. T. swallowed hard. “Now the church would like to have a TV station of its own. And why not? I’ve said for years that there is too much crime and sex on television, and that it’s about time the Lord had his chance for equal time.”

Old Thumbtack’s eyes darted around the room, looking for some signs of support. Now he was talking very quickly. “Sometimes you have to put principle above profit; that's the way I see it. So effective immediately, the Friends in Faith Church will assume ownership of this television station." Then, without another word, C. T. Thornton took his seat.

There wasn't a sound in the studio. No one could believe it. Thumbtack Thornton had just given away his television station. And he did it just to avoid being sued by Reverend Billy Joe Hargis. I looked at Morris Chiles; he gave me a champagne-loopy smile and said, "Rick, my man, the Lord works in mysterious ways."

Larry the Loon, looking as if someone had just shot his dog, got up and stammered through a little speech about how grateful we all were to his dad, and how we understood his dilemma and would try our best to make the transition to the new owners as smooth as possible.

But no one was really listening. We all understood that we had just lost our jobs. Unless, of course, we could suddenly grow silver-blue hair and wear shiny suits and cry on cue about how the Kingdom of Heaven was in trouble and could only be saved if God-fearing viewers kicked in part of their paychecks.

chapter forty-three

SINCE I WAS A KEY PLAYER IN THE EPISODE, I WASN'T ABLE TO COVER Festerwood's Trial of the Millennium: *The State versus Norbert Fagan.* The trial pitted F. Lee Fenneman against Prosecutor Bartholomew M. Tibbert, age twenty-eight but not looking a day over seventeen.

Tibbert was known to the courthouse media as "Plea Bargain Bart" for his most prevalent legal strategy adopted after he lost his first four no-brainer felony cases. Once, Bart brought the wrong case file to court, and, as a result, he called the wrong witnesses to testify against the accused. F. Lee was the defense attorney in that case as well, keeping an uncharacteristically discreet silence as witness after witness told the startled Bartholomew and the confused jury that the accused bore absolutely no resemblance to the man on trial.

Tibbert came to court ready to throw the book at Nutsy. He charged him with kidnapping, felonious assault, child molesting, arson, illegal weapons possession, public drunkenness, and ninety-three counts of disobeying a police officer. As for F. Lee, he was true to his word and donated his services in the interest of freeing his client from Festerwood's corrupt, vigilante legal system. Of course, the fact that Justice TV planned live, gavel-to-gavel coverage, and that all three networks, plus CNN, were going to be there, may have convinced F. Lee that he would soon be the new Gerry Spence.

Some of us were a bit surprised that the presiding judge, T. Corrigan Thomas—the "T" stood for Thomas—allowed cameras into the courtroom for the first time. In the past, Judge Tom barely tolerated reporters in there; he said he found them to be a nuisance, especially when a case was dragging on and threatened to run past his regular 3:00 P.M. tee time.

Judge Tom was sixty-four years old. He took the bench as something of a retirement project fifteen years ago, and he treated everyone who appeared before him as if they were gum on his shoe. But Judge Tom had never presided over a Trial of the Millennium before, and it was clear that the prospects of national fame were having their impact on him as well. First, he gave his courtroom its first paint job since the French and Indian War, then he set about to give Festerwood the first sequestered jury in its history.

However, the judge had to alter his plan when the two motel proprietors in town informed him that the trial would come during the high season in Festus County. It was scheduled for the same week as the Tri-County Milk Bottle Collectors Show and the Festus County Invitational Bowling Tournament—every room was booked. The county commissioners also pointed out that feeding twelve people breakfast, lunch, and dinner over an extended period would pretty much exhaust the county budget. So Judge Tom reluctantly abandoned his plan, but, for dramatic effect, he ordered that the jurors be given round-the-clock police protection during the course of the trial, which pissed off everyone—especially the families of the jurors and the cops.

All of the networks had enlisted the on-air expertise of their by-now legal celebrities. Gerry Spence was on ABC; Alan Dershowitz on NBC; CBS hired Johnny Cochran; CNN had F. Lee Bailey; NBS had Geraldo Rivera; and WHOE, which had not yet been delivered into the Lord's hands, had Lester LeDetz, a local ambulance chaser whose chief qualification for the job of TV analyst was that he worked *pro bono*—for nothing.

However, LeDetz did stand out from the rest of the commentators when he concluded that Plea Bargain Bart was presenting a textbook prosecution and had Fenneman on the run. That led one of the network commentators to remark that the textbook that Tibbert was using must be *Dick and Jane* and that the prosecution would be just as well off having "Spot" as the lead counsel. Later, it was learned that Lester was Bart's roommate in law school. Actually, LeBetz never earned a law degree, but he was part-owner of The Law Firm, a bar located in a downtown alley near the courthouse.

In one of her last acts at the old WHOE, Teri was responsible for lining up LeDetz as the station's legal expert after spotting his tasteful newspaper ad that read, *Have a Snort with your Tort!* Had she bothered to look, Teri would have seen that the accompanying picture of the blind woman holding the scales of justice had been altered slightly to show a shot glass on one scale and a beer mug on the other.

The trial didn't last long. Tibbert's first witness was Police Dispatcher Thad Barrett, who stuffed his three hundred pounds into the witness chair and proceeded to recall how he took Nutsy's 9-1-1 call that fateful November night. Tibbert even played the tape of that call, but the voices were practically unintelligible. Nutsy's speech was slurred from drunkenness, and Barrett, who normally turned his eight-hour shift into a continuous banquet, was chewing rather loudly. Dispatcher Ted didn't sound particularly alarmed by Nutsy's call, but under Tibbert's prodding, he said he felt a "crisis may be at hand."

When F. Lee got his crack at Barrett, it suddenly became show time. "So, I take it you dispatched the Festerwood SWAT team to this crisis on Ralston Street, Officer Barrett?" Fenneman sneered.

"Well, no . . ." hedged Barrett as he squirmed in the solid oak witness chair, which suddenly looked very fragile under his bulk.

"Did you send for sheriff's deputies, Officer Barrett?"

"Well, no—"

"Did you send for the state police?"

"Well, no—"

"Did you send for the National Guard, Officer Barrett?"

Tibbert sprang to his feet. "Objection, your honor! Counselor is goading the witness!"

Normally Judge Thomas would sustain such an objection, check his watch, and say, "Get to the point, counselor." But for this trial, he stopped the proceedings and called the attorneys to the first of what would be an Indiana state record for sidebar conferences. In each case, Judge Tom made sure that he was in full view of the courtroom camera that was mounted just above the jury box. Those sessions gave the network analysts plenty of time to keep score on the trial, with all but one concluding that it didn't look good for the prosecution. The one holdout was Lester LeDetz on WHOE, who called every one of the fifty-six sidebar conferences "a turning point in the trial."

F. Lee was back in Barrett's face. "Well, Officer Barrett, who did you dispatch to this 'crisis at hand'?"

"Officer Lem Talbert."

"Officer Talbert and who else?"

"Well, just Lem. He was the only one on patrol that night."

Fenneman was addressing Barrett, but he turned to look at the TV camera to say, "You mean to tell the court, Officer Barrett, that you sent only one patrolman with no backup to this so-called crisis at hand?"

Barrett squirmed and the chair creaked. "Uh, well, Lem—Officer Talbert—figured he could handle the situation himself."

"And what, pray tell, would cause Officer Talbert to arrive at that conclusion, in light of what you told him about the danger ahead? Surely, he caught the alarm in your voice?"

"Well, uh, actually, at first Lem and me wasn't all that alarmed."

Fenneman's eyebrows shot up nearly to the top of his scalp. "Oh, really! You felt no alarm at first upon receiving a call from a man who informed you that he was holding his wife hostage? I take it you get this type of call every night?"

Barrett's forehead was hemorrhaging sweat. "Well, no, not every night. But from Nutsy—I mean, the defendant—well, he usually calls every year at about this time."

Now F. Lee was in his element. He had this witness on the spit. "So, I gather that for some years now you have summoned the full might of the Festerwood County police force to take up arms against Mr. Fagan?"

A long pause. "Not exactly."

"Well exactly what *did* you do?"

"Always before, the patrolman on duty would just take Nutsy—Mr. Fagan—down to the police station, and he would either let him sleep it off or charge him with some kind of drunkenness violation."

F. Lee gave the jury a look of mock puzzlement. "But, Officer Barrett, I take it in light of *this* year's police response, that the officers who answered past calls at Mr. Fagan's residence routinely stormed the home behind a fusillade of small-arms fire?"

Plea Bargain Bart knew where this was going, and he leaped to his feet. "Objection! Defense counsel is badgering the witness again!"

Judge Tom sighed. "You may answer the question, Officer. Did the defendant give you guys a hard time during those previous incidents?"

"Well, no, I can't say that he did."

"So, if it pleases the court," Fenneman said, "would you enlighten us, Officer Barrett, on why you and Officer Talbert felt compelled to treat this last such incident differently?"

"Well it was different!" Dispatcher Thad sat up in his chair. "When Lem got there, he saw this big television truck parked out front, so he figured this must be big. That's when he radioed back for help."

Fenneman mercifully let Barrett off the hook, but he was locked and loaded when Officer Talbert took the stand.

"How is it, Officer Talbert, that these TV people arrived on the scene before you? Our records indicate that you didn't arrive on the scene until forty-two minutes after the call!"

The short, wiry Lem Talbert was perched on the edge of the witness chair, looking as if he might burst into tears at any moment. "Well, I was on dinner break at Dirkie's at the time, and my supper hadn't come yet."

Fenneman's voice oozed sarcasm. "So you didn't want to face this crisis on an empty stomach?"

Talbert shrugged. "Well, I figured it was just Nutsy Fagan—and that he would keep until I finished supper. It was catfish night."

From that point on, Plea Bargain Bart's case resembled a slow-motion train wreck. At one point, he called me to the stand, even though to everyone else it was clear that I was siding with Nutsy for a lot of reasons, one of which was the fact that he had extended my allotted fifteen minutes of fame to nearly half an hour.

Tibbert asked, "Mr. Roberson, are you saying you were not alarmed when the defendant pulled a shotgun on Kathy Kellogg and her crew?"

I tried—and failed—not to laugh. "Actually, Mr. Tibbert, I was able to ascertain that the weapon in question was made by Mattel. Now, had Mr. Fagan brandished a Daisy Air Rifle, I would have been very concerned, indeed, since you can lose an eye with one of those things."

Dennis Fronzman took the stand and explained that he and the chief were concerned about the erratic and explosive behavior of Sheriff Slope, and that's why we all spirited Nutsy to safety out the back door. When Father Mike was called to testify, his testimony about Nutsy's inherent goodness and innocence was so convincing that a hapless Tibbert looked like he was ready to join a monastery and take a vow of silence. Even young Horace did nothing to hurt his uncle's cause, although he did cause some commotion when the bailiff pried the Game Boy from Horace's sticky hands. About the most damaging thing that Tibbert could extract from Horace was that his uncle was "pretty boring."

But Tibbert did have one joker up his sleeve: Kathy Kellogg. She gave the prosecution its only legitimate shot at a felony conviction—in the guise of attempted murder. Fronz, Father Mike, and I had all testified that Nutsy's outburst with the toy weapon was no big deal, just a slightly injudicious reaction to Ms. Kellogg's insensitive inquiry into the origins of Nutsy's nickname. Unfortunately, she brought along a heavily edited videotape of the incident in which her question was magically removed. As a result, the tape showed Nutsy leaping up, holding his Mattel; Father Mike restraining him; and Kathy screaming and ducking behind a chair, out of camera range. She calmly explained to the jury that she did this out of fear for her life, because she assumed that Nutsy's weapon was the real thing.

F. Lee, just as calmly, asked whether this tape represented the only footage her crew had taken of the incident.

"Yes, Mr. Fenneman, that is the only tape. We were about to start the interview when the defendant went into hysterics for reasons I cannot fathom, other than those relative to his mental state of the past week."

F. Lee turned to the judge. "Your honor, I would like to introduce into evidence another tape of this interview that shows considerably more than Ms. Kellogg is suggesting to the court."

The tape had arrived in the mail the previous afternoon. The package carried a New Jersey postmark and was addressed to Fenneman. After viewing the video in his chambers, Judge Tom gave it his blessing and, with the courtroom lights dimmed, *The Kathy Kellogg Chronicles: The Lost Episodes* flickered on the court's circa-1934 movie screen.

This time, the jury plainly heard Kathy Kellogg ask, "Mr. Fagan, why do they call you Nutsy?" and her obscenity-laced tantrum when she discovered that my earlier interview with Nutsy was being aired on *Inside Affair*. Through it all, courtroom spectators could see the heads of the jurors in silhouette as they revolved back and forth between the screams on the screen and the loud, anguished noises coming from the witness box.

When the lights were turned on, Kathy Kellogg was standing—her hands tightly clamped to the top rail of the witness stand—looking ready to pounce on someone sitting in the second row behind the prosecution table. It was Buddy Tellman, her photographer that fateful night, who was at last getting even for years of insults from America's sweetheart.

Buddy sat there with just a hint of smugness on his face, as if to say, "What can they do to me?" Fact is, they couldn't do a thing. Buddy had just been dumped by NBS, as it exercised its constitutional right to downsize its news division. I never knew what Buddy's working relationship with Kathy Kellogg was, but I suspect it was such that every major television newsroom in the country had a copy of her performance for their very own private viewing.

Kathy Kellogg—looking for all the world as if she was about to implode—glanced at Fenneman, the jury, the judge, and the audience, and, in the same clear, dulcet tones that had elevated her to the top of her profession, she shouted, "This is sick! This is a goddam outrage!"

chapter forty-four

It took the jury all of sixty-five minutes to reach its verdict, and that included a one-hour lunch at the county's expense. Norbert Fagan was found innocent on all counts.

Prosecutor Tibbert saw the bulletin announced on a television set over The Law Firm bar. He had sent a subordinate to represent the state, since—within an hour's time—he had consumed five Harvey Wallbangers and would soon set the meet, course, and pool record in that category.

For Nutsy and Marie, the Ralston Street episode proved to be quite lucrative. F. Lee saw to it that they became multi-millionaires through the movie and television deals he set up for them, based on their best-seller *A Call for Help, An Answer from Hell.*

Indeed, an ABC movie did quite well in the ratings, with Woody Harrelson as Nutsy, that girl who played *Blossom* as Kathy Kellogg, and Kevin Bacon as me—although I thought he was too old for the part.

I liked the big screen movie version better. *Rage On Ralston Street* starred Tom Cruise as Father Mike and Brad Pitt as me! Brad Fucking Pitt! I saw that one three times.

With the money they made, the Fagans got their dream home—a farmhouse ten miles west of Festerwood—and even bought the restaurant that Marie worked at. They turned it into a gourmand's delight, thanks to some of Nutsy's hidden talents as they applied to chili, sloppy joes, cream of celery soup, and lemon meringue pie. Best of all for Nutsy, Marie took him to Florida every winter, putting him up at a hotel at Disney World for a week, while she headed to Daytona for her yearly sabbatical—assuring multiple orgasms for one and all.

Suffice it to say, Sheriff Slope dropped out of the race, making Chief Penny the new sheriff and Dennis the new chief of police. To further augment his and the Fagans' income, F. Lee sued the city, the county, and the sheriff for more money than they were remotely worth. To almost everyone's surprise but mine, Sheriff Slope paid up immediately with a personal check for ninety thousand dollars. Before anyone could ask where that came from, old Slope was off to warmer climes and, hopefully, more forgiving voters. As for Father Mike, as expected, he became the new pastor of St. Bonnie's.

WHOE's call letters promptly changed to WZKL—The Station That Puts Prophets Before Profits—and there to redefine himself once again was the amazing Thaddeus Bodine, formerly T. Clayton Bodine, formerly Clay Bodine. Now in his *Thaddeus* reincarnation, he became senior anchorman of the *Eyewitness to the Lord Good News* news, a half hour of all the news the secular stations ignore. Now, for the first time, Festerwood viewers could enjoy stories about students who get straight A's without the need of a pager; banks that do not get robbed; wives who don't drop bowling balls on their sleeping husbands' heads.

Bodine was now sixty-seven years old but in no position to retire as his many creditors frequently reminded him. And I must say Clayton—I mean Thaddeus—was clearly in his element, with a booming baritone that seemed to be coming straight from the Pearly Gates and hair the color of a Christmas snowfall. He was still looking up the hard-to-pronounce names, but from the Old Testament now.

Larry the Loon also survived the transition, mainly because that was the one condition that C. T. insisted on. Reverend Hargis agreed, with the understanding that Larry's job as operations manager would be limited to keeping the soda and candy machines filled and conducting tours of the station for area Bible study groups and church choirs.

Many of the old WHOE staffers found work in smaller or similar size markets, but most of the engineers survived—mainly because Reverend Hargis couldn't figure out what exactly they did. The engineers even successfully resisted the Reverend's efforts to get them to sign his Contract with Christianity, which mandated that they not smoke, drink, swear, or engage in any activities that might violate the church's moral code. Thumbtack interceded to suggest that Billy Joe look upon his engineers as guardian angels with a pension plan and union steward, since they were the only ones on the premises capable of carrying out the Christian broadcast message of "Let There Be Light" and keeping it on through the broadcast day. As a result, the Reverend Billy Joe Hargis adopted a more accommodating and diplomatic "Don't Ask, Don't Tell" approach to employee behavior.

However, there was one part of the code that was written in stone: No employee was allowed to make any un-Christian comments about any member of the Hargis family, especially during the engineering department's interminable coffee breaks. That, of course, was aimed specifically at references to Dawn Rae and her weekly show, *The Glory Raes of the New Dawn*, in which she unleashed her sparrow-in-heat soprano on the full range of Gospel Golden Oldies.

Obviously, Ira Grossbaum didn't come through with his big plans to make Dawn Rae a national celebrity, so she settled for local stardom instead. It was a good decision, since, in time, Dawn Rae's show became syndicated on the Christian television circuit, attracting a new generation of male viewers who no doubt appreciated both her vocal range and the astonishing vistas created by her newly consecrated bosom that had taken on Partonesque dimensions following elective surgery.

Dirk Tubergen struck it rich. A TV station in Chicago saw his work on Nutsy's front lawn and hired him to be their weekend anchor and investigative reporter. It was funny, in a way. I inadvertently had helped get Dirk the job I had always wanted.

The great salt scam dissolved like an April snowfall. Plea Bargain Bart—still smarting from the beating he took in the Nutsy case—decided not to convene a grand jury based on what he said was flimsy evidence. My mother threatened a long, noisy city council investigation if Tad Tyler didn't step down. So he did, stating that he would pursue new challenges and spend more time with his family—which delighted everyone in the community, except his family.

As for Norma Flescher, she just sort of disappeared, and not a word of the scandal was heard from her. And while no one felt inclined to file a missing person's report, several Florida snowbirds from Festerwood reported seeing her in Fort Myers. These were folks who prided themselves in never forgetting a face, and it's a good thing, since Norma had apparently undergone a cosmetic makeover of *Cosmopolitan* proportions. She was blonde; she was tan; she was forty pounds thinner; she was driving a Lexus (presumably from Tad Tyler Motors); and she was living in a well-appointed condo on the beach (also presumably courtesy of Tad Tyler Condos International).

And hardly an evening went by that I didn't see Kathy Kellogg on late-night TV, extolling the wonders of a psychic call-in service. I definitely thought, by the way, that these were a cut above her diet pill commercials.

chapter forty-five

IT WAS MID-MARCH, WITH JUST A HINT OF SPRING IN THE AIR. THE ground was still salted with frost, but the winter wind had lost its bite and the dingy clumps of snow that lined the Festerwood streets were slowly melting away. In four short months, my life had changed drastically. I had just about exhausted my savings, and I was only two paragraphs into my long-deferred dream of writing a mystery novel. I had almost decided to take my mother's advice and apply for a teaching job at Festerwood Community College.

"I trust you aren't driving anywhere tonight, Rickster? These extra-inning ballgames can be murder."

Dex Feasal set another bottle of Iron City beer on the bar—the brew that made Pittsburgh famous. And since it was now available in Festerwood, it was being priced and marketed as a foreign import.

The Cubs were playing one of those endless exhibition games on television. It was now the twelfth inning, and I was averaging about a beer an inning. "Don't worry, Dex," I said, "I'll quit as soon as the Cubs score."

Dex emptied an ashtray. "Shit, if that's the case, you'll have to watch the conclusion of this game from the Betty Ford Clinic."

Of course, I knew Dex wouldn't cut off his best and most reliable customer of the past couple of weeks, even though I was costing him a fortune in corn curls and trail mix. I had become a fixture at the Ramada Inn bar, ever since Hybernican Press signed me up to write the definitive account of the Ralston Street saga. That was three months ago, and the deadline for a completed manuscript was yesterday.

I had assumed by the publisher's lofty-sounding name that this was a class organization with superb literary taste—*Hybernican* suggesting the name of a publishing house that would unveil the lost works of Proust and Camus. It was later when I learned that the founder of Hybernican Press was Hy Bernican, whose most prominent best-seller was *The Wit and Wisdom of Jeffrey Dahmer*.

It seemed that Hybernican Press specialized in so-called "instant books," usually involving lurid murder trials and written by a local reporter who covered the case. He or she would be hired to augment their meager salary by writing an account of the saga ten seconds after the jury's verdict, so it could be in a drugstore paperback rack near you while the public still had a vague recollection of the event. So instead of a six-figure advance, Hybernican put me up in the Ramada Inn for nine days with twenty-five dollars per diem to get this sucker cranked out.

I adhered to a strict writing routine. Up in the morning no later than 10:30, down to the dining room for a "Slamma Jamma" breakfast, a quick shower, a thorough read-through of the morning newspaper, then down to the bar to watch the Cubs game with Dex.

Someone had punched up a Jim Reeves song on the jukebox. His easy baritone floated across the room. *Hello walls, how'd things go for you today?* That—combined with the beer—put me in a nostalgic mood. I got to thinking about Teri. I hated to admit it, but there was still a spark there. I had heard that Teri and Boyd Nelson had run off together to revolutionize television news in sunnier climes, Mobile, Alabama, to be exact.

She called me one day out of the blue to inform me that she and Boyd had rocketed their station to number five in the ratings, just behind the *Bewitched* reruns, pre-colorized of course. She said Boyd wanted to offer me a job; I told her that I was reconsidering my career goals, but thanks anyway. There was a pause at the other end, then she said, "Well, then, how about Morris Chiles?" It was thoughtful of her to call.

Dex snapped me out of my reverie. "Damn it!" he shouted. "Do you think we'll ever see Sammy Sosa hit the cut-off man in our lifetime?"

The Cubs' Uzi-armed right fielder had almost sent the team's bat boy to an early grave trying to gun down a runner at third, several blocks away from his throw.

Dex was as agitated as I've seen him in some time. "Hell, those Latino outfielders never hit the cut-off man. They're a bunch of glory hounds."

"What about Clemente?"

"He never hit the cut-off man, either. Hell, Sosa couldn't throw my crippled grandmother out at third, even if she tagged up first."

It was usually at this point in the game that Dex would bring up a slightly delicate subject.

"So, how's the book going?"

I dug a handful of trail mix from the bowl in front of me. "I'm pretty much at the point I was three days ago."

"The title?"

"Yeah. How does this sound: *An American Folly in Festerwood*?"

Dex looked at me wistfully, a sure sign that he was about to get serious. "This book ain't gonna happen, is it, Rickster?"

"I don't think so, Dex. I'm suffering from a major case of bullshit block."

The trouble was, this book deal was the only thing I had going. All of the news directors at the major-market television stations who burned up my phone lines after the Nutsy affair now seemed to be permanently away from their desks or in the longest meetings in recorded history with no time to get back to me. Obviously Nutsy was no longer news, and I was no longer in their Rolodex. And the major publishers that had been panting for my firsthand account of the ordeal suddenly decided they would prefer to hear about it from Nutsy and Marie.

"I'm bailing out of this project, Dex. This isn't a story that deserves to be told, drunk or sober." I started to pay my bill, but Dex waved me off.

"I agree, Rick. But listen, this is your bartender speaking. Don't give up on yourself. I mean it."

On my way out, I was stopped by the Ramada Inn night manager, Larry Fedders. "Oh, Rick, I didn't know you were still here. Some guy named Fred Hogan has been trying to call you."

I assumed Hoagie was just keeping in touch and was prepared to clue me in on how he was adjusting to those seventy-five-degree temperatures, unsalted streets, and Florida skies where the sun actually shines—even in March. So I was surprised to see an area code listed on the message that suggested he was calling from somewhere in Indiana. I could only hope he wasn't placing a call from jail.

Since the Ramada Inn had been my home away from home for several days, I was greeted by an alarming array of smells when I opened my apartment door. The only scent I could instantly recognize was spoiled meat. But there was also a subtle bouquet of soiled socks and a faint trace of stale bed sheets. The first thing I did was to dial the number of Hybernican Press, which I had been led to believe was near the University of Kansas. I was only mildly surprised to hear the automated operator inform me that the number was no longer in service. It took three more phone calls to learn that Hybernican Press had filed for Chapters 11 through 23 and that I needn't advance any further beyond the title.

I had just hung up when the phone rang.

"Rick, it's Fred Hogan."

"Hoagie! Christ, I wondered what happened to you."

"Well, I've found honorable work, my man. Believe it or not, I have become a bona fide television news consultant."

"Right. And I'm Bob Woodward."

"No, I mean it, Rick. Look, you and I have seen how screwed up things have become. And what have we done about it? I slink out the door with my tail between my legs, and you wind up making heroes out of the very people you despise. I say it's time that the good guys fight back."

"With what, Hoagie? You and I both know that we're outnumbered here. The consultants have every news director in the country shivering in their boots. The tabloid shows are setting the standards for what used to be journalism. Are you forgetting? Nutsy Fagan was a goddam national news story! And then you have people like Teri, people who don't have any journalistic experience at all. They're telling news departments what stories to run so she can promote them during ratings months! And they are getting away with it! What kind of—"

Hoagie interrupted. "I know. I know all this, Rick. But somebody has to try. Don't you think it's time we stood up for ourselves? Time to correct a few things? Look, I have a couple of clients lined up. Nobody big. No major markets. Just a few UHFs in little towns in Nebraska and South Dakota, places like that. But it's a start. Maybe we can make a stand there and, who knows, maybe in time we could turn this thing around, not to where we used to be—that was no good, either. I mean, maybe we can take all the new hardware—the helicopters, the radars, the satellites—and use them to cover some real stories, stuff that makes a difference. If not, we'll still be doing news and having fun. What do you say?"

It was late afternoon and a sudden shower was thrumming at my apartment window. A few employees at the insurance company next door were dashing for their cars, using suit coats and purses as makeshift umbrellas. I knew Hogan was right. I still loved television news, and I wanted to be part of it. So far, I had skated by, making wisecracks from the sidelines while others changed the rules. Or, as in Nutsy's case, I became part of the problem. If I was serious about making a difference, now was the . . .

"Rick? Rick, are you there?"

"Yeah, Hoagie. Sorry. My mind sort of drifted off."

"Listen, there's someone who wants to talk to you."

There was the muffled sound of a telephone receiver changing hands, then a voice that I never expected to hear again.

"Hi, Rick. It's Jeanette. Remember me?"

"Vaguely. I believe you are the girl who robbed me of my innocence."

She chuckled. "In more ways than one, I'm afraid."

"But what are you doing there with Hoagie? And by the way, where exactly is *there*?"

"We're in Terre Haute, at our flagship station."

"*Our flagship station*? You and Hoagie? Wait a minute, Jeanette—you're not telling me that you've joined Hogan's consulting firm?"

"Why not? I'm good at this, you know."

"You're good, all right. But not at this. Hoagie hates your style of—"

"Who said that was my style? Look, Rick, I'm a technician, not an ideologist. People like me, we're sort of like media consultants for politicians. We don't have to believe in what our client says or what he stands for; we just have to make sure the public is buying it. In this case, Fred wants to take television news in a new direction, and I know how to get the job done. Period."

"But you were so sure about what you were doing. I mean, what about *Fast Attack News* and phone-sex features and—"

"That was then, and this is now. And if this doesn't work out, then it's on to something else. But right at this moment, I'll put everything I've got into making this happen." There was a brief pause and her voice softened. "It would be so nice if you'd join the team. We could work wonders together."

"Put Hoagie on, would you?"

"Sure. See you soon?"

Hogan was back, laughter in his voice. "Surprise, eh?"

"I'll say. She is good though. Almost had me convinced before. I think she may have got the job done this time."

"Then you'll join us?"

"Not sure, Hoagie. Give me a few days to think about it. Terre Haute, right?"

"Right. The only Fred Hogan in the book. We'll have fun, Rick. See you soon, I hope."

I hung up and, for some reason, I started to laugh. The more I thought about things, the more I laughed. I mean, it was funny. Here was a chance for me to get out of Festerwood at last, but not as a reporter on the way up. I would be leaving to become a news consultant! And all because some poor soul got drunk one night and missed his woman and called the cops. It had nothing to do with me! That was the funny part—I was just along for the ride. In a way, I had become a victim of my own profession. The more I thought about it, the more I laughed.

I opened the window to get some air and was slapped by a gust of cold wind and a shower of needle-like rain pellets. That was funny, too. Everything was funny. I leaned out the window and turned my face into the stinging rain. The wind flattened back my hair, and my shirt was soaked. I was gasping for breath. I looked down on the parking lot next door, where more employees scurried over a pavement ponding with rain.

And I shouted at the top of my lungs: "Hey, Festerwood! Listen! Listen to me! I have a bulletin from WHOE *Fast Attack News!* The jury has returned its verdict and guess what? You won't have Rick Roberson to kick around anymore!"

A few people looked up, but most of them just kept running to their cars. It didn't matter. I just stood there—soaked to the skin— laughing like a madman.